THE
PORTRAIT

EMINA TEMEL A.

Prime Seven Media
518 Landmann St.
Tomah City, WI 54660

Printed in the United States of America

Acknowledgment

I would like to express my deepest gratitude to my beloved sister Felek whose unwavering support, encouragement, and belief in my journey gave me the strength to bring this story to life. This book would not have been possible without your inspiration.

To my dear husband, Bilal, for his endless support and belief in me. Your encouragement has been the light guiding me through this journey. In every moment of uncertainty, you stood by me with patience and love.

And a special thanks to my dear friend Danny, thank you for your friendship, encouragement, and the steady support you offered without ever asking for anything in return. I am lucky to have you beside me on this creative journey.

I also extend my heartfelt thanks to my family, my friends, and to you, my dear readers.

SESSION 1

"A person's homeland is the place where they are rooted. Where they feel at home is where they find calm."

Qasim stepped into his village, weary but excited. The locals had gathered to welcome him and he waved to Abrohom, his Christian neighbour. Not expecting Qasim to arrive so soon, Abrohom mouthed and cried out with delight. While watering his flowers, he threw the pitcher aside to run to Qasim. The pitcher fell and rolled after him, the water inside flowing down the stairs, following him as he waved his arms back and forth and ran. The elderly friends hugged tightly before speaking and stumbled to the left and the right as they gave each other rough back pats. On a crisp autumn day, Qasim returned to his village; this time, he intended to stay.

Qasim, the dark-haired young man with a moustache, hollow cheeks, and grey eyes, was a man of faith and national consciousness.

Britain became the de facto ruler of Iraq. The constitution included certain representations of democratic elements as a system of rule. He was a member of the party. Even though he kept his political relationships separate whenever he came to the village to see his family, he always had a passion for revolution in his heart.

He continued his struggle with the dreams he couldn't get out of his mind, even in the village.

He had such high regard for the Barzani administration and used it as a model that he named his newborn son Mustafa for the oldest and Lokman and Idris for the twins. He was inclined to do anything with his closeness to the Barzani administration. He had the guts to give his life in the name of his revolution and people.

Despite the turmoil in Iraq, besieged by crises from all sides, Qasim would fulfil his duties to the nation and the party. He would dedicate the rest of his life doing agriculture and animal husbandry. He would breathe the air of his village, which was vibrant daily, and spend time with his family and neighbours. He would read his books, listen to his music on the radio, and drink the coffee and tea he had brought from Iraq. He would reside nearer to his aspirations. He didn't have any other plans aside from that.

He was sweltering as he kept a watchful eye on his luggage, which showed that he had left his revolutionary friends behind. He took a deep breath, carefully opened his luggage, and took out his possessions one by one. He was a bookworm, and the majority of the contents of his backpack were books. He also had a battery-powered radio with him. He picked it up first, then his books, and walked towards the house, drawing strength from the ground beneath him.

The twins were bouncing and playing among a few scattered garments and the remaining books flipped upside down in the wooden suitcase, believing that their father Qasim had purchased them new toys. When Qasim returned and carefully placed his books in the cupboard, the children immediately sat down, looking innocently into their father's eyes and refraining from misbehaving.

For eight days, they had travelled across enormous mountains and plains with their friends. They reached Midyat by pushing the mules that were about to die of hunger. Qasim was fortunate in that he owned a home in the village. Despite his repeated invitations to his home, his revolutionary comrades preferred to settle in the city centre. That's how they would arrange their family to escape out of Iraq. They didn't want to squander any further time. In truth, the youngsters were eager to begin a new life in the difficult living circumstances of the border camps.

On the one hand, he was exhilarated by the prospect of farming in his village; on the other hand, he was weighed down by the melancholy of being away from the revolution while also grappling with love. He missed his buddies when he was with his family, but he missed his family even more when he was with his revolutionary friends. On the other hand, a cloud of grief accompanied him wherever he went.

He wished he could have a small shop like his neighbour Abrohom and tend to his vineyard seasonally as Abrohom did. He fantasised about going to his shop in the morning, returning home to his kids in the evening, and becoming contentment with his family.

Qasim was a man of few words, often perceived as abrupt. If he said "yes", it meant yes; if he said "no", it meant no. He never accepted anything that didn't make sense, and he never broke his word. As a result, he spent little time with the locals except on occasions of condolence, celebration, or during the vineyard and harvest season.

It was time to sweat in his idyllic village. He needed to re-target, revitalise, and rebuild his ties to his neighbours. He should have spent more time with Abrohom, his best friend and neighbour, who hadn't sought him out while he was gone.

Greenvillage—It was a small village of around twenty houses, largely inhabited by Muslims and Christians. Muslims' homes were often built with masonry buildings plastered with mud brick. The geometrically formed dwellings were rectangular, with elongated windows that were longer than the width. The homes were enclosed by waist-high walls made of stones of various sizes. The ground floor was visible from the outside on the sloping land, and a barn could be seen underground from the side of the house. Again, stone steps were used to alter the majority of the mud brick dwellings. The barn's entrance would be distinct from the stone stairway leading to the house.

During the summer, people slept on terraces and climbed onto the rooftops using wooden staircases. In the summer heat, this was the only way to sleep comfortably. They would fall asleep under the velvet sky.

The adobe dwellings all had doors painted the same shade. Its metal doors were painted blue as if everyone in the village had used the same paint can. The colour matched the blue sky perfectly, and the doors creaked with the pleasure of people who came and went.

This community featured a small mosque for Muslim residents. Nonetheless, the mosque's minaret towered over all of the houses in the village. The dwellings were either single-storey or double-storey, with some being higher than others. The village headman's house was one, and the imam's house was the other.

There were houses where the mud bricks had cracked in places, the soil had shifted, and the heaped stones had become visible. These stones were used to make it sound like human labour was required. These stones were all shaped by hand. Ploughs were used to defend in front of the earth-coloured nests, but they were rusting and awaiting work the next time.

The houses of the Christians were coloured differently. Vaulted entrances were found in houses that were as pristine and striking as the wings of a white dove. Balcony arches were delicately embroidered with lace-like designs. They were built entirely of the region's large white stones, which were meticulously arranged. These two-story mansions would become more resplendent over time, glowing golden and amber under the sun's embrace. The windows of the homes, like the entrance, were in the shape of vaults and were evenly spaced. These houses had lofty, open ceilings and were embellished with inlaid beams and arches. Sarcophagi-shaped houses would be cool in the summer and warm in the winter. Everyone had a village room in their home that could accommodate fifteen or twenty people. The villagers would rest their backs pleasantly on thick, filled pillows as hard as stones.

They would meet daily in someone's home, layered on the mat, to debate history and politics. Typically, one of the dengbejs (storytellers) would recount the incidents and stories they had witnessed for a long time while unleashing his scorching voice. Because of the emotional intensity of the words, everyone in the room would take a deep breath and remain transfixed after the dengbej sang until their final breath.

All the Christian inhabitants of the village adhered to the Orthodox faith, which made it simple for them to live according to their principles. Additionally, a member of the clergy resided there.

As opposed to Muslims, Christians preferred to work harder and often pursued multiple occupations. Even when Muslims rested during the midday heat, Christians continued to labour in their vineyards and gardens in the scorching sun, and if they didn't own a vineyard, they dealt with silver and gold works at the market. Even those who had a vineyard also worked on their silver and gold trades. As a result, Christians maintained a better financial standing than Muslims.

The village women adorned themselves with brightly coloured and patterned festoons that rivaled spring flowers, wearing their finery regardless of whether it was a feast day or not.

Material concerns were one of the central preoccupations that peasant women noticed, and they competed fiercely with one another. They used to compare one another covertly and make their spouses compete to be more extravagant than the other...

They were pitted against one another for reasons other than materialism and ostentation. Boys symbolised continuity, lineage, and family honour. It denoted strength and effort. The youngster proposed money as a contribution to the home. A son is a wonderful blessing for every family.

The village also had a mud pond, which resembled a swamp when it rained. Children would play on the pond's edge, and they would capture tortured frogs in the pond. Despite the fact that the frogs wailed in their hands, the children would inflate them like balloons. The mothers of the children would avenge the frogs in the evening. When warts appeared on their hands, mothers realised they had gone to the pond, and the children received a mother's loving punishment. The wild youngsters of the hamlet, on the other hand, ignored their instructions and would squirm around like they were swimming in the lake again, splashing unclean water at each other. The snobby kids, their hair strewn across the soil, mistook the pond's edge as their playground.

Another fall had withered away, leaving spring to take its place.

The village was flooded with light, the whitewashed cottages shining like incandescent bulbs. The mosque's roof shimmered in the sunlight like a golden nugget.

The daisies were withering; although the April rains had made them more colourful, it was time for them to leave; nature would replace them with other flora. The rain had stopped, and the clouds had dispersed.

With the sun shining brilliantly after the rain, the rainbow stretched valiantly to show off its vivid hues to the village. Yellow, green, blue, red, and purple are all colours that appeared. A bridge in the sky was built by pure colours that could not be obtained in any mixture.

Each house had one or two mulberry trees beside, behind, or in front of it, but their shade was insufficient to keep the dwellings cool. The small birds had made their nests in the mulberry trees, singing from morning to night. People would come to life when small owls made an occasional chirp. Goats bleated in their barns in the early spring, and roosters announced the daybreak to the household. In the distance, donkey braying could also be heard. The creek was a little far away, but when viewed from above, it seemed like a green line dividing the land. The pond frogs croaked all hours of the day and night. The sounds that mixed with nature injected soul and life into the village.

Fatma poured the hot tea and summoned Mustafa for assistance. She was pregnant and couldn't gather the strength to move. Qasim stood up, fearful that his son's tea would burn, and instantly removed his own tea from Mustafa's hand.

Qasim, sitting cross-legged on the mat in the comfort of his trousers, considered counselling his boys, who were seated across from him. Mustafa, his eldest kid, was six years old, and his twins were four.

"'Compete for the good, my children, at all times and in all things in this life." This is how it is worded in Surat al-148th Baqara's verse. "Don't be less or more than your friends. Never deviate from the correct path. Kindness will always point you in the correct direction."

Fatma's eyes widened as she heard from the kitchen door. According to Fatma, Qasim could not have imagined that he would read books other than to read the nonsense of the unbelievers. She was surprised when he cited an example from the baccarat era. She seemed thrilled that Qasim was reading the Qur'an, and she listened more intently, her chest thumping.

The kids nodded as if they understood what he was saying.

Qasim longed for a daughter so badly that he practically prayed for one. Fatma writhed in agony for days. The midwife had not left the house since the early days of May because Fatma was about to give birth. It was obvious that the birth would be challenging. The locals began to weep for the woman who gave birth as the anguish lasted for days, believing that the mother or baby would die during childbirth. Noon turned into evening, evening into night, night into morning, and morning turned into noon once more.

Qasim sat hunched on his house's stone steps. He took the silver sheet off his belt. He removed the fig leaf that had been placed in his layer to absorb moisture. He wrapped a cigarette with a tobacco leaf and rolled it. He raised it to his dry lips with a shaking hand.

Abrohom accelerated his feet, entered the garden gate, proceeded to the stone stairway where Qasim was, and took the dinner plates that Aziza had cooked for dinner. He would never let his next-door neighbour and old friend Qasim alone. Qasim panted and yanked on Abrohom's arm, rocking it up and down to offer him his seat. Abrohom rolled a cigarette, and they both blew smoke in response.

The kids were having fun in the courtyard. The children's screams blended with Fatma's groans. Fatma gave birth to a flank, and the groans stopped.

The local midwife and a helping woman approached Qasim, who was wrapping and smoking tobacco in the courtyard with trepidation. The helper, who had turned pale, grasped the midwife's skirt and gave her a comforting look.

When Qasim saw them approaching, he leapt to his feet. He became apprehensive since the women were about to deliver the awful news.

"Can you tell me what happened? How is my wife doing? Has the baby been born? Come on, speak up!"

The women exchanged glances, unsure how to explain the situation.

"God has given you a daughter, Qasim Agha."

Qasim flew into the air with a benediction as he heard the news. He screamed with delight. He even forgot about his wife for a moment.

"How about Fatma? Is she okay?"

"Yes, yes, she's resting now, thank God."

The midwife and the assistant were surprised and smiling when they realised they had received more gratuity than they had anticipated. They moved their breasts to get to their residence, happy to hear the jingle of money.

The birth of a girl on such an important day made Qasim extra pleased than he already was.

"Thank God, this is a miracle!"

He started shaking his early Qasim pooch after taking it off. Abrohom, the Syrian neighbour, observed Qasim dancing halay in the courtyard, and he chuckled. He walked up to the edge, which was scarcely longer than his legs, and knelt down, praying, "May God raise her with her parents, my friend."

"Come on, Bro, let's dance the halay together."

Abrohom was surprised and looked at his old acquaintance.

Some people shortened his name to "Abrohom" and dubbed him "Bro."

"Just today, a year ago, a young female student companion named 'Leila Qasim' perished in the killing of Saddam. Our revolution's first martyr was the first to die. God gave me a daughter today. A year has passed, bro! Leila is no longer here, and a new Leila has emerged. I'll give my daughter the name "Leila" if my name is Qasim. Leila must be her name.

Mustafa and Idris, the twins, would not leave the baby's cradle for a second. Leila was adored by her brothers. Idris took the baby's little hands in his and waved them around as if he were doing the halay with her. If something occurred to the newborn, Mustafa removed the twins from the cradle.

Qasim seized one of his rams' by the horns and dragged him to the guillotine stand. They sacrificed beside Abrohom, his close buddy, and the fertile meat was distributed across the hamlet.

"People make sacrifices because they have sons, and yet you…"

Qasim grinned beneath his moustache, dominating his daughter in the same way he possessed his sons.

Fatma was depressed because of this girl who had caused her so much pain. She avoided breastfeeding and did not hold her sobbing infant in her arms. For the second time, Qasim noticed this movement. The baby was forced onto Fatma's lap and forced to breastfeed. Fatma had covered the baby's mouth and nose so that it would choke on the day when Qasim was not at home, but the baby Leila laughed at her mother as if she was being tickled. Fatma has been terrified of this baby girl since she was born. She had refused to be strangled. Even getting close...

When Qasim discovered Fatma had ignored Leila, he broke his silence, saying:

"Look at me, Fatma; listen to me carefully. If something happens to this girl, I'm not going to let you live, just so you know."

It is unknown whether Fatma nursed Leila and raised her involuntarily out of respect for her husband or out of fear.

Aziza, their Christian neighbour, had also given birth to her sixth child. There were two more sons born after Leila... Benjamin, Turabdin, Yausef, Gabriel, and Samuel were the Syriac family's five boys at the time.

"I gave birth to twin boys at the same time. Let's see if that woman, Aziza, can demonstrate this talent. She was the mother of five sons..."

She gave Leila a spiteful glance. "Why did you become a girl!" she exclaimed.

She'd go and say this; she'd sit up and count the five sons, Fatma.

"Please give me a son. Daughters arrive and bear their father's surname. We have boys, Mr. Qasim, and they keep your name alive. "Do you not want that?"

"I have three sons and a lion's share of a daughter." he replied. Then he added, "What else do I need?"

"One more for a boy..."

The wheat they had set aside for planting was scattered on the earth, and it penetrated it by turning green. In a week or two, the stalks would be taller than most people. It feeds on the ground yet is controlled by the light and blooms toward it. The braided spikes sprang from their skulls with awns, braided like a girl's braided hair that couldn't be cut. The milk they'd stashed inside was about to burst forth.

They would converse about their love while reclining in the shadow of the mulberry trees that adorned the hills, their heads turned to the golden fields.

It would inspire artists; even if it could not be perfectly captured in paint, nobody would tire of looking at it.

It was a source of income for the farmhands; it was the largest booty on the property. Wheat, bulgur, stuffed meatballs, and flour - the foundation of wheat bread - are all essential ingredients in the kitchen. The means the ears were used to make food, fodder for animals, and even adobe dwellings, and straw was added to the mud brick to make sturdier shelters.

In the meadows near the end of May, golden-yellow ears glistened in waves. Virgos could no longer bear their height and began to sag. It was now harvest season for the locals.

During harvest season, the people assisted one another without receiving any cash assistance. Someone, the local headman, employed a paid worker who was unable to assist anyone due to their weight. No one wanted to help him because of his degrading demeanour.

The newborn girl in the carved wooden cradle was sucking her lips, closing her eyes, and sleeping. He couldn't stop staring at his daughter; he wouldn't take his gaze away from her.

Qasim would take his books from his niche and read them to his daughter Leila while he was at home. He couldn't bear Fatma's nagging, and Qasim's reading became louder as Fatma's humming became audible. Qasim was very disturbed by Fatma's displeasure with every issue. He had no choice but to get used to it. And he didn't expect her to change anymore.

He frequently reads to his daughter Leila to lull her to sleep. Rumi, Ehmede Xani, Melayê Cizirî... Father Qasim continued to rock the cradle with his toe until he was certain his daughter was sleeping. He carefully rose, softly lifted the books he'd read to the load, and placed the embroidered cover over them.

hile rolling cigarettes on the patio, Qasim contemplated an Iraqi revolution. He couldn't get away from the instability and arguments within the party committee, so he went to Iraq several times. Qasim could not be at ease in the village during this time. The revolution, for which he would give his life, fell short of his hopes. He had suffered the loss of close friends and acquaintances. Regardless, he did not give up. He remained active in the endeavour to leave his family behind and bring about the revolution.

He felt compelled to confide in his wife, who served him a cup of mirra alongside the coffee pot.

"I'm glad I didn't drag you along with me. Otherwise, you'd be crushed like me," Qasim explained. His voice was caustic, and his heart was angry.

"Does it make a difference? The Christians wreaked havoc on us as well. Would I plough the land alone? Would I pasture animals? Would I make yoghurt and butter and sell it? Which one am I going to catch? They have absolutely everything..." Fatma nodded and pointed to her next-door neighbour. When it came time for Qasim to speak, he delivered it all in one breath:

"A little excess, my carefree head... What is wrong with my children, thank God?"

"That infidel wife, there's a well in front of your door. Let the muck fall, and I hope the birds and animals get messy! Until I get to the creek's headwaters and carry one gallon on one shoulder and the other on the other. I have a herniated disc and can no longer carry myself..."

Fatma was expecting a child.

Qasim put his palm to his head, his head aching like a church bell. Fatma punctured Qasim's head with her pointy beak, exactly like a woodpecker to the tree. He couldn't find solace in the house he arrived at on the first day, so he sought refuge in his revolutionary fantasies. This agony would not have been bearable otherwise.

"They have grape fields and silver shops; all the bazaars are always theirs. They have a minibus and wine cellars, so they can drink the root of my faeces! I wish they had visited their relatives in Germany. Why didn't they leave? Even if they had departed, we would have inherited their property. Muslims would stick together. Even the imam's wife brought him bad luck because of them."

"Fatma! Do your ears pick up on what you're saying? If you weren't pregnant, I'd put you in your place! What are you on about? I was not left behind because of these neighbours. Whatever you required, thank you; didn't they help?"

"Would I take bread from Aziza's hand? According to the imam, it is haram! God bless..."

Qasim's rage flared, and he clenched his fist. He stepped out of the adobe house, the blue-painted metal door rumbling behind him.

On the one hand, he was consumed by a desire for a revolution that he couldn't shake. The command centre had devolved into petty rivalries, and the revolution's preparations stalled. The revolution was on the brink of becoming corrupt. As Qasim brooded, he would remove the tobacco from its silver coating and begin rolling it.

He had a son named "Mesut" five years after Leila. Even the names he gave his sons reflected Qasim's deep respect for the revolution's commander, Mustafa Barzani. He named his children after the Barzani family.

The age difference between Leila and Mesut was five years. He would have Leila do the housekeeping despite the fact that she was a child.

It didn't matter if they had boys for Qasim or not. Leila was her father's favourite child.

Fatma almost fell at Qasim's feet in order to become pregnant again and have another son. She couldn't sleep at night with Qasim. Her avarice had gotten the best of her. Qasim was becoming increasingly detached from her activities. Qasim would sleep in the garden if he could. Fatma was acting like a desperate lady, not allowing her husband to breathe.

"Do you really want us to have another son, Mr.? They work our fields, herd our livestock, and bring us money. Daughters, on the other hand, cause problems for the family. Let us have sons; they will carry on the lineage, while daughters belong to other families when they get married..."

"Shut up, woman, that's enough!" he said with a scowl.

Fatma's jealousy and never-ending demands exhausted Qasim. He made his bed separately, and he stopped sleeping with his wife from that day forward.

It was around midday. The sun cast a soft glow over the patio like a curtain, though it couldn't produce heat. Fatma swayed and talked as she led Mirra to Qasim.

Qasim sat on a wooden stool at the top of the stone stairway, admiring the shimmering leaves in the shade. He increased the volume on his portable radio, which was powered by thick batteries.

The radio turned to music after briefly providing the day's news for around five minutes per hour. Qasim eagerly awaited, he could hear the smouldering music. It was inevitable that he would enter other realms when listening to Ayşe Şan on the radio. The magnificent scenery's background music was a crystal clear sound.

Qasim, the revolutionary dreamer, straightened his legs while listening to the news on the radio.

"Mustafa Barzani died in George Town Hospital on March 4, 1979. His body will be sent to Tehran." Qasim's throat clenched, and his eyes welled up with tears. He would like to go back. He'd see his buddies, share his pain, and find relief from his grief.

He cleared his throat when he noticed Abrohom's shadow. Abrohom called him, asking about the news. Qasim also asked him to get ready immediately and drop him off at the Midyat bazaar, and from there, he would go to Tehran for the funeral.

This wasn't the last mission of Qasim, either.

He donned a brown color shalwar suit with a white shirt over it. He tucked the hem of his shirt into his baggy bag and tightened the elastic. He strapped the comfortable shoes on his feet and tightened the laces tightly after wrapping the pooch around his head. He threw himself from the balcony.

Abrohom leaned against the garden gate early in the morning and asked, "Qasim, if you're ready, shall we go?"

"I'm always ready, Bro; wait a minute, I'll be right back."

He fetched his sickle from the barn, closed the door, and began clearing the weeds in the garden. He approached Abrohom, who was expecting him. Abrohom had also come prepared with the scythe. The locals were joined in the square by two neighbours and two close friends. Lots were drawn with the justice of Qasim. They would each travel to their respective fields in turn.

Wheat was collected in the summer, and grapes from the vineyard were harvested in the autumn. They were becoming a workforce, an activity, a necessary labour to be done for the peasants.

They made their way to Daniel's pitch, one of the Assyrians, in the first row.

Qasim was not a dengbej; he couldn't sing, but he became part of the chord as the people sang his words, humming in unison.

They did not deviate from their ancestors' traditions. They held sickles in their hands and stood apart. They sang while mowing the field. They would put the sickle to their ears and pull it to themselves at the first syllable of the word; in the last syllable, they would breathe, drop the sickle a little, cut it with a single move, and collect it in their palms.

> *"I am a successor, Oh Mir, Oh Mir*
>
> *Yezdanşer was the Prince of Botan, Oh my Mir, Dear my Mir*
>
> *I wander among the tribes, Oh my Mir, Dear my Mir*
>
> *I own the mother-of-pearl sword. Oh my Mir, Dear Mir*
>
> *The successor is not afraid of squares, Oh Yezdanşer!*
>
> *I am Mir's successor, so let's see who's brave."*

They were silent for the time being, but nature's symphony continued: the birds in the mulberry trees were chirping happily;

cuckoos provided rhythm with their intermittent "coo" sound; and the stocky, hard-eyed small owl would join them with its haunting cry. The lambs bleated, and the crickets never stopped. Surprisingly, one's mind was at peace.

They gathered the severed ears in bunches in their palms. They took small steps, setting their hands aside. The Virgos were grouped in groups behind them.

They swung the golden straw bunches in the direction of the tractor. Women wrapped their shawls in an unusual way, indicating that they were workers. There were also peasant women among them, whose task it was to transport the crop stacks to the machine. As the gear wheel rotated, the spike bundles they threw into the machine shook. The thresher was separating the wheat from the chaff, and the wheat trembled as it passed through the sieve.

When things lightened up and came to an end, the traditional halay was performed in the evening, and the villagers returned to their homes with boiling enthusiasm. Although the villagers stood in solidarity in the field, their houses were independent and separate from each other.

Qasim went to the city with the money he earned from the harvest income. Fatma cried until the evening that he would not return.

"Your father cast me aside because I bore no more sons..." she lamented.

Idris and Lokman, the twins, were identical. They were two reflections in a mirror facing each other. Even if Lokman choked on his words all the time, it was difficult to tell them apart; Fatma would get them mixed up. Whoever uttered someone's name first would know that the person who nodded was that person.

Despite their similarities, they gradually distinguished themselves by expressing their identities and characters.

Idris would construct a path for the ants to follow in a single line on the bumpy dirt with his finger; Lokman would dip his hand in the ants' paths, disrupt their order, and torment any insect he picked up in countless ways. The twins would unite together to defend the ants. When the twins, who were left in the dust, fought and cried, they were thrashed with their moms' slippers.

Idris and Lokman were constantly fighting, competing, and playing games. The one would hold the other's throat, while the other would misstep and attempt to overturn the other. They would sit in their corners and act as if nothing had happened as soon as they heard Qasim's footsteps. Fatma had always worried about them with their father, but it didn't take long for them to resume up where they left off and play games again. The child's mind holds no grudges against anyone or anything.

When their mother's patience ran out, she would scare them by shouting, "Oh, here comes your father."

The twins were drawn into corners right away. But over time, the twins became immune, and they refused to believe their mother. Qasim would not give his children a single flick, but children who were scared of his stare would remain silent in their reverence for their father.

A horse neighing was heard a few hours later. The kids went into the garden and saw: Qasim was pulling the bridle on the horse, and the majestic horse was imitating it, swinging behind its delicate slim.

Mustafa yelled with delight and dashed to his father. In wonder, the twins trailed behind him.

"My son will ride a horse now, and he will not fall behind his peers."

The horse was a robust, heat-resistant Arabian horse with thin legs. They named it "Auburn" His hair was a delicate hazelnut colour. It had a silky texture. It had a fluffy, long tail, with a jet-black mane to match. Qasim elevated his son's foot and supported it with his hand. Leila had her finger in her mouth and was staring at them.

"Leila, run, girl, come, and I'll put you right next to your brother."

Leila leapt up to them. Her father carried her onto the horse and handed her over to Mustafa, saying, "Hold on tight; let's go around the village together."

"Daddy, me too, me too," the twins cried. "Let your brother get used to it. He'll take you around a lot, too," he remarked as he handed the bridle to Mustafa. "Come on, girl, don't be afraid. Sit up straight and hold tight," He said, holding the saddle's edge in one hand. Okay, that's all there is to it. Don't be afraid; your brother is right behind you, holding you firmly."

Mustafa joyfully yanked the reins of his horse, fiercely grabbed Leila with one arm, and cried to the twins, "Come on, catch the stirrup!" as if daring them to a race. The twins chased after that horse like it was a game. In the garden, they were circling.

"Brother!... Slow down a little, slow down a little!" Idris pleaded.

"Come on, you useless little kiddos!"

Lokman slipped in the mud. Idris rolled over him as well.

Leila burst out laughing; Mustafa was secure in the care of his brother.

Mercifully, the brunette slowed down. Mustafa went on a tour with his brothers. The brown hair was likewise cheerfully neighing. The twins were panting, their tongues hanging out.

On September 12, 1980, a military coup took place within the Turkish Armed Forces' chain of command. The parties were disbanded. Hundreds of films and videotapes were prohibited. The peasants were cautioned by the headman.

Qasim rushed home and dug a hole in the garden for his books, wrapped them in black plastic wrap, placed them carefully under the scooped soil, and rolled a large stone on top of it. He, too, pulled his fingers through the dispersed soil, shook his hands, and wiped them on his shalwar.

When Leila saw her father's uproar, she knew something was amiss. He dashed into the backyard. He scaled the apple-adorned tree. He climbed up from branch to branch like a cat. The apple trees began to shed their leaves, and the apples, together with the leaves, were spread on the ground. Above them, apples dangled. Leila pretended to be invisible and stood there for a long time.

He observed the rays as they moved through the branches. He didn't take his gaze away from the dancing sunshine for a long time.

The Gendarmerie jeeps rolled into the village. Gendarmes dismounted from the back of the jeeps and lined up in formation, marching down the only asphalt street. Muhtar had dazzled them with his remarkable eloquence.

Whenever there was a quarrel or an incident in the village, the headman would appear when things had calmed down. As a result, he would not have to intervene with anyone or choose sides with anyone. He was just concerned with his income. Muhtar was a man for all ages.

The expressions on their faces suggested that he had persuaded the gendarmes and commander to abandon their search for the village. They inquired about Qasim, who was stationed in Iraq. The headman declared that he was no longer merely a poor farmer.

The folks avoided the blow cheaply and without losing their lives. However, just in case, the tapes were not made public for some time.

Şiwan Perwer and Ciwan Haco were popular Kurdish singers then. There were other peasants who thoroughly wrapped Şiwan Perwer and Ciwan Haco's recordings in nylon, and buried them in the courtyard's open, stone-covered latrine hole. The majority of the peasants carefully concealed any items they feared would be prohibited in this manner. They didn't have time to dig a grave as quickly as Qasim.

Leila was still scared to leave the tree; when she got hungry, she reached the end of the branches and plucked the apples one by one. She bit it and spat out pieces on the ground. She noticed a curly yellow-haired boy lad amusing himself and laughing loudly underneath her. He was Abrohom's third son. Yausef had a bright smile on his face and curly hair, and he laughed joyously at Leila. Yausef, the third child, had a tranquil build. Leila was likewise the third child born, although she was the fourth. Yausef was a year older than Leila, but she could create two Yausefs from her body.

"Hey curly! Do you want an apple, too?"

He nodded eagerly.

"Then pick up the apples on the ground instead of taking care of me," Leila remarked, and it was evident how awful she was from that day forward. The curly head continued to mock her. Leila must have been influenced by her mother because she discriminated at that age.

"Shall I tell you in Syriac! What are you still looking at from there?"

"Come on down, cowardly cat. The soldiers are gone; you can get off."

With his eyes concentrated on his waist, he challenged Leila. Leila, on the other hand, had forgotten the gendarmerie had arrived; she hadn't even noticed them departing. The scent of apples charmed her and whisked her away to another world. Leila attempted to descend but couldn't see where to place her feet; she was stretching like a spring when she clutched the weak branches.

"Jump, I'll catch you," Yausef said.

He stretched his arms out and calculated how far Leila would jump, sliding left and right.

Leila rolled over and swayed down the stairs, but she couldn't get her foot on the cluster of trees. As he emitted a faint cry, one of the brittle twigs he was holding split and fell on Yausef. Yausef was clinging to the dirt floor while giggling at Leila.

"But you're big and heavy, fat!"

"No, you're weak, curly head!"

Leila stood up, dusted off her shalwar, and ran towards the house. Yausef felt something stir within him from that time forward. Leila studied the wall with a glint in her eyes till it turned.

The love of the two neighbours' children began on such a day when the sun was at its peak and continued to blaze the soil with all its power. A spark penetrated the lovers' hearts. The sun, the star of the sky, departed tiredly towards the evening, leaving its place for a cold night.

Fatma usually emptied herself by grumbling and talking. Her spouse didn't listen to her and didn't meet her expectations, so she vented her rage by chatting endlessly. Qasim didn't frequently take her for granted, yet a single glance was enough to calm her down. Fatma's nagging trembled in the face of Qasim's gaze.

Fatma refused to speak to Qasim for days out of spite, but Qasim was so used to his pestering that when she remained silent this time, he felt something was missing, which irritated him. All of Qasim's mercy would be shattered if she opened her mouth.

The houses of Qasim and Abrohom were directly opposite each other. Fatma had the eastern side of the home closed up and a door installed on the west side. The Abrohoms' home faces south. There were just two steps between the two buildings, and a wall was constructed with stones of various sizes that did not extend beyond the length of the leg.

Qasim had returned with the books he had revived from the dead. He carved out a concealed compartment in the niche and hid his books inside. He took his radio and went to the terrace after selecting one.

Just beyond the wooden staircase was the broken window. Fatma used to water the apple trees and the flowers on the stairs, her basil, through this broken window, the reason for which is inexplicable. She pulled the hose from the inside, extended it to the apple trees, closed half of the hose end with her finger, and sprayed the water to hit the apple trees with pressure. Especially that broken window that had been a watchtower for Fatma. From there, she peeped at the Assyrians' house; who came, who went, who did what? He followed them step by step. She would overhear conversations through that broken glass.

"I saw women coming to help Aziza. They were washing their carpets in exchange for money. This is how the house cleaning fashion trend is beginning."

"The woman has five children; there is a difference of one or two years between them. What else can she do!"

Fatma exclaimed:

"I got pregnant too. I also gave birth. I also have five children. Do I ever run away from housework!"

"But Aziza was coming to help you before, without even asking for money!"

"Let her name be cursed, that infidel. As if she needs money! Bread and water come from the lake, oh, she's in a good mood. She used to come to me to flaunt her gold and smack it in my eyes. As if I don't know her at all!"

"This stupidity, this nagging, will get you killed, woman! Well! Stop competing with Aziza right now..." Qasim's neck veins were swollen with rage, and his eyes were bloodshot. Despite his rage, he restrained himself.

"Oh, I did; either I'll be adorned with gold like her, or..."

"Damn your obstinacy, Fatma! It is much more difficult to persuade you than to persuade a believer to abandon his religion!"

Qasim had given up on it; it would have been better for him if he hadn't spoken to her; he felt more at ease alone. A world would discover a way to work from sunrise to sunset. At home, in the garden, in the field he would start and repair whatever he could get his hands on.

"Mom, are you going to cook that one for us tonight?" the girl Leila, rejoiced.

Fatma did not even glance at the tears of the chicken struggling to get rid of it. She snapped at her daughter, "Go home quickly. Don't go outside. Don't tell your father about it."

Leila was disappointed; she entered the house and played with the rubbish in her hand. Without disturbing the rhythm of the steps, she proceeded by swirling her shoes that remained on the ground. She sat on the edge of the terrace. She was looking from the hall to the house of the Abrohoms. Her eyes were looking for the yellow curly head among the gamers. If she saw Yausef, all her resentments would pass. She grimaced and crossed her arms, tears streaming down her cheeks.

The terrace that followed the house was also connected to the east side by a staircase. It was lined with flowers from old oil boxes on the stone staircase. The stone staircase was connected to the terrace from the south side, and from there, it met the stone stairway on the west side. The terrace was quite large, like a balcony without railings.

The wooden staircase leading to the roof became the decoration of the terrace. When the sun returned, Qasim would sit next to the stairs, throwing down his stool. His greatest pleasure was drinking Mirra coffee, listening to music on the tape recorder, reading his books - sometimes even reading and arguing with himself repeatedly - and rolling up his addicted tobacco even though he knew it was harmful... Occasionally, he would reach out for basil and comb it, allowing his strong and beautiful scent to turn into a feast of fragrance.

After the song ended on the radio, the news started. A female voice announced the news then a male voice came out: "If millions of citizens are deprived of their national rights in any country, democracy and freedom cannot be talked about in that country. We must never forget these people who have been deprived of their rights. A people that oppresses other people cannot be free..." the commentator announced. Qasim thought these were repeated in 1960, and nothing had changed 20 years later. Then a heart-touching song echoed on the radio.

He noticed his shy daughter.

"What happened, Leila?"

Leila shrugged.

"My mother told me not to tell you. So I can't say what it is."

He turned up the radio's volume a little more because he thought it would make Leila happy.

"Do you know what these words mean? Do you want to listen?"

Leila shrugged again, her arms tightly folded and sulking at the stone on the ground.

Qasim did not reach his daughter.

"Leila, let me read you a book."

Leila immediately got rid of her grip and knelt beside her father.

Meanwhile, the twins were also arguing about who was victorious and who was defeated when they approached the home pathway.

They came home by jumping over the fence from the side. Their minds were still in the game, arguing heatedly. Someone had to support one side, or the defenceless side would be pathetic.

An hour or so later, Fatma hurriedly entered the garden. She started talking as soon as he entered, never shutting up.

"Lokman, Idris, get up and bring me water. I will cook."

Qasim realised that he was doing some shit and said:

"Where did you go?"

"Nowhere."

"I saw her going next door, Dad," said Lokman, one of the twins, betraying his mother.

"Oh yeah, I went to the next door, Mr Qasim, to ask about their condition."

"One of our next-door neighbours is Syriac and the other is an imam. Since you don't go to Aziza…"

Idris, one of the twins, was also in favour of honesty:

"My mom goes to cook and clean for them once a month, Dad," he said. Even when the children were playing, they noticed their pheasant-like mother.

"Sir, it was my turn today. I brought them chicken and cooked it. No, it is good. He is the servant of Allah; he guides us, washes our dead and brings them back to our loved ones. He is a holy man, Imam Saleh…"

Qasim closed the book in his hand. Leila looked at her father, startled.

"He has three wives; however, are you serving as a maid to them!"

Fatma tossed a threatening glance at Leila. It occurred to use her for her sin.

"They give Leila a Quran lesson."

"What are you sending her for? Why did you not tell me!"

He dragged Leila to his side, not quite sure that he was hurting her:

"You were supposed to tell me everything, my daughter; why didn't you tell me you went to the Quran lesson?"

"They don't teach me, Dad; I'm going there to care for their babies."

The words in Leila's mouth were heavily echoed in Qasim's head.

"Are you sending this little girl as a babysitter, huh? Get in quickly!" Then he raised his hand to Fatma, but that hand remained in the air.

Mustafa entered the garden with his horse Auburn:

"What is going on here? Your voice could be heard from the beginning of the back street."

He pulled the reins of his horse and led it to the stable. The argument between the parents continued inside.

"If you defy me again, if you go to that house as a maid again... If you take my property out of this house without my knowledge again. Don't ever come back to this house. These doors will not open for you. You go and stay as a servant in Imam Saleh's house ..."

"My dear Mr Qasim, have I been dishonest enough to deserve these curses? All because it is thawab and for good..."

"Look, she's still talking!"

"It's not only me; all villagers go there, except Christians... Every day is a woman's turn. Going and cleaning, cooking for the hodja. It is a merit; how else can we reduce our sins in this life?"

Qasim knocked out whatever he could lay his hands on. He threw the items in the hall and left the house. Mustafa and Leila ran after him, reaching out to him at the garden gate. Mustafa grabbed his father's arm:

"Please, Dad! Why are you so angry..."

Qasim was ashamed of his eldest son.

Fatma nodded threateningly to her daughter; she thought Leila was out of her mind. She knew that Leila was a daddy's girl. She distanced her daughter and brought her closer to her father.

Apart from the adhan, Imam Saleh had another obligatory service: spending time with his wives. He spared only one day of the week to rest, except that he spent every day with a wife. He was quite fair in his own way.

"I am the mullah," he said, "listen to me."

He used to preach that polygamy is better for the men, insisting that a woman kept him vigorous.

"Your wife who doesn't wake you up three times a night deserves a second wife." He declared every Friday.

The poor peasants were lured by lust and discovered that their minds mocked their sensations and obeyed everything this "holy man" said. However, because there were few single and mature women in the hamlet, they could take a second wife and conduct their businesses. When it came to sex, the village's mullah, a feeble old guy, was no ordinary man.

He had some more time after the Friday prayer. When he had the chance, he would go to the headman's side. He travelled the gravel route to the headman's house this time. After learning that he was exempt from praying due to his weight, the headman obtained permission from Imam Saleh to worship at home on a chair.

"Hah, I had just prayed Imam Saleh, welcome."

Imam Saleh, who enjoyed playing cards with the headman, passed by and drank from the tea that had been brought. They delivered their statements as if they had taken over the village and established their own regime. They gave charity in their own manner.

The priest had marriage authority but was not married; he was devoted to the scriptures. When two clerics passed each other, they glared each other beneath the brows as if they were enemies.

"Is the pastor a child molester or gay? He doesn't have any girlfriends…"

As the laughter of Imam Saleh and the headman echoed through the village, Qasim pushed the garden door open furiously. The two big men of the village, who turned their heads to the rustling of the door, saw Qasim in front of them, and their facial expressions suddenly changed.

"You are fond of worms. You are not worth a penny, guys."

"What have I done now, Mr Qasim!" Muhtar tried to save himself from the turmoil. He backed away, rubbing the ground.

"Is this how you will guide our people, huh? Our villagers already have a little bit of mind in their heads. Are you taking it from there and putting it somewhere else!"

"Infidel!" shouted Imam Saleh, "Help me, someone is killing people."

"I'll tear you apart, man."

The villagers immediately rushed to the noise. The village headman's courtyard was full of villagers. Assyrians and Muslims alike forcibly rescued the drowning Imam, who was as red as a tomato, from Qasim's hand.

"Mr Qasim, be kind; what are you doing?" they shouted.

"This heretic treats our wives like his servants. He gives false sermons to them. The peasant women cook and clean at his house rather than cooking at their own home!"

Qasim was forgetting to breathe in his anger. He did not need to attack further because the villagers also marched on the imam hiding behind Muhtar. Some villagers were taking cover among them; they did not want the fight to escalate further.

"Yes!" one of the villagers agreed. "they read to our wives in case they have children. Or are you laying your hands on them!"

"How dare you!"

"You are all infidels, messing with the infidels…" Pointing at the Assyrians in the spot with his finger, and added, "Separate religions should not be together; they are poisoning each other," said the imam, behind Muhtar while Muhtar's turban was broken. Muhtar was hiding him with his weights and his belly.

"Know your limits! Sinful scum! That's enough that you insult us; you are the one who poisoned the villagers!" said the priest, sneaking up behind them. He made a cross on the cross.

"May God forgive our sins!"

"Since you came to this village, our wives have not been at their house. They are exhausted from cleaning your house… They say it is for good fortune, but we are awake, you snake man!"

"And if they don't make you feel comfortable three times a night, you say get married!"

"You snake imam…"

"Perverted imam, get out of our village…"

The imam was sweating and looking at the villagers with fear as if he was out of breath. He regretted calling for help.

Muhtar stopped the villagers:

"My dear villagers. Calm down a little bit," he said, raising his fat hands, "we're all brothers."

Among the attackers, Assyrians did not accept insults and wanted to put the imam in his place. The elders hid an iron power behind their weak appearance; the younger villagers could not crush them, and they could not reach Imam Saleh.

"Get out of here, Saleh! You turned us all against each other."

"Even our children no longer play together anymore. They said 'sin' and remained strangers to each other."

"Before you, we did not know what the distinction was! Now look at us…"

"Get out of this village!"

"Go away, Imam Saleh!"

Muhtar crept forward, raising his arms, silencing the villagers:

"My dear villagers, friends, listen to me… Our state does not make mistakes for us. The state sent Mr Imam Saleh to our beautiful village as Allah's guest. Wouldn't it be unfitting to fire the guest who came to our house!"

"The guest who comes to our house should not disturb the peace of the family, headman," said Qasim, he could not restrain his anger.

The villagers approached a little and walked towards the headman and imam.

Muhtar has also been booed together with the Imam. The headman's eyes fell to the ground; the ground they stepped on was the only built asphalt road in the village, and he deduced that it belonged to him.

"No, no… You guys, get out of here. You are now on my property!" he said, swelled with courage, pushing the villagers on the road and spreading them out into the street. Qasim spat to the side, unable to help to look angrily. They desperately withdrew from the headman's garden.

Imam Saleh could not leave his house for several weeks. No one attended Fridays for a while. He was left alone with his hands, cursing Qasim because there was no one to preach. Once again, he acted as if he had left the microphone on, saying what came to his mouth to Qasim.

Qasim and Abrohom sat in the courtyard chatting and witnessing what was said. Abrohom caught Qasim, who was jumping to his feet, and grabbed her by the shoulders:

"This demon makes people hurt, Mr Qasim, don't do it... Don't obey the devil... Let him see what he is."

Although the headman warned the imam out of his own fear, the imam did not listen to the headman. He told Imam Saleh that he had left the microphone on.

He criticised, "I won't get involved after this." The headman had a falling out with the imam, and they never played cards together again.

Imam Saleh's wives also got into each other because of their housework. No one enjoyed their day, burdening the other with the task. While he was trying to separate the wives who were fighting, it was thought to be the hair of his cloth, and the imam's beard was also taking its share. He was changing from shape to shape due to being pulled.

The wives had an idea, promising gold-loving women in the village of gold in heaven, inviting them to clean their homes again. Imam Saleh told the men, "Do not be sad because you do not have a second wife in this world. Fulfill your faith. Seventy hours, with their white skin and virgin bodies, will be waiting for them in heaven", and he aroused lust in men. They defined Qasim among themselves as an infidel. They were both afraid and distant from him. Imam Saleh continued to play with the villagers' minds again until the next rumours reached Qasim's ears.

❧

Mustafa had grown into a burly young man with muscular shoulders. He was taller than his father. His eyes were amber, inherited from his mother, and the dimple on his chin from his father...

The father and son acted together, supplying the necessary provisions of the house. They would ask for a girl from the village behind the slope. Mustafa spent time with his father. Together, they would go to condolences, visit the sick, and wish 'good luck' for ceremonies.

The school in the village provided education only for the first five years. To continue, he had to go to the school in the district. Lokman did not continue to study after school in the village. Lokman did not like to go to school, despite his father's forcing. Qasim also divided the work, saying, "If you're not going to school, then you're going to graze the animals." The price of not reading would be to graze the animals for Lokman.

On the other hand, Idris went to school; he used to go to school in the village with his sister Leila.

Fatma prepared bread with tomato paste for her children in the middle of the day. Leila quickly consumed her share. Lokman finished seven times as if someone was competing with him. Idris shared his bread with his sister. Lokman tripped and dropped Leila. The tomato paste bread in her hand was covered in dust. Leila raised her face and glared at Lokman:

"Wait, you'll see... If you dare, act like this when my father or brother Mustafa arrives!" She shrugged her hands. Since she could no longer eat the bread, she threw it into the courtyard. Small cattle rushed for bread as if out of hunger.

Mustafa wouldn't put dust on his sister; he didn't know how many times he punished Lokman for this. Sometimes, Idris would suffer from Mustafa's beating due to the disadvantages of being an identical twin. Although he said, "By God, I am not Lokman," his twin, Lokman, acted as a jackal and said, "No, brother Lokman is lying, I am İdris, he is Lokman!"

Mustafa started shaving them differently, but soon, Fatma interrupted:

"God gave me two identical boys. It wouldn't be right to differentiate between my sons! What, like criminals! You're shaving someone's head!" She beat her knees and cried out. The next day, she shaved the twins and compared Idris to Lokman.

Leila was brunette, with leek hair, protruding cheeks, and was slender, sprawling like a pheasant.

When her eldest brother Mustafa once said, "You're going to look like my mother, not now but obviously soon, you'll be thin and tall like her", Leila winced as if possessed.

"Oh my God forbid!" she cried out; she clung to the bread ever since starting to eat more than ever. Leila had become a chubby little girl who no longer looked like her mother.

It was unknown whether Fatma was so weak because she talked too much or if she was so weak from running all the chores of the house as she complained. Caring for five children with her husband, especially twins, made it even more difficult to do housework. Fatma was straightening up, the twins bickering and knocking everything down. Fatma took her anger out on Leila:

"Get up, girl; you're like a cow; you don't do housework either. I'm tired of cleaning all of you."

Qasim would say, "I think you look so weak and sickly from taking the neighbour's sin," causing Fatma to have a nervous breakdown and pretend to be unconscious.

"Something fat and brunette… How beautiful is that! She moves so slowly that she cannot do housework, so she hires a helper."

"The woman is very healthy and has a calm disposition… She gets help when the children are one after the other; what's wrong with that?"

She muttered, cursing at her Christian neighbour in a fainting trick. Qasim regretted what he said and threw himself out.

Squatting in his usual place on the terrace, he took the silver sheet off his belt and rolled up tobacco.

"What happened to the people of the village: this hatred, these curses, indifference to one another… Can I not find peace anywhere…"

Qasim blew his sadness into the sky with his cigarette smoke.

The sun reflected on the village like a golden tray, and under its command, the clouds were thinly accompanying. By noon, it had warmed the village and melted the morning frost. Between warming and not warming, the air was filled with the rich scent of fruit mixed with straw. The animals were bleating and jingling as they went to graze. The donkeys were braying as if they were waiting to be rescued. The birds had been chirping since the early morning without interrupting their conversation.

Qasim's dressing style never changed; it was the same in the village as it was in Iraq. His white cotton shirt, brown trousers and belt with a few rounds around his waist… Above all, the "pushi" (scarf) on his head deepened his gaze even more.

He opened his eyes with a bright idea that suddenly came to his mind, lowered the extended pole of his radio, bent it, and inserted it into its socket. After making sure he had left it in the shade, he slowly descended the stairs. He went to town to sell a couple of animals.

He returned with the red-billed partridge in each of the wooden cages he held by the rings in both hands. They stuck their heads out through the wide opening of the cage and looked in the direction they were going. The partridges were calm and dignified.

"What is this, Mr. Qasim? You bring animals every time you come; you don't bring anything else. Wouldn't it be better if you bought me a gold bracelet instead of wasting your money?"

"No matter how much I buy for you, you can't get enough, woman. Besides, these are my companions, from whom I can escape from the nagging and take shelter."

The twins ran and seized the cages.

"Kids, don't scare them… Look how they get aggressive."

"In this cold winter, where will you fly these animals?"

"They will always be with me; we will sleep and wake up together during summer or winter."

Fatma was jealous; she looked enviously at the partridges. She could no longer remember when she slept with Qasim and woken up with him. From that day on, she started to dislike birds and held grudges.

When the winter cold started to make itself felt, Qasim did as he said. He heated the soil in the stove and placed it in the cages of the partridges. He renewed his partridges' water every day and changed their feeders regularly. He would smile at them and chat with them.

The twins were screaming, trying to catch the partridges he had left in the room. The chirping and gaze of the children frightened the partridges. They were flying back and forth, leaving feathers. Fatma almost had a nervous breakdown.

"You ate meat; you went mad again! Sit down quickly at once. Sit down, I say! You'll stick to the stove; you'll be in trouble. Look, they're still not listening; my God, who are these kids attracted to? What sin have I committed, my God... The smell of these birds will suffocate me..."

Qasim was never even there. He snapped the partridges into their cages with his finger, picked them up and placed them on the warm earth. Each one moved in his cage, rolling on the ground. In their cage, it seemed like a pastime for them. They found their faces on the ground left and right. They stared at Qasim gratefully, necking in circles, and the red-billed partridges, born singers, thanked him with a crowing. They flapped their black-striped wings and played with the hot earth again.

"Do you know why these partridges have red beaks and feet, kiddos?" Fatma said, and she had caught the attention of Qasim.

"The Prophet who was martyred in Karbala. They covered their faces and feet with Hussein's blood. That's why their beaks are red."

Qasim turned his face away and covered the cages of the partridges with the blanket he used.

"They are the biggest betrayer of their friends, Mr Qasim; why did you bring them this home on purpose? They will bring misfortune..."

Qasim replied with harsh calm:

"Not them, but your nagging will bring bad luck. Repentance... Don't lose my patience, for God's sake. If you don't want to see them, go to the next room."

"What do you mean by betrayer..." said the young Mustafa.

Qasim took a breath, and as if he had a responsibility to reply to his son, he cleared his throat and replied:

"Actually, they look like us... The hunters of this region especially raise partridges that they take when they go hunting. When the partridges start to sing in their cages, the partridges flapping their wings freely in the air hear their friends and come to their aid. Thus, the free partridges fall into the trap of the hunter. The hunters shoot them with rifles and cook them for dinner…" He couldn't continue; he interrupted, "They're just like us… Friend of another class, traitor to his own class…" Qasim sighed:

"We're not helping ourselves anyway…" He curbed his thoughts about his experiences in Iraq and here.

Since Lokman scared Leila with a snake, Leila was afraid to go to the bathroom in the courtyard; she couldn't sleep for days because of constipation. Whenever Leila went to the toilet in the courtyard, she was afraid to even crouch right, as if the snake would show its head through that black hole. Lokman had said so and added that they pee standing up because of this to Leila. Mustafa caught Lokman, turned him over, and took him to the courtyard.

"Come on, show me where that snake you made up is!"

"Brother, let me be your victim. By Allah, I will never say such a thing again. Get me out of here, brother…"

"Then you will wait until Leila feels no stress. You're going to protect her, understand?"

Once she had this fear in her mind, Leila could never do her defecation again. She would only partially wash herself, and she would run away from there. She was afraid and even had trouble falling asleep. Even if she felt desperate at night, she kept to herself until the morning.

"I am not afraid of snakes!" said Idris as a warrior, "we already go snake hunting with Turabdin all day. We kill them with our sticks and count them. Whoever kills more gets something from the other. Sometimes ice cream and sometimes balloons from the peddler who comes to the village…"

"You snake hunters! Then you will be standing at the door. You will be the watchman for Leila."

The twins were blown away. They always tried to play games, and Leila didn't trust them.

"That's why she's fat!" Fatma said, "God forbid, she will explode at this rate."

Leila was unable to hold back her tears. Qasim built a small bidet on the side of the house. It was delayed for a while because the cement was not enough. Mustafa appeared in the garden on Auburn's back with the air of someone who had won a battle. He called Leila.

Saying that hedgehogs kept the snakes away, he collected three hedgehogs from the mountain with his friends. He released the hedgehogs into the garden from the sack he was holding. As soon as Fatma saw them, she collapsed to the ground. She had fainted from fear. When she woke up she grumbled:

"You turned this place into a zoo with animals! Oh my God, what am I suffering from... First the horse, then the partridges crowing nonstop, now these rats... But when it comes to gold..."

"They are not rats; I also brought them from nature, and didn't buy them."

"How will they protect me, Big Brother Mustafa?" said Leila.

"Do you see those spines on their back?"

Leila nodded.

"The moment they sense the snakes, the hedgehogs curl into a ball and immediately roll over them. They also have more powerful weapons; they shoot their spines like bullets. They knock them out instantly. And we can easily take the partridges out into the garden and release them. They will be comfortable, and you will too. Is that okay?"

Qasim was proud of Mustafa and kissed his hair.

"Well done, son. If I die, I won't be left behind. I know you will lead this family much better than I do."

Leila had calmed down a bit. Still, she couldn't get the possibility out of her mind.

Yausef had loved her too since he was a child. He would not play with his own siblings, he would prefer to play with the twins to be closer to Leila. To see her more than ever. He would join the twins in the field in front of their house, share their marbles, and play. It didn't matter whether he won or not, just seeing her was his victory.

Aziza cooked "bellog", an Assyrian meal, for lunch. She invited the kids to her balcony with stone balustrades and carved railings. Yausef persistently pulled the twins and Leila out to the balcony. Idris and Leila were acting shy. Lokman was playing by pulling the rubber of the slingshot in his hand. Aziza first washed the children's hands with the well water she poured into the ewer. One by one, the children crouched, palms open, and scrambled. They sat at the table shyly. At the table, there was also mint "ayran" beside "bellog". The children were both very hungry and very thirsty. Yausef and his brothers hungrily chewed the "bellog" they were holding like meat. Aziza urged the twins to eat:

"C'mon, guys, help yourself."

They were silent as if they would like to be asked one more time.

"Let's eat," said Aziza again.

"Tsk…"

"Don't be shy, help yourself, eat please."

Lokman shyly took one and ate it gently. Aziza relaxed a little more and boldly insisted to her:

"Yes, my dear Lokman, why don't you eat?"

"I am not Lokman, I am Idris."

"Leila, my dear, what about you?"

"I am not hungry."

Leila lied, though her stomach was growling. "I wished to God" she begged inside herself. Idris was ashamed, looking at the table on the one hand, turning his face to the other side and saying, "tsk".

Aziza refused to insist. "Because of their mother. She definitely told them that my food was haram. Otherwise, why aren't they all eating my food…" she sighed. She did not offer again.

Leila regretted that she said that she was not hungry. She wished she hadn't been so shy.

Idris was starved of embarrassment, he regretted that he was not acting as assertive as Lokman, he was looking at Lokman with envy.

"Oh, if only Aunt Aziza would propose again. How those 'bellogs' would scatter in my mouth, how could the mint 'ayran' cool me…" she imagined.

Yausef handed the piece to Idris and then to Leila's hand.

Seeing the neighbour's children sitting on the terrace with embroidered railings from the back window of her house through the nylon opening, Fatma wailed:

"Come home quickly. What are you doing there? Devil's offspring! I will beat you up; nobody can save you from my hands…"

Aziza had come to the kitchen, leaving the blanks she had carried. She frowned when she saw Fatma.

"They are Fatma's children, Fatma. Can't they play together?"

"No, their religion is different! Come on, I say to you, nasty ones! If you're going to play, play in your own garden!.."

Children were not aware of this distinction and classification at that age.

Fatma gradually poured the poison inside her into her children.

"Which of you went there first?" he asked, waving his slipper in the air.

The twins pointed to each other: "he!"

Idris said, "You are lying. You ate; you didn't even look at me!" They fought with a clamour. Fatma's slipper hit both of their butts.

"Look at you! You devil... Did you eat that woman's food? Go wash your mouth..."

Leila started to do the opposite of what her mother said that afternoon when she was hungry.

"Don't go to that infidel's home again! Her food is haram, don't eat there, it will poison you!" however Leila had eaten her food once and realised it wasn't like that. It was not haram at all; pretty tasty food, she thought.

Aziza even made her swing by hanging a rope from the arch of the house. She always loved Leila like her daughter, as she did not have a daughter of her own. Whenever Leila went to her, she would be beaten with slippers or sticks by her mother at home.

"Let me see you next to that woman again; I'll burn your lungs... Daughter of the Devil!" She herself could not understand the reason for this hatred towards Aziza. Her mother was always disturbed by the presence of her Assyrian neighbours. Fatma was always angry with her father and with Leila herself.

espite her plumpness, Leila was agile and graceful. With her success in school, she had conquered her father's heart. Her mathematical intelligence and her teacher's satisfaction with her aroused his paternal feelings. He used to say he would send his daughter to high school, to Midyat. He was very happy to be the father of a daughter.

"I know my daughter will be a great person," he said, "I will send her to middle school and high school in Midyat and then to university."

"The girl sits at home and straightens her dowry. Why are you sending this girl to school? Read and let be a bitch? It is a sin; it is forbidden... Oh Lord of repentance..."

"What are you talking about, woman! For God's sake, don't say a word anymore..."

Even if Fatma was silent momentarily, she would still interfere with almost every conversation.

Leila had already begun to dream of going to Midyat with the red minibus of the neighbour Abrohom. They would go to school with Yausef, warming their souls. When she saw Yausef, her heart rhythm quickened, she felt as if her heart would explode.

When Leila was only five years old, the only answer she could get from her mother to the questions "What is this, what is that" was "Don't touch".

Leila couldn't think of anything worse than being alone with her. Since Mesut was born, the housework had been left to Leila. The mother once said, "I do all the family's laundry, cook early in the morning, turn on the stove, then do the laundry... Why are you sending this girl to school all the way to Midyat? Look at me; I can't keep up with anything," and cried to Qasim in front of his sons.

Qasim said, "My daughter will be a big person, don't get involved with her," and just smoked his pipe as usual. He had switched from tobacco to a pipe, which he had brought back on his last trip to Iraq.

Qasim no longer enjoyed spending time at home other than reading a book or listening to the radio. When he was condemned to spend time at home, he would start repairing whatever he could get his hands on. The day ended like this, and when a new day started, he would apply the same routine again.

Leila, on the other hand, could not stay close to her father; she had to listen to what her mother said.

"Damn, girl. Get up and help me. Go wash the bed where Mesut peed, and lay it in the sun! Since you were not born a boy, get up and do housework! Damn, I wish I had a stone the day I gave birth to you!"

Leila used to take her father's face; she didn't take her mother seriously. She professionally escaped from Fatma's slippers, which were flying at the speed of fireworks.

Still, out of the desperation of being the only girl in the house, she couldn't help saying, "I wish I had a sister; she would have helped me, and we would have beaten you".

Leila headed to the backyard; her favourite thing about housework was sweeping the backyard. She took the broom in one hand and the dustpan in the other and began to sweep up the brushwood. Then she scattered it around again, swept it again. It could go on like that all day until she got to see Yausef. Leila waited patiently. Yausef appeared at the door with his brothers. Leila lowered her head, speeding up her sweeping. She ignored Yausef as if she had never expected him there. Leila's heart was stirring, and the pain in her soul dissipated.

Leila returned home and cooked mirra for her father. Qasim told her to buy a handleless cup for herself too, and they would sit together and talk about literature and history. Leila served coffee to herself and her father as well. While mırra left her bitterness on her palate, her eyes darkened. Qasim started to tell what he had read in the manner of a historian:

"Some women have brought peace and tranquility to their country. For example, Queen Elizabeth the I. She ruled her country for forty-five years and kept its golden age alive."

Fatma stuck her head out from the inside and muttered her envious words, "Who is that woman?"

"She was the queen of England, Ireland and symbolically France. Even now, there is a woman and a queen at the head of England, and her name is Elizabeth the II."

"I hope to see you there one day, Daddy."

"Why not, my dear? Improve yourself; read, research, listen, watch and travel... Work hard for this, my dear. Travel the world, know that there are other people besides us."

"Is your daughter a bitch, sir? What about marriage, children... Why don't you teach them to her?"

Qasim likened the murmur of the woman sitting just beyond him to the hum of a fly. He sighed and continued talking to his daughter without turning to his wife.

"Queen Elizabeth I never married. She had no children. She became the mother of the people. You get married one day, or you don't; it's up to you, my daughter. Don't listen to anyone, if you are sure of what you know, only you can shape your life. Don't let anyone interfere with your life."

"Muhtar's wife is so rich, but he has no sons." Fatma said, as if talking to herself, "You keep giving birth to girls; what's the meaning of your life Behiye..." "They have put their seventh and last daughter's name as 'Bese', so they wouldn't have any more daughters. Let's see if the girls really end up or not..." Fatma giggled.

Leila tried to reason with her mother's discontent:

"How happy you are! If only you knew how to be grateful! Look, God gave you healthy sons, even twins! You have a hardworking daughter like me, who does the housework. What more do you want from life!"

"Oh you, like the stone on the door. That stone at least serves as a seat for me to rest. What are you good for? Your tongue is like a worn-out shoe," she continued, muttering, "You think your father will always watch over you, huh..."

Qasim ignored them as usual and puffed on his pipe. Qasim started coughing, whether intentionally or because of his damaged lungs. Thus, ended the mother-daughter argument.

Butter was pressed from milk and yoghurt was formed from milk. Sometimes wheat was added to the leftover yoghurt and thus *mehir* was cooked. Children would put molasses in it and eat it for dessert. The cheese was made and stored under the ground in a barn. Since the refrigerator did not exist then, electricity came recently, and they used the ground as a natural cooler. The soil was dampened so that the cheese jar could stay cool. Mud was plastered around the lid of the can, so bugs would not be filled.

Leila would take yoghurt and butter to Midyat with her mother's insistence and sell them to the women at a prearranged location in the market. The woman, who was against her attending school, did not show the same attitude when Leila carried those buckets and had them sold in Midyat bazaar. Leila held her breath as Yausef approached her on the minibus.

"Yeah, fat one, let's get the fees."

Leila rolled her eyes and said, "Aren't you ashamed to ask me for money?"

Yausef said, "No, why should I be ashamed? Business is business; friendship is another thing."

Leila scowled and turned her face towards the window. Yausef unable to resist, "Then give me a kiss," he whispered. Leila was about to faint, but she didn't break down.

"Oh really? Come closer and I'll give it to you."

Yausef brought his face closer and extended his cheek. With all her might, Leila slapped his face with a "crack" sound echoing through the minibus. Those in the minibus sighed to these teenagers who stepped into the youth; on the one hand, they liked that the boy was slapped, so they laughed.

Abrohom was driving; the minibus swayed left and right as he looked behind him in the rearview mirror, all he could ask was, "What's going on, guys?"

"He asks for money from me, Uncle Abrohom."

"No, misunderstood, Dad."

The father said, "My son..." They carried a multitude of potential meanings from this word: anger, decency, a reminder of customs... The passengers could choose whatever they wanted.

"We're going to rematch this, fat girl."

Yausef moved to the front seat, resting his hand on the front seat, occasionally glancing over his shoulder at Leila. She was staring at his reflection in the glass. She couldn't help but smile when she found Yausef's eyes in that reflection.

Leila shyly leaned on the stairs, staring at her father while Qasim was sitting on his stool by the stairs as usual. Qasim realised later that she was sitting next to him.

Qasim noticed his daughter, "What happened, my dear?" Leila didn't make a sound.

"Listen, let me tell you a historical event," said her father, Leila's shyness dissipated.

She nodded, leaning against the wooden ladder and eyeing her father curiously.

Qasim must have been influenced by the book he was reading because he told the Epic of Gilgamesh by living it. He stated that the flood legend in the Epic of Gilgamesh inspired the Odyssey, the first two books of which were sacred and even mentioned in the Hellenic period.

Words (kelam) were sung long and consecutively on Yerevan radio.

"Dad, what are these songs about? You listen every day..."

"Derweş and Adule... Love, struggle, betrayal..." Qasim brought the book from the niche in the wall. He handed the book to his daughter, nodding for her to read.

"Come after you read this; let's discuss it."

Leila found this task enchanting; she could think of no greater pleasure than reading a book with her father. With her chubby fingers, she turned the pages and began to read aloud.

"Derwish is A Yazidi boy, Adule is a Muslim girl... They belong to different faiths, just like Yausef and me..." She muttered to herself and finishing the book within a few hours. She delayed doing housework, which did not resonate with her mother. Qasim still sat in his seat, lost in his book. Leila's expression turned somber.

"Derwish acted a little selfishly... He didn't consider his brother, his friends... all for Adule... Why did he burn the engaged young people with him?"

"It means that love hit him on the head..." Qasim said, laughing mixed with sadness.

"Derwish's father, Evde also fell in love with Adule's aunt, but they could not reunite. Don't people of different faiths ever meet?"

Sighing bitterly, he gazed at his daughter through the haze of his tobacco cigarette:

"Of course, they will..."

"Well, but how?"

"By challenging their families... Believing in themselves... Struggling..."

"It doesn't mean there can be no peaceful reunion..." thought Leila, and continued:

"He challenged the agha by drinking bloody coffee, but isn't it foolish to fight with a sword and shield against the 1700-strong Arab army with twelve people and to think that he will dissolve them?! Shouldn't they be riding horses in the treacherous terrain? The horses' hooves broke, and therefore, they were defeated. Most of these lands are like that; if they were people of this land, they should have known. And as a result, Adule becomes someone else's wife, as the laments say."

"Still, this is our history, and it's all ours, with its faults and sin... There's no harm in learning... We just need to know so we repeat the same mistakes."

"If I were Adule, I would not reach anyone; I would throw myself off the cliff for the love of Mem and Zin. In addition, while one side dramatises the events in the war, the other side plays victorious and enthusiastically describes its victory. However, both are the same. Why is there pain in defeat and joy in victory?"

His daughter's careful, courageous and critical approach was flattering and sought to preserve his seriousness.

"These are the books that should be in every library. Our experiences should not be ignored... Look, Leila, if something happens to me one day, I want you to take care of these books as you would yourself. They are my greatest wealth, and if they gave me all the land, I wouldn't trade my history and literature."

reparations for the wedding of Muhtar's second eldest daughter had begun. The villagers were very excited about the wedding, which would last forty days and nights. Everyone except Muhtar's daughter. She wasn't satisfied to be a married woman who did not like the groom.

No one in the village did not know that Muhtar gave his daughter in exchange for three oxen.

Aziza had sewn a dress for Leila that she had embroidered with her own hand. Despite Fatma's reluctance, Qasim gave a bucketful of butter to Abrohom's wife for her daughter's dress.

Aziza said, "I love her like my daughter. How can I accept that? You are so kind, thank you."

Qasim insisted, and when they didn't take it, he left it at the door. Of course, that bucket did not return empty; it was handed to Fatma with a basket of grapes.

"I know; she filled this basket to spite us and sent it away. That's to say, our land produces more than yours. Here is to say that our vineyards produce beautiful grapes... Don't I know that Christian woman..."

Qasim could not stand it, glaring at her, "Be a human, human!" he said.

Fatma directed her anger at Leila:

"Get up girl; what will we put in the basket they brought us because of your dress? It's not worth it now. It is shameful."

"Put me on. I'll be rid of you."

Qasim smiled vaguely.

Qasim told them to put a duck in the basket. Leila got the most beautiful mottled duck. She also made a bow around its neck with a red ribbon, put it in the basket and handed it to Yausef, who was waiting in the garden. Yausef went up to back stairs, and grabbed Leila by the hand:

"We'll play hand in hand tonight, right?"

"If only my mother didn't come between us and play..."

"What are you waiting for, Leila? Come home soon; we'll go to Muhtar's house," Fatma shouted at her daughter in the backyard through the broken window.

The two young lovers panicked. Leila withdrew her hand from excitement. Yausef lost his balance and fell to the ground with the flower pot. Fortunately, nothing happened to the creature in the basket. He got up from the ground and shook himself. He could hear Leila laughing as she covered her mouth with her hands.

While Leila continued to laugh, she put back the fallen flower, the soil that had been spilled in her pot, and placed it on the ladder.

"Thank God my mother didn't see this. Otherwise, you couldn't imagine what would happen."

The duck's feet were loosely tied, so it got untied. The duck got its chance and immediately fled, and Yausef chased after it. Leila was watching him with laughter.

In the afternoon of that day, they went to Muhtar's house on the main street.

The headman used to take his daughters and give them away only after he taught them at the school in the village. He looked at his daughters as property. He gave his eldest daughter in exchange for five acres of vineyard. No one else wanted the bride price in the village anymore, but Muhtar insisted that a girl without a bride price would not be worth much. When Muhtar continued this tradition, other fathers with daughters would take a face from him. Because of this bride price issue, Qasim brought all villagers who thought like Muhtar against him. He used to lash out at them many times and even fight. But for the girl's father, money and goods were sweeter. There would be no morality.

While Hatice, the daughter of Muhtar, was shedding tears softly, the women of the village thought it was customary. She was crying, wanting nothing of this arrangement, but everyone whispered that the new bride was very coy.

The preparations lasted for days and were mostly holidays for the children. All the village children were screaming and laughing from the bride's house to the groom's house; They went from the groom's house to the bride's house. The ground table was set, and the guests were fed first. Even the headman could not calculate how many lambs he had turned; he was already thinking about when he would plough the field with oxen. The village's soil was unsuitable for tractors, and mechanisation had not yet become widespread.

Since the groom was also from the village, every street in the village was festive. The groom shaved, tipped; took a bath, tipped; shoes stolen, tipped; shirt soiled, tipped; drummer and zurna player also got their tips. The headman had already paid all the wedding expenses, except for the oxen, which were paid by the groom. He didn't even put his hand in his pocket for the bride's preparations.

The bride couldn't walk because of the weight of the jewellery she wore, and no one understood that she was so weak from crying.

"Muhtar's daughters are also very cute, my dear", the village women said, "should they not get married and die at home?" they were told.

Although Muhtar had a lot of money, he never bought a horse because he could not ride because of his excess weight. Mustafa's horse was very useful in the village. They decorated the horse beautifully.

The groom tipped again. The bride struck the money with the back of her hand.

"She wants more," they murmured, and the groom held out two full gold coins. When the headman took a side glance at his daughter, they forced the "delicate bride" onto the ride.

Old women were sticking their heads out of the evenly spaced windows of their one-story adobe houses and clapping their hands. The children roared forward to play. The youngsters were rallying rhythm with arbane and tambourines in their hands. The drummer was at the forefront, beating the drum with all his might in a sweat. The children, who did not like the noise very much, scrambled away from the drummer, covering their ears. They threw candy at the bride through the window. The children, attacking here and there like chicks scurrying out of the coop, gathered candy on the ground, causing the crowd to stampede.

They arrived at the wedding square. Most of the elders were lined up in chairs, looking happy. The elders had rosaries made of olive seeds, and they uttered Salawat as they drew the rosary grains.

They served buttermilk (ayran), which they shook in sheepskin for three or four hours by crushing ice. The village guests drank the cool buttermilk and prepared to dance halay.

Men were dark coloured; some were striped, linen baggy pants and white linen shirts. The belt on their waist was patterned, mottled and mostly dark in black, navy blue, brown and green. Some wore vests, and others did not because they could not withstand the heat. They were dressed in pouffes on their heads. They were shaved like a groom and splashed cologne on themselves.

The women and the girls were all dressed in a wide variety of sequined and tulle local clothes. Muhtar's previous daughter had the same outfits at her wedding, but at this wedding, her outfits were swapped with each other. The women wore shimmering dresses with sleeves that swept the floor, over plain suspenders, with wings that stretched from her sleeves to her back and were tied there like ribbons. The dresses were vibrant and brightly coloured. The front part of the dress, which was worn over the top, was embroidered throughout. Only the bride wore red, and the rest wore whatever colour was available in nature. No matter how sleek and shiny their robes were, their shoes were, on the contrary, shrivelled and covered in mud. Their faces were covered with powder and makeup. Their heads seemed detached from their bodies. Unmarried girls, whose lips looked like red roses on their porcelain-painted faces, were looking at the village's single men with charcoal-black eyes. They were passing in front of them with their distinctive features accentuated.

Single youths were glowing like lightbulbs. Thin girls looked sickly, so the plump ones for girls' flesh were acceptable. However, Leila was unaware of this; she was gaining weight despite her mother.

Sweat dripped onto the drum, which the drummer was beating incessantly. The drummer also looked as if his face was swollen and bruised, almost like he would explode from blowing. While they were resting a little, it was time for the Kemenche player. When the girls in kaftans and bindalis lined up, the festival of colours took place. Men, too, appeared on the folkloric scene in shalwar and white linen shirts.

They were dancing halay, and there were a few people between Yausef and Leila. As Yausef swept them away, he added another, taking them to the other side. One turned out to be very stubborn.

"Get away from us."

"Why?"

"Get out, I'm telling you."

"In exchange for a bottle of wine," the peasant said with cunning. Yausef agreed. While he was about to pass another one, this time, Leila told him to pass to the other side. Just then, the music ended. Leila and Yausef stood there for a while. They followed the Kemenche player with their pleading eyes. After tucking the tip into his belt, the kemenche player continued from where he left off, and the youngsters continued to jump at the same level they had left.

"Jump, fatty, jump, you'll lose some grams," Yausef was grinning, even happier than the groom on this wedding night.

The lyrics of the songs sung at the wedding were often either erotic or political.

The commander and a couple of gendarmes were there to control. His fear discouraged the villagers. To avoid the trouble of the gendarmerie, they tried not to venture into other topics, while singing as much as they could.

n the village, scorpions could come out of unexpected places. That's why the beds were always shaken before they were made. Scorpions love closed places. Especially, no matter what, they would hide in closed-toed shoes and wait for human feet to sting. The peasant, who shook his shoes madly in the air, would crush his toes when he was not convinced; to see if there was a scorpion in them. A girl had been stung on her feet by a scorpion when she had unwittingly put on her father's big shoes. Her body turned petrified, and her tongue numbed. She was passed through the hands of experienced women without being brought to the hospital immediately. The peasant women had treated the girl in their own way.

When they encountered a health problem in the village, they first tried to be treated with folk remedies. If that didn't work, the patient woul be taken to the health institution in Midyat by the minibus of their Christian neighbours, and if there is no solution, they would be taken to the hospital in Mardin by car. If no solution was found in Mardin, they would go to Diyarbakır Training and Research Hospital. Whether they understood it or not, the candidate doctors would make it up somehow. Still, if there was no treatment there, they would immediately surrender to the hands of intern doctors in one of the training and research hospitals in Istanbul. Now that place would be the last stop for human health. Finally, they were brought to the cemetery with shapeless obelisks.

Samuel, who was only seven years old, fell ill with measles and his short life was completed before he could be brought to the hospital in Mardin.

Aziza had been distraught for weeks. She couldn't help herself not to cry and scream. Losing her youngest son was a devastating tragedy for her and Abrohom.

"Oh well! One boy was missing from the family."

Mustafa was harsh on his mother:

"Mom, what are you talking about? What if it was one of my brothers? If they were happy with this condition, what would you say?"

"God forbid, my child," she said, looking at Leila, spewing hatred. Qasim came in; it was hot. He sensed the gloomy air, but first, needing rest, Qasim sat cross-legged on the ground.

"Mustafa, son, we will go to pay our condolences with your brothers; get ready soon."

Mustafa lowered his head and nodded.

"It looks like your funeral; God bless. What happened to you on Earth!"

"Okay, no more Fatma! Now is not the time! And yes, it is our funeral. They are closer than my own relatives. Do you get this? Now, go and make tea first, then cook for your neighbour. Let Idris and Lokman distribute tea to their condolence guests," said Qasim solemnly.

"She doesn't care; because they are Christians, she thinks I should cook alone," said Leila.

"If I ever catch you, I'll pull your hair out, girl!"

"Fatma! Have some consideration!" said Qasim, as if "I am here; how dare you speak such a thing to my daughter."

She started to cry, saying, "Sir, don't you see what she's saying to me right in front of you?" Trying to take advantage of Qasim's emotionality, she turned to take her anger out on Leila again.

"Get up, girl; you're not saying that your father is here; my father is thirsty; let me get him a glass of water for this funeral!"

Leila got up from her seat with fury and poured water from the can into the glass. While walking angrily, she handed her father half a glass of water. After the father drank the water, he returned the empty glass to his daughter, who was waiting.

Father and sons left for the neighbour's funeral.

Leila deliberately rubbed her feet on the ground as she passed in front of her mother, scattering dust clouds up the rug.

"How dusty these rugs are. Leila! Let me look at this outside when your fathers leave for condolences."

In the village's small church, the ritual was still going on. Qasim was with Abrohom.

In front of the condolence house, village-style plastic chairs were gathered from the neighbours and arranged in a circle so everyone could see each other. The heat obviously warped the chairs from the summer. Everyone was there except the Christians. The villagers were seated on plastic chairs of an assortment of colours. They had the traditional pooch on their heads, protecting them from the cold and heat. They were waiting in the shade of the apple trees on a bright day.

Silence prevailed. Others were playing the snare drum with their fingers on the plastic arm of the chair. As if they were waiting for someone to speak.

Despite her mother, Leila did as her father said and made tea quickly and prepared it in a large aluminium teapot. When the trump card under the teapot in the garden started to burn out and go out, the smoke was coming out, and it was moving towards those waiting for condolences in front of the next-door neighbour. Leila blew on embers with all her might, making it burn again. The twins had gone to collect tea cups to serve tea to the villagers. When Muhtar saw Leila there, he twisted his moustache and could not understand the fast growth of the girl. Even when he saw her at the second daughter's wedding, he noticed her immediately.

The headman turned towards the tent, raised his hands, and greeted the villagers. When the headman lost his balance in his chair, he fell to the side, and the leg of the chair under him broke. The people beside him grabbed Muhtar by the arms and lifted him with difficulty. When some villagers laughed, the canine tooth they had made of gold appeared. He had invested in his teeth.

Qasim warned Muhtar, "This weight will cause trouble, Muhtar. All of them are diseases. It's a shame."

"Look at you," he said, waving his hand in the air. The headman was so overweight that his baggy trousers were slipping down, his shirt and underwear were coming up, and his thick waist was exposed like a pumpkin.

Qasim and the notables of the village were discussing politics there too. They talked about whatever came to mind, from pulling the agenda to how we could work the land.

After the mass, Yausef also helped Mustafa. They poured tea into the tea glasses lined up on the tray. Leila was also eating tea as it ran out. Yausef and Leila's hands accidentally touched each other, and they were startled, as if tea spilled on their hands.

According to the number of Muslims, food aid was also given to the condolence house. Muslim neighbours did the same. Sugar, flour, wheat, bulgur, chickpeas... They shared whatever they had in their houses. This was the custom... Just as they did at weddings, the customs of this village were adhered to without any discrimination between Muslims and Christians, and they shared the means at their disposal.

Leila's body lines had become obvious. Leila's world would have crumbled if she hadn't run into Yausef one day. Her desire for intimacy curled up like cabbage leaves as she walked in. Getting over her mother and meeting Yausef required a lot of somersaults and pink lies. She was bored while waiting in this house, where she spent her time outside of school, to the point where she felt suffocated.

She was disregarding all the customs she had learned so that she could spend time with the boy. She was a Muslim girl. Her breasts were prominent, she was almost a woman now, she came from a feudal family... Leila let these concerns go one ear and out the other.

One of their neighbours said they often saw Leila and Yausef in secret places. Fatma burst into a fury; she held a stick and waved it at Leila, who was doing her homework next to her father.

"I will kill you! What are you doing with that Syriac boy? I will cut your legs to pieces!"

Leila jumped up and hid behind her father.

"Stop it, woman! How dare you, even in front of me!"

Qasim looked at the girl behind him, with a look to see if what his mother said was true.

"There is no such thing, Father. We are in the same school as Yausef, he helps me with my homework because he is in the upper class".

"Homework, huh! Why would you make an infidel do homework when you have siblings? I'll show you now!"

"Stop, woman, stop."

Grabbing the stick from where he was sitting, Qasim broke it in two with his knee.

"This girl is so spoiled. It's all because of you... When she becomes a bitch tomorrow, you'll beat your knee, not your daughter!"

"Fatma, be decent! She comes and goes with my neighbour's son, whom I love like them, even more than my relatives. They are still very young. What is she going to get so angry about!"

Qasim gave the necessary answer, but Fatma could not keep quiet. She was muttering to herself.

"So you take shelter behind your father, huh? Do you think he will always be with you? One day you will get it... You'll see..."

Leila felt that she had let her father down and kissed her father on the cheek, "I'm sorry, Daddy."

"I know you didn't do anything bad, girl. Just be careful, don't give the villagers supplies."

Fatma's murmur continued:

"Trust your daughter; let us get in trouble and see! I wish I had given birth to a stone instead of giving birth to you!"

"Fatma, if you don't shut up, I'll get up and put you under my feet," he said with a wink at his daughter to show that he wasn't serious.

Before time stood still, she created another event and handled the situation.

"Come here, girl, set the table. Am I going to put some food to fill your stomach too!" she said and continued, muttering, "One day you'll get to me. I will end your life. Not even Azrael can save you from my hand."

The red minibus was running and waiting, Abrohom would collect the villagers going to the city or the children going to school every morning and take them to Midyat. On his return in the evening, he would take the grown ones and bring them to the village. The minibus was an incomparable blessing for the village. In sickness, he was always at their disposal on a visit. Abrohom also went to the silver shop, sometimes alone, sometimes with his son Benjamin.

"Yeah, Bro let me call her. Leila! Come on girl, run, don't make your uncle Abrohom wait too long!"

Leila's skirts caught fire; she tied her shoes casually and jumped. She ran back to the house as if she had forgotten her lesson notebook.

"Beware of the pressed carpets; I will cut off your feet!"

She walked around the rug with one foot, staggering around the bottom of the wall, reaching her bag, hooking it on her arm, and jumping around with the other foot, again in the same direction, around the rug.

"Don't tell me to sit next to that boy. Sin! It is not permissible in our religion!"

She ignored her mother's call. She kissed his father's hand and ran to the bus. When she got on the red minibus, she sat next to Yausef, who was empty, and she stuck to Yausef and stuck her tongue out to her mother.

Qasim laughed wearily at her daughter's battle with her mother.

"For God's sake, Fatma, what comes to your mind..."

"You always spoil her. Look, she went in front of you and sat next to that Christian boy. You know manners, you know our traditions..."

Qasim opened his hands and looked up with a pleading look to Allah.

Yausef and Leila's arms caressed each other along the short road, warming themselves in their dreams. They looked in different directions and grinned, enjoying their shirts touching each other. They followed each other's movements with their ears.

While walking around with his hands in his pockets in the Midyat market, Lokman found money on the ground. Instinctively he hid the money with his foot, and as he bent over it, his father's teaching came to his mind. When he finds the coin on the ground, he should raise it in the air and say, "Whose money is this" three times so that the owner can be found, but if the owner is not found, then the money would be his own without being considered haram. Lokman peeped around him with Jinn and saw many pairs of feet. He squeezed the coin in his palm, raised it to his chest, and muttered:

"Whose money is this, whose money is this, whose money is this."

No one's spirit even heard.

He transferred the money from his hidden palm to his pocket. He put his hand on the money he had put in his pocket. He wanted to make sure it was there. His pockets, which were raised at the edges, radiated warmly to him like a mother's breast. Confident of the money in his pocket, he rushed out of there and burst into Abrohom's silver shop.

Abrohom noticed her as she was about to lower her silver boxes.

"My son, Idris, here you go."

"I am Lokman, Uncle Abrohom."

Benjamin was also dealing with the other two customers, eyeing Lokman out of the corner of his eye. He didn't even say hello.

"I'm always sorry to confuse you, my son. Here, what do you want?"

Lokman glanced at the hand-embroidered filigree silvers on the hanging window. He wanted to buy a gift for his girlfriend, he thought. Abrohom showed him the pendants. Lokman felt like testing them all by touching them. On the one hand, Abrohom expressed his concern that Lokman was suffering.

"Lokman son, are you looking after your animals in the pasture or your twin?"

"It changes sometimes," he said, focusing on the pendants. At that moment, he was living the love again.

"Your animals always go astray, they enter our vineyard, my son. They plundered the grapes. Because of them, we won't be able to do the vintage this year. My son, watch your herd carefully. By Allah, I will not be able to step foot in the house because of my lady's nagging."

Lokman seemed to like a pendant. His mind was still on Muhtar's daughter, whom he was in love with.

"If I see your father, I will tell him, actually, but I can't find the opportunity to tell him. Anyway, leave this issue to me. Don't take this as a complaint, son. My problem is not the vineyard or garden, I worry about our peace with my lady."

"This necklace, Uncle Abrohom, how much is that?"

"My son, did you hear me?" He put his hands on the counter and sighed, "I think you're going to gift it to your girlfriend."

"No to my mother…"

Abrohom laughed.

"Okay okay, let's keep your money in your pocket. Instead, buy a sherbet with it."

Abrohom adjusted the chain to fit the pendant, wrapped a stylish gift and handed it to Lokman:

"Don't forget, my son, our peace with my lady you know…"

Lokman forgot even to thank him and ran out of the shop.

"I think everything you said was in vain, Father. Look, he didn't even care about it."

"What should we do, son, other than to warn him?"

"It would be a lesson to them if we injured one of their goats. That dog especially lets his herd graze there. Idris is not like him. I don't think Idris does that."

Indeed, to distinguish the twins, one had to pay attention to their characters.

"Okay, Benjamin, now is not the time. I'll tell Qasim privately. A customer has arrived. Let's attend to them."

Leila and Yausef began to meet frequently. On the mountain, on the slope; in the city, in the village… They flourished as young people, alive like blooming flowers, fluttering like butterflies. Surely they would find a place to meet. In order not to be caught, they would not return to the same place. Sometimes they would look into each other's eyes without speaking and smile strangely.

"Now, when you sin and commit and then confess to the church, to the priest, all sins are erased?"

"How it is believed that all sins committed during a year are erased in one night, on the Night of Power…"

"You know they won't get us married easily, right? My mother said that if a Muslim woman marries a Christian, it's a sin. We will either convert or sin."

"Then you will be my most marvellous sin, my sin that I can't get you out of me easily…"

Leila's face was changing strangely, she liked what Yausef said very much.

While they were waiting for the minibus, giggling after school, Idris pulled his sister by her arm and took her to the side.

"You see him very often. If my mother hears..."

"He won't hear if you don't say it."

"If you are not careful, someone else will tell her, not me. Watch out, Leila, you will make me your murderer."

"Don't be too hard on Leila, Idris. She is the last person I will harm."

"You shut up. If you do something to upset her, you're already..."

"What, me?"

"I'll circumcise it, even from the bottom."

Yausef's father was driving the minibus, approaching them and stopping. One by one, the young people sat down on the minibus. They did not talk to each other in the minibus that was going on the dirt road of the village.

The apple trees in the garden, which Qasim looks after like his children every day, turned green with the arrival of spring. Birds chirped,breaking the stillness of the village with their sounds.

He was fixing the radio and hadn't heard any news of the sizzle in days. When you put the tape in your hand to one ear, you hear the sound, and when you say it's okay, the frequency disappears again. After a while, as a result of perseverance, he succeeded and started listening to the 13.00 news on the radio. The article talks about Saddam Hussein's atrocities and his chemical weapons.

"A chemical weapon?" said Qasim in surprise, the radio sizzling again, unintelligible. In the end, he decided to go to Muhtar's house. He walked on the only asphalt road in the village. Neck and crop, he went to Muhtar's house with steps running down this road. Muhtar's door was wide open. Half the villagers were there, sitting next to each other. They were listening to the news on Yerevan radio.

When Qasim spent his time reading at home, he would be the last to know what was happening in the village. He learned that two hundred people had died in Halabja the previous day. He could not hear any villagers for a while from his heartbeats; he could not believe what he heard. The announcer, who voiced the Halabja

Massacre, confirmed it by mentioning the name of Saddam Hussein. Blood gushed into Qasim's brain. He heard that more than five thousand people had lost their lives. More than seven thousand were injured. "The smell of apples…" said one of the villagers. Qasim did not understand; he looked at the villager with questioning eyes.

"Saddam threw an apple-scented chemical," said the next villager.

The marrow in his bones seemed to dissolve. His throat tightened, his eyes burning. Qasim was shaken to all his cells, he left immediately and ran home. Cold sweat was running down his face, being soaking into his collar. He picked up the axe he had grabbed from the side of the house and walked towards the garden.

Fatma watched her husband with astonished eyes. Leila had milked from the goats when she saw her father like that. She dropped the bucket on the ground and ran after him.

Qasim lifted the axe with all his might and slammed it into the waist of the apple tree. He wailed as if taking his anger out on the tree. He was screaming and swinging the axe to the tree's trunk. Leila was surprised by what she saw, seeing her heroic father crying for the first time. She covered her ears and looked the other way not to hear her father's cries of pain. The tree fell with difficulty. Fatma caught up with him, "My dear, are you crazy? What are you doing!"

Qasim, so that the whole village could hear, shouted "He threw chemicals in Halabja… Saddam… He killed innocent people… He killed… Again and again…" He was saying on the one hand and lowering the axe on the tree's waist.

Fatma could not untie the connection between what she heard and Qasim's actions. Mustafa appeared and tried to prevent his father at that moment, but it was too late.

"What does it have to do with the apple tree, Daddy!" he said.

"Chemical, apple-scented..." Qasim shed tears as his shoulders shook. Mustafa hugged his father's waist and rested his shoulder on his chest.

After that day, no more apples would come into the house.

"In Iraq, which was under the rule of King Faisal until July 1958, Abdulkerim Qasim and his friends carried out a military coup and ended the reign. He sentenced the king and prime minister to death. The people were hopeful when he invited General Mustafa Barzani to the country. The disagreement between the two disappointed the public. Unfortunately, hopes were dashed to this day," Qasim sighed to his closest friend Abrohom next to him.

Qasim was very upset and he could say something wrong.

"Please be patient Mr Qasim. Nothing will change if you get yourself ill," said Abrohom.

Abrohom could spend less time with Qasim, as he went on his minibus daily to the silver jewelry shop in Midyat. Although he said he would always support him in everything, he was sure he would not find a cure for Qasim's problem.

He would often stop by Qasim's every evening and tell the news about the situation in the city. He used to express hurtful words in his speeches. No matter what Abrohom did, Qasim's face was not smiling.

Qasim didn't listen to anyone around him. He would like to go to Iraq again, and he couldn't bear to stand up anymore. He was ill for weeks from the failed results of the revolution.

His ideals, which had not been realised for years, greatly saddened Qasim. Using his family as an excuse, he gave up the revolution and tried to re-establish life in his village. He also took credit for the reasons the revolution did not occur. He blamed himself for days; he was exhausted.

After the felled tree, the courtyard looked barren. Easter was to be celebrated in April of that year. A bittersweet feast passed after the massacre. Assyrians continued their own culture in silence.

Leila had sneaked up to Aziza and had black writing on her head. They laid eggs and dyes brought by the chickens from under them. First, the egg pierced the bottom with a needle, and Leila watched and applied it. They poured the egg into a bowl, put it in a shell state in vinegary water and waited. They prepared the paints and drew and painted shapes and patterns on the eggshell. She loved painting too much.

Leila was quite happy; she had never thought of her mother at that moment, and she was content with the present moment. She took home the eggs she painted and the products she made. She was hiding them behind her back. She was going to gift it to his father and brothers. After hanging the laundry on the roof, Fatma went down the wooden stairs to the house. When she saw Leila bouncing like a gazelle in the garden, she called out:

"Where have you been? I hung these laundries and now I have to go look after the herd!"

Leila was afraid to hide her easter eggs behind her, unsure if they were broken, praying inside that they didn't break.

"Nothing. I was around."

"Where are you going without telling me? Hold on, what's behind you?"

"Nothing…"

"Show me, show me…" She caught up to her and pulled her hand away. One of the eggs fell, and Fatma stepped on it:

"What are you doing with these eggs? These are wicked things! Let me see the others."

She cracked all the eggs into pieces, unable to contain her anger. She grabbed the hair of her daughter, who was taller than her now, and slapped her on the cheeks.

"Will you be a bitch in this family!"

If only her father had seen and heard Fatma beating her by the hair at that moment. Fatma knew that Qasim would take all his anger out on her.

Leila both had her eggs and had her share of beatings.

Qasim was dealing with the partridges. Heartbroken hearing the cries, he jumped out of the henhouse.

Leila was moaning in pain. Noticing the eggshells crumbling on the ground, he hurried to Fatma. He grabbed her arm. He squeezed.

"What have you done again!"

"My lord! She goes there without telling me. Now that she's a teenage girl, there are teenage boys. What will we do if someone rapes her? Don't you ever think about that?"

Qasim was enraged, his sunken cheeks tense.

"If you touch my daughter again, I will divorce you, do you understand? I swear I will…"

Qasim saw the smashed-coloured shells on the floor, Fatma was afraid she would be beaten, so she covered her face with her hands. He wailed.

"Do not beat me, sir. I am the mother of your children. I was educating our daughter so that she wouldn't be harmed."

"You are not human! May God not be pleased with my deceased elders; they made you my wife."

He grabbed her daughter's hand and pulled her around her neck. He kissed Leila's hair. The crowing of partridges could be heard:

"You know, Dad, I didn't love that woman as my mother for a single day, and I won't," she said, sobbing, "I will never be sad if she dies. I hate her."

Qasim is squeaky. "Your mother is your mother, even if she is bad... A daughter does not fail to show respect to her mother and father; she does not hate them. Hate separates us; love unites us. Agreed, dear?"

Leila pressed her lips together and did not say anything. She nodded.

The decorated partridges kept crowing to calm Leila.

"Look, these partridges... The oldest one rules the others."

"Which one? How do we know which one is old and experienced, Dad?"

"The one with the big head, the adult partridges, have bigger heads than the others."

He managed to make Leila laugh.

"When there is danger, the male partridge will fight to the death to protect his female offspring. If there is no male partridge, the female partridge will... Even in animals, such is the instinct of protection."

"We just painted eggs with Aunt Aziza, Dad; there was no one at home, I swear."

The red-billed partridges were flapping their black-striped wings and adding sound to their chirping.

The next day, Lokman, one of the twins, was walking home in the village square, whistling, with his hands in his pockets. When Aziza saw him, she called out from her balcony:

"Idris, my son?"

"I am Lokman, Aunt Aziza."

"Oh, well, sorry, dear. Come and take these plates home. You will eat after."

Lokman rushed up the stone stairs two by two from the vault's entrance.

"God bless you, my son. Let's enjoy ourselves. Is pouring okay? I also put it for Mr. Qasim. Say hi to him a lot."

Lokman entered through the blue-painted steel door with a plate in his hand. He took slow steps, containing Easter buns and rice pudding. He walked carefully so as not to spill the rice pudding in the bowls.

"What have you got?"

"Aunt Aziza sent it."

"My God, why do my children always go to the next-door neighbourhood?"

Qasim seemed to hear the hum of flies. He nodded as he read the book. Leila was reading the Turkish composition Mustafa had written under her arm. She felt herself under her brother's wing.

Idris went for a jog and poured the tea.

"It was a holiday dessert… They don't eat meat for fifty days. I wouldn't feel alive if I didn't eat meat."

The twins greedily spooned the rice pudding. Tea was brewed and brought. They served tea with Easter buns.

"Don't eat too much. You might get poisoned. God bless…"

At her third buzz, Qasim could not stand it; he opened his mouth:

"What are you talking about there again? These blessings are sweets brought according to their beliefs. They respect you; why don't you respect them? Why this hatred?"

Day after day, the cough made it difficult for Qasim to speak.

Fatma stared blankly; she had never thought of the answer to this question. Because even if she thought, she couldn't find the answer. They didn't stay quiet, and they made up talk:

"The Halabja Massacre is still being mourned, and Christian families are worried about the holiday. They have everything, of course, do they ever worry about themselves…"

He threw that "I can't bear you out now" look and took his tea. He got up and limped forward to the coop of partridges. After him, Leila, little Mesut and the twins took their tea and muffins in their hands, floundered like partridges, and followed their father. Mustafa was there, cross-legged on the cushion, looking at his mother in amazement:

"Why are you upsetting my father on purpose, Mother? Can't you say a bad word about them for once?"

Mustafa regretted what he had said at that minute. It was not known which aspect of Fatma had sprinkled so much liquid. She cried and cried.

"You have all become fathers. What am I in this house? I'm not worth as much as a piece of trash. I'm mommy, mom! Who carried you in his womb for nine months!" she was hitting her chest mercilessly, "I'm fed up; I feed you from morning to night, I wash your clothes, I take care of all your troubles again. Not even you, but the animals as well. Your father has no job; he always goes to those birds, and he doesn't even listen to me. What am I, huh, what am I…"

Qasim could no longer remain silent to Fatma's shouts and rebellion and turned to Mesut:

"Son, run, call your brother to come here. Save Mustafa…"

The summer heat was long. It would take courage to sleep inside the houses, just in the season when the snakes heat up. Sleeping in the house was not considered very safe, and since it was a pleasure to sleep on the roofs, a throne was prepared on the roof of almost every house.

Leila would take it out at the hour that Aziza was on the roof, while making the beds, and pull the mosquito net around the throne. She watched her next-door neighbours, her beloved family, wondering what they were doing, eating, drinking, even talking.

"I wonder if Yausef told his mother or siblings about me..." she thought.

She memorised Yausef's every move. She always followed what he was laughing at, what he liked very much, and what he wore. That's why she didn't make the beds right away. She acted slowly and slowly. The longer she lingered, the more she would see her beloved, even for a second.

She tucked the bed sheet under her knee under the mat, keeping her eyes on the roof. Yausef was helping his mother while his other siblings were helping with the domestic chores... Aziza's sons would help, as she had no daughters.

"Oh, how nice... So he will be a good husband and help me in the future. We will lay the cover of our bed together and do everything together," Leila dreamed.

She met Aziza's eyes and couldn't help but smile. She dreamed that she was her future mother-in-law. How lucky was Leila! She already loved her so much, and so she did. They called each other from afar and asked how they were. Fatma had already heard about them:

"Leila, shake the beds well, spread them a lot. God forbid there will be a scorpion or something..." she interrupted.

Aziza did not show her emotions that she had lost her child because of a scorpion. She just saluted Fatma. Although Aziza saluted, her greeting remained in the air. Fatma came in and continued cooking where she had left off. She started talking to herself.

"Their throne is iron; ours is wooden... Even their beds are different, posche!"

Abrohom had carved separate wrought iron for himself and his wife and had his sons sculpted and welded a larger wrought iron throne.

Leila had memorised the colour of their beds and duvets. She wondered which way Yausef was looking, which side he was using. She wanted to go under the same colour satin duvet under the same sky. Thus, they would cover the sky and the same quilt over them. Side by side, they would feel each other's breath; they would close their eyes with happiness and open them with happiness.

The stars hung sluggishly in the velvet dark blue sky.

They fell asleep at night with the croaking of frogs and woke up in the morning with the bleating of sheep.

She poked her head out from under the mosquito net and looked in that direction to see Yausef on the roof. She was curious if they had woken up too, or were they still in their beautiful sleep... In the dark of the night, she couldn't see what he was wearing, but this time her eyes were alive because she could see with her bright eyes during the day.

In the heat of that summer, the villagers got through the hot sun season by taking a nap in their homes to avoid being scorched. When September came, activity started again in the village. The first month of autumn also had its share of sun, yet their faces burned gently.

The wheat used to be dried in the warehouses since May. In the first week of September, they boiled the wheat and ran like every year.

As soon as the village children left the school, they would run towards the area where the smoke was rising. They had already brought stone plates from their homes. If the way to get rid of the children surrounding the wheat-boiling cauldron was a big colander for each child of the neighbourhood, they love very much, two large colanders of wheat were placed on the plates and bowls between the children's hands. They added margarine and salt to the gifts and ate them hungrily.

The boiled wheat was dried in the sun for two days. They made stuffed meatballs by breaking some of it on a mortar stone; and reserved some of it for edible bulgur. Some of it was taken to the mill and turned into flour, the main consumed bread in the village. That's why wheat flour was essential for everyone. After the wheat mill, mortar stones formed a decoration in front of the doors. The unboiled wheat took its place in the barn to be sprinkled on the field again.

On the one hand, they cut the noodles to mix with bulgur. The dough was kneaded. The young and unmarried girls of the village came because their fingers were thinner than the other women, and they helped each other in a collaborative fashion. They gathered the kneaded dough in their palms, dipped their fingers in oil, shrunk it with their thumb and forefinger, and turned it into a wire. The young girl who cut the thinnest noodle would become famous in the village. Her praises would circulate even in the surrounding villages. It would be the subject of the Dengbejs and take its place in the words. Women with adult sons would insist that she was the bride they were looking for and would go after him. The fortunes would be lined up at the door.

Young and virgin girls cut the noodles as if they were competing with each other. They competed fiercely to reveal all their ingenuity.

The cut vermicelli was put in a sacca and fried. Rice was mixed into bulgur. Bulgur pilaf was a must for the main course at least three days a week. The young girls swelled their breasts with the praise they received and went home with their hips twisted.

Mustafa was jogging with his friends. None of their horses were as fast, agile and noble as Mustafa's horse Auburn. They were strolling behind the hill. They were young lads, each sitting proudly on their horse. From the village streets they passed randomly, they saw young girls coming from the opposite direction. They were returning from helping their neighbours and cutting noodles. In order not to look at them—it was considered rude to look at them—the young cavalrymen passed by, turning away.

One of the girls had a porcelain face and attractive eyes and received so much praise that she walked proudly and confidently among the other girls. With her glass eyes, she sighed at Mustafa, sitting upright on a velvety-red earth-coloured horse with strong arms, and parted her voluptuous lips. She managed to attract Mustafa's piercing gaze on her. The sun-haired girl, who separated from her other friends with her beauty, was embroidered in Mustafa's heart.

As if his eyes were enchanted, Mustafa dragged his eyes to the same spot, thinking that the girl was smiling at him, turned his face towards her, and then looked again. The girls had passed them, and the pretty-faced, rose-lipped girl turned around again and smiled. Mustafa replied, too, his white teeth showing.

When his friends crossed the street, they showered Mustafa with "wow ". They teased him and made fun of him. They rested on the stony creek that quenched the thirst of the villagers.

Mustafa and his friends rode to the village at every opportunity, rested by the stream and shared their news with each other. The subject came to Mustafa as if his mind was not there. His transducers were turned up enough to hear almost the entire area, but he could only hear his friends.

Women were carrying water on donkeys to their homes. They kept telling each other about the vaguely blond-haired, blue-eyed girl.

It matched the description of the girl he saw. They kept saying, "Sileman's daughter, Sileman's daughter"...

Mustafa heard the women talking twenty paces away rather than the purring of his friends. It was as if the murmur of the creek was also confirming the women.

"Soon, his fortune will open. I haven't seen anyone cut noodles that well either."

"She is a good girl, by God."

"It is so. Fortunately, she will find a husband."

"I think she will get married in a few months. No one misses that girl."

Fire burst into Mustafa's brain, lava came out of his ears, his eyes froze, his heart would burst. He had learned that he would miss her if he didn't act quickly for the girl he liked. That girl should have belonged to Mustafa. Right now…

He woke up to his friends making fun of him.

"Oh man, what are we saying, where is your mind?"

"He's definitely obsessed with that blonde."

"Sorry, guys. The fire fell down the chimney. I have to find that girl."

His friends fell silent, questioning Mustafa with their eyes: "Right now?"

He thought he would miss the sun-crowned blonde beauty if he didn't find her. They hurriedly put their heads together with their youth strategy and came up with a plan for Mustafa. It was about to be evening. They had little information; a good noodle cutter, blonde and Sileman's daughter.

It was not difficult to find her in the village, they found her as they laid eyes on her. The village was small, everyone knew each other. Even if the bird was asked, he would show Sileman's house.

His friends whistled to Mustafa, and they gathered back to the point where they had met. Whirling around on his horse, the shrewd young man said excitedly:

"Her name is Suheyla."

"Where did you learn that right away?"

"Thanks to the girl at the fountain," he said, laughing at his cowardice. They also learned about Sileman's house. After that, it was up to Mustafa.

He waited for Suheyla in the village as if lying in an ambush. She must have had siblings because three young girls were leaving the same house and going to another house. The young girl dropped her scarf, Mustafa bent down, took the colourful scarf and called to the girl, "Suheyla!"

Everyone froze, he shouldn't have said that name, but he did. They thought that if their father heard, they would be beaten until the donkey came out of the water.

Still, he did not lose his composure, and Mustafa called her, "The most beautiful girl of the seven villages, Suheyla."

Suheyla left her sisters behind, and they fled a short distance, covering their mouths with cheesecloths/scarfs, but even Mustafa could hear their giggles.

Suheyla froze where she was but still looked over her shoulder with confidence. Mustafa got off the horse and started his first conversation with her. They were released into the gravitational pull of love as if they had known each other for years.

Mustafa has never been this close to his mother, he mostly prefers to be with Qasim, plays with his father, does business with his father, and goes on walks with his father. Fatma was proud to have her eldest son with her.

To avoid breaking this spell, she listened to Mustafa with both ears.

"She is such a beautiful girl that she raises the dead, mother. I want to marry her if my father consents. I think you'll love her too."

"How do you know? You've already changed into a girl you don't know well. I'm your mother, no one can replace me."

"Mother, my dear mother. She is so talented that she helped the whole village and became the best noodle cutter. I heard this with my own ears. Tell my father to ask for it from me, please…"

Fatma was already delusional when it was said, "Who cuts noodles". The boy almost begged his mother to persuade him to talk to his father. He was so caught up in her love that he gave up his courage, pride, and depth.

Now it was Fatma's turn to play her sneaky tricks.

Controversial gossip was inevitable for women while waiting in line at the tandoor. There were large rose-patterned, flower-printed festoons on them. They reflected the vivid colours they received from nature on them.

"If we get our son married, it will be a hassle my dear Qasim. Besides, he likes Mustafa... It will be more suitable for him." While saying that, she stuck the dough she had opened on the heated wall in the tandoor. Embers glowed calmly red at the bottom. The women gathered in the tandoor looked at each other and smiled.

"So, do you have a girl in mind?"

"All the girls of this village want to marry a warrior like Mustafa."

"No, neighbours, the girl I have in mind is not from this village. Down with your luck."

"Is she prettier than the girls in our village, Fato?"

"In spades..."

"May God not make you regret it, what shall we say..."

"I found the moon and am not grateful for the star."

Qasim was not in a hurry to marry his son Mustafa.

"He's only nineteen... There's time... Don't be in a hurry, woman... It's like you're going to get married. What a thrill..."

"Mr. Qasim, if a bride comes to our house, she will help me. Also, Mustafa is an adult man among his friends. Let's ask for the girl before he goes to military service next year. Preparations will continue slowly. You open one eye, you look, the time is over…"

While the carpet was being washed by hand, the spirit of Qasim was brushed, folded and stepped on, just as the carpet was brushed until it felt like it was folded and rinsed with the foot. He was short of breath.

"They say that she is the most beautiful girl in the other village, my dear."

In the house's cupboards, satin-faced quilts of all colours were lined up in rows on the flowery and patterned floor beds. Leila and her older brother Mustafa listened to Fatma, who was leaning her back on this load. Mustafa was listening to his mother's excited expression, his ears fluffy like a bowl.

"You haven't even seen the girl yet, woman!"

"Don't be angry, my dear. Can't I see, I saw with the eyes of the heart? Mothers feel it. Besides, you don't know what it means to be the girl who cuts the most beautiful noodle of the year. The fingers are so thin that the body is just like a pheasant. She has blond hair, almost indistinguishable from spikes, and has glassy eyes, you say this is our sky. She has skin like white cotton, a piece of the moon, she makes the angels jealous of her."

Even Mustafa could not think of such details; after the appetising descriptions of his mother, he embraced the girl; he loved with a higher love.

Leila, "I wonder if my mother would do the same for Yausef? She's blonde too, like Suheyla," thought, sighing.

Qasim rebelled with a scowl:

"Shut up now."

"Besides, the atmosphere of the house changes a little, sir. It will also cure your sadness, these wedding preparations…"

Qasim was manipulated momentarily; it would be good to see his son's elderness; he would disperse the clouds of despair from the house.

"Okay, okay."

He felt like a weak soldier surrendered; his gun raised.

"Brother."

"Yes, darling."

"You call me your sweetheart; I will always be your sweetheart, forever, right?"

Mustafa implied that he did not understand.

"You're not going to love anyone more than me, are you?"

"Your place can never be denied, Leila; you are the most sensitive point of my life."

Leila laughed awkwardly.

"Will I like her?"

"Certainly."

"What's her name?"

"Suheyla."

Before heading to the village behind the hill, Qasim researched the family thoroughly. Some people knew them from the village and told him briefly that the family were good people. They informed me that they would go to ask, and they answered, "They can come".

The demand has begun.

Qasim asked Abrohom to use his minibus. Abrohom had decided to close his shop that day, as he had announced that Qasim would be with him anyway.

Fatma wore her print dress from the ballot box. Her *fistan* smelled heavily of naphthalene. She had put a lot of naphthalene in the dowry chest to protect them from moths. She tied her golden belt. She put on her jewellery. The smell of naphthalene glided around like a skunk.

In any case, Mustafa wanted to go with his horse Auburn, thinking that it would be cooler...

Aziza was also prepared. She wore a simple tailored dress and enough Assyrian jewellery. A light blush was applied to her pale face and high cheekbones. When Fatma saw her, she was startled as if she had stepped on a snake:

"Why is that woman coming with us now?"

"Because they are our neighbours and closer to our family... and we will go in their car. If you complain, you will go on foot yourself!" said Qasim seriously.

Fatma did not make a sound.

The sneaky one has a hard job. She has to remain insidious for the rest of her life. Once its deception is exposed, it will neither reassure nor inspire mercy. Fatma had used her sneakiness well in the first months, but Qasim did not respect any of her words anymore and did not play any tricks. For her son Mustafa, the situation had changed. Her son's happiness came first. To hide her anger, she grits her teeth and rolls her eyes, staring straight ahead without a word.

Qasim scratched his head, and dandruff fell like snow from the roots of his hair; embarrassed by the white powders on his dark shirt, he got up, changed, and put on his white shirt. He wore the pouffe he wore on special occasions. He wiped his shoes with Vaseline and made them shine.

Leila also wore a frilly pink sequin dress that fell to her knees. She spun around with joy, watching her skirt rise. She was examining herself like a princess in the reflection of the glass.

Both twins had their hair straightened with lemon. Mustafa came sluggish, dressed just like his father. His trousers were slightly wrinkled. Qasim had also polished his shoes with Vaseline.

Mustafa prepared the horse Auburn like a bride: she wore a colourful pom-pom saddle on the horse's head and decorated the strap with ribbons. The Auburn looked very pleased with her colourful adornment. He brushed his mane and gave it a silky look. He stroked Auburn's hair once more, letting his breath rest. He shared his excitement with his horse. He put his foot in the stirrup and mounted the horse like a warrior.

"I hope that woman does not like my bride for her own son. I'll strangle him on the spot" was murmuring Fatma.

Qasim followed. The capricorn tugged at his hand. Capricorn was stubbornly kicking its feet back, not advancing with Qasim but resisting.

"Whom are you strangling?" an exasperated Qasim asked.

"Nothing... I just don't know... What if these Assyrians don't give the girl away because they are with us... That's what I was thinking" said Fatma.

"If so, they shouldn't give the girl away anyway. There is no need for another Fatma in this house!" he cut her off.

Qasim sat next to Abrohom in the driver's seat.

She warned Leila, who was walking squatly to the minibus:

"Come here, girl, we'll sit together," said Fatma. In her other hand, she held Mesut tightly next to her. Fatma glued Leila to her side.

She tucked the biscuits and delights (locum) she had bought from the peddler in Leila's hand, pulled it from her shoulder and put it in front of her.

Aziza sat in the back row out of courtesy, naming her later son "Samuel" after their deceased son. She took Samuel on her lap and looked ahead with a smiling expression. Fatma spread out in her chair, spelled "Bismillahirramanirrahim " at length. "This woman is always giving birth to a boy," she thought in her hateful feelings. It was obvious from her gaze.

On the raucous road, they passed the back of the hill. Goat was bleating and stomping in fear.

"I'm out of my mind; let me open that window" Fatma slid the glass to the side with her hand.

Mustafa was walking around in front of the house, aware that he was being watched from the window. The shuttle was parked on the side. They got off, straightened their clothes one last time, and headed for the door.

Aziza was also carrying a jug in one hand, filled with the blood-red sherbet:

"I made sherbet from the roses in the garden, neighbour. I hope they like it."

"So that means roses are blooming in my garden. Damn, you… I hope she doesn't poison my bride…" she muttered barely audibly. To Leila:

"Take those jugs from her hand and deliberately drop them on the floor, spilling them all on the floor. Who knows if it's magic … Come on, run and grab those jugs."

Leila shrugged, did not do as she was told, followed her father. "You'll see in the evening", Fatma nodded as if threatening her with her gaze.

They were planted at the door. Mustafa was at the back, holding the goat's collar now. The girl's father, who opened the door, introduced himself:

"I am Sileman, My Mir, welcome. You are welcome too, sir. You've given me the honour of being over my head."

They greeted each other with approving looks. The girl's four uncles were also there. They separated the men's room from the women's room. The men sat cross-legged in the place shown to them. They were all lined up like a rosary. The women were also taken to a separate section and sat crouched in the same place shown to them.

Village news would begin wherever at least two people gathered and continued until evening. Sileman:

"You've come to my senses, My Mir."

Sileman was addressing Qasim as "My Mir" and Abrohom as "My Haji" for whatever reason.

"As you have heard, we are a well-known family. Our relatives are located in fifteen villages. Our fields are endless."

"Do you rest your head on the pillow at night peacefully? That's important. Or can even a single sock from a person's possessions take him to the next world with him?"

"Of course, my Mir, of course. It's not all about the harvest. If a person has no honour, what good is it to be the owner of this region? After all, we will rot under the same soil."

Qasim's eyes lit up; obviously, this man was someone who didn't brag about his existence, knew where to talk, and he thought so.

Sileman got ten points from Qasim in his own way. He wasn't counting on it. Looking at Qasim's thin and weak body, he couldn't help but wonder if this revolutionary could handle the bill.

"All three of our three girls are beautiful. You came for your son Mustafa, isn't it, Mir?"

He showed his son, Mustafa swayed slightly and clasped his hands. His palms were coldly sweaty. Sileman eyed the groom-to-be out of the corner of his eye. He was well-built and handsome, and you could tell how valiant he was from his eyes.

"Have you done your military service?"

"Not yet; next year, if I'm lucky…" Mustafa replied in his newly seated voice.

Qasim caught the attention of Sileman, who shook his head so that his son would not be crushed under the harsh stares:

"We came for your daughter Suheyla."

"Yes, but she has an elder who is almost the same age as Mustafa."

"We came for Suheyla, you know that," Qasim repeated, "and I would like you to know that we will not accept it without her consent."

"Qasim brother is my soul. He is a man of his word. There is no more honest person in the village than him. We intend for your daughter Suheyla," added Abrohom.

The girl's mother, referring to Leila, asked Aziza, "Your daughter, how similar?" She loved Leila. However, Leila and Aziza were both brunettes.

"What a deal, ma'am. She is my daughter," Fatma interrupted. Leila liked that her mother owned her, and she was flattered for the first time. She was ready to forget all her anger towards her.

The woman bit her tongue as she was about to say, "Oh, sorry, but with her beauty…" she fell silent.

"Yes, I am blonde and my body is white, like porcelain. My daughter looks like her father. This is our daughter, what should we do?

Leila was convinced that her mother would never change, and she stopped forgiving her.

Aziza smiled, and stroked Leila's hair. Fatma was an absorbent woman, but she described herself as having yellow hair and a white body like porcelain; she just was brown-haired.

She provoked Aziza by saying, "We are in our religion, our faith, alhamdulillah," but there was no discomfort on her face.

Although her eyebrows warned her to sit beside Leila with an eye movement, Leila walked across to the girl with rose-pink cheeks and a well-behaved seat.

"Suheyla, is that you?"

She lifted her face and smiled; her dimples hollowed out in her burly face. She had a ring that went from her nose to ear. Her face looked delicious and creamy. As Fatma predicted, the young girl was a piece of the moon.

"My name is Leila."

"I'm glad, Leila."

"You know, my brother is very handsome and very nice. He is my favourite brother. He teaches me to ride a horse. We always go for a walk with Auburn."

Suheyla looked happy.

"You've already seen it, you know, I don't need to tell you. But there are many more beautiful aspects of my brother that you do not see or know. He is like an angel. He is very brave and very strong…"

Suheyla's heart palpitations could be heard.

"If you agree to marry my brother, we will be good friends too."

Suheyla was lowering her eyes from her shyness.

Fatma called Leila to her side again.

"Come, my daughter, do not disturb our daughter, be cool," she said softly, and when Leila looked towards her, she sharpened her eyes and whispered, "Come here, now is not the time."

Laughter could be heard from the men's room, which meant everything was going well. Fatma took a deep breath and gave thanks. She moved and swayed in her seat, jingling her showpiece gold jewelry every time.

Sileman knocked on the door of the women's room, called out to his wife. Fehime got up from the ground and hurried to the door.

"Let our daughter bring the coffee. Let the young people see each other. Then talk to your daughter about what she says…"

The coffee tray was also decorated, it was shown in front of the elders, and the coffee was distributed. She had put a lot of salt in Mustafa's coffee, that was the custom. Even though Mustafa's hand trembled, he took his cup without overflowing, and his eyes met Suheyla.

Suheyla's head was wrapped in a hand-embroidered crown. It was quite remarkable with its silver ring. She walked up and left the room delicately.

Next to the girl, who was taken to a room according to an arranged procedure, her brother's wife, aunt, and Leila were next to Mustafa. They smiled as if they were seeing each other for the first time. The youths exchanged glances without speaking.

Yausef was in Leila's lapsed dreams. She imagined herself at the betrothal ceremony with him.

When Suheyla went to the women's room, she kissed Fatma's hand again and put it on her head. "A drop of water, mashallah, mashallah…" they sobbed and fawned at Suheyla.

They knew that the men's and women's rooms were separate, but when the decision was made, they sat all together, so they sat in the same place. The women were a little bit shy and sat in the doorway. When the chairs were not enough, they fell on the ground.

"What did you decide? Shall we interrupt today?"

"Well, lord, neither the officers asked, we did not give our daughter," said the girl's mother, coming forward.

Here it is, so there was a Fatma in every house. The girl's father cleared his throat.

"Well, after the youths saw each other, let's talk about more. These are fateful things. Since the young people have liked each other, if we agree on gold, we will be relatives (dünür) tonight."

"Gold! Yes, of course..." Qasim agreed although he disagreed.

"Of course, for the girl's assurance... This is in every religion. Isn't it so, Haji?"

Abrohom: "We have it banned by the churches; there are no such things..."

Only Qasim had heard it; it had gone in one ear and out the other from the others sitting in the hall. Abrohom they did not consider.

Sileman's brother handed him a piece of paper with a number on it, and he refused:

"No need," Qasim said, tilting his head, and Sileman began reciting the list: "A twisted bracelet worth a kilo of gold."

"Alas, ten sheep are gone," Fatma bit her lower lip. Sileman continued without breaking his composure:

"Two meters of chain. A choker set..."

"Five cows from there..."

"There will be two sets, the ring, bracelet, necklace, earrings, etc. Apart from these, there is also the girl's shopping expenditure at the bazaar."

"Half more of the field... Alas, we will starve to death this year." Every time Fatma was calculating in her head, she bit her lower lip until it bled. She was shaking her head from side to side.

Abrohom looked like his emerald eyes would pop out of their sockets. He had neither heard of nor was familiar with such a list.

Qasim accepted what Sileman said normally. He was still a novice for his first son, and the lovely Abrohom had never taken a bride.

Qasim had relied on his knowledge, but he brutally confronted the lack of knowledge around here.

"Okay, by order of Allah…"

"There is one more thing, forgive me… We have been protecting our traditions for years."

Qasim and Abrohom, and the young boys had their eyes on Sileman.

"And the bride price is 50 thousand…"

Qasim's face fell.

"Everything is okay, but what the hell is this bride price?! Everyone in our village knows I am against it, even though all regions know. Haven't you heard that?"

"We can make beauty like this."

"What are you saying, for God's sake, will you bargain with me for your daughter?"

Sileman's brothers stood next to their generation as if preparing for a fight. Sileman stopped them with the back of his hand.

"Mr. Qasim, Mr. Qasim… I loved you like a brother. You know, too, that raising a daughter is not easy."

"Your daughter is not a commodity, she is a person… It is not easy to raise a son too, especially in such an era! Do you understand me? I'm sorry, I don't want to waste any more time with this attitude." He nodded to Abrohom and his sons.

There was a commotion among the women.

"Mr Qasim, please don't do this to our young people…"

"I didn't know that you were so impulsive." Sileman's tone changed.

This time Abrohom spoke:

"Right, he is not an impulsive person. You touched on the subject that he never liked. You used to say honour, Mr Sileman, when a person's dignity was worth all the land…"

"Yes, I'm saying it again." Five people couldn't contain Qasim, who was wearing his shoes at the door.

"My Mir, for God's sake, don't be stubborn; let's sit down again. Look, is it worth her tears?" Sileman said, pointing to Suheyla crying in the doorway.

Qasim's eyes were dark; once he turned his back, he would never look back. He was even more stubborn than any of his goats when he was right.

Mustafa was whatever his father said to him. He untied his horse. He jumped into his saddle at once and spurred his horse. Sadness caught in his throat. He galloped back to his village. Abrohom used the minibus and took the children.

Abrohom, who got into the driver's seat, looked at Qasim and frowned.

"Come on, drive Bro, we're not here to buy animals."

Leila pressed her face to the glass and watched Suheyla cry. The twins sat down resentfully. Aziza was very upset but could not console Fatma. She was worried that if she said something, it would be misunderstood. Fatma's embroidered manuscript had slipped; she was speaking as if she was talking to young kid Mesut.

As she entered the house packed with scraps, she continued to murmur:

"It's always the bad luck of those Assyrians... I saw how the snake-eyed Aziza looked at my bride, sighing. It was worth the evil eye!"

"Well, enough of you!"

Qasim left the house and walked quickly away from the village. Abrohom just left the minibus and saw that Qasim was going the opposite direction. Although Abrohom followed Qasim, he signaled that he wanted to be left alone, leaving Abrohom behind.

Qasim stream crossed over the stones and sat on a high rock. He prepared his pipe and lit tobacco. The village houses looked like birds' nests from afar.

"I want him. I will not marry anyone. Kill me better!"

Suheyla was weak from crying for hours. Their uncles sat until evening and then dispersed to their homes.

She stood in front of her mother.

"Why did you play with my destiny? Do you not fear Allah at all? Better kill me. Or I will kill myself. And my sin will be on your neck," she said.

Suheyla's eyes did not close that night; the moon's brightness was dull, and bruises were under her eyes. Her siblings didn't even blink so that she wouldn't hurt herself.

"Suheyla, Suheyla…"

"What?"

"You can continue to cry tomorrow. You should sleep now. I really have a headache and I can't sleep because of you."

"Let my funeral leave this house until the morning. I cannot live without Mustafa …"

"Okay, my sister, water flows and finds its way. Let's sleep. Then we'll talk about it to our mother again."

"You sleep. I will continue to prepare my dowry."

She was embroidering a cone lace angrily.

"You're not going to hurt yourself with that needle, are you?"

Suheyla continued to cry.

"Okay, okay, please be quiet a bit."

The young girl was doing cone lace in the moon's dim light; she did not know how to get tired.

"If my father does not give me to Mustafa, you will bury me with this dowry."

His sister was already snoring.

Suheyla's mother could not stand her daughter's tears. She tried to persuade Sileman.

"Very arrogant. Why should I give my daughter to the son of a revolutionary-dressed man!"

"Maybe that's how it was understood due to tension, Mr Sileman, this girl will hurt herself, and we will be disgraced in the real world."

Sileman frowned deeply.

"Nowadays, daughters don't listen. There is also an oldest one… Isn't it a sin to get Suheyla married before the older one first!"

"I am sure she will find her lucky one soon."

Sileman looked at his wife suspiciously:

"Or are you tempting them, huh?"

"No sir, nothing of the sort…"

"How do you know that she will marry too…"

"Everybody has their grant, I mean it, sir. The girl also means visiting of luck. They are a holy piece; every prayer is answered. Please, don't upset our daughter Suheyla. Good luck with her life."

Sileman was silent.

Fehime clung to her husband on the yacht:

"Sileman, let the children get married. We have enough goods."

"Don't get involved, woman. Get away from me. Old thing…"

"My lord. Don't act like that. It's enough for the girl to get the gold. It doesn't stay open. Our groom candidate is tall and handsome; he can do everything he can for our daughter."

The jealousy was evident in every part of Sileman.

"If this girl hurts herself, we will be in trouble. Forget the bride price. It is enough to buy a separate house for our daughter. We get their gold from him somehow."

"You say so…"

"Yes."

"Come here; let me see you."

Qasim was unhappy that he had spoiled the situation. Fatma looked to cheer him up.

Of course, no one was in the mood to be happy, but Qasim sensed something wrong. Thereupon, Fatma found a topic to change the subject:

"His fiancee's expectations will never end later on. The Indian jewellery set is a compulsory thing, her mother said it first. She finds many materials to add to her bridal bundle. Let's see what happens. You are brave, Mr. Qasim, don't be stubborn for our young gentleman. We can afford them all. Finally, she will stay with us; the gold will be ours already."

Leila couldn't stand it, "If I have a mother-in-law like you, I will drown her in a spoonful of water."

"What a pity. Unfortunately, it's not your mother-in-law; it's your mother. I'll be mannered. Who did this girl take after, my God? What was my sin, you gave me such a girl!"

"Stop it at once. We don't buy a woman from the slave market, Fatma. If only they accept this…"

"Mr Qasim, don't worry; we will find a way. The girl will be ours, the jewellery too."

Qasim gave a gaze to his wife. He knew what Fatma sensed.

A bit later, Muhtar leaned on the door of Qasim:

"I wish you had told me earlier; I would have handled it. Let's meet them again, I insist, Mr Qasim. For God's sake," he said.

Qasim had softened. All was about his son's happiness. Because Mustafa, too, wasn't happy and couldn't sleep at night. He agreed to go to Sileman's house again. With the headman, too, this time.

Abrohom prepared the minibus again and honked to give attention. The Family took a seat as they sat before, and they went with the same excitement. All the effort as on the day of the girl's betrothal ceremony.

The previous regiment reappeared at the door; on the other hand, the girl's side was more excited and ostentatious this time.

"Cough cough…" Qasim coughed, indicating they were coming.

The door opened. There was also the bride-to-be Suheyla at the door. Her cheeks were red, and she was smiling with hollow cheeks.

"Well, welcome, My *Mir*. You've come to my head. Here you go."

This time, he hugged him tightly as if greeting a close friend who had come far away. He hugged Abrohom similarly, and they froze for a while. They took off their shoes and went.

Sileman and Muhtar shook hands, followed by Sileman's brothers…

Qasim was standing confidently upright in front of his door.

"For God's sake, Mir, don't turn your back on us. Since the young people love each other, we must reunite them."

"You were calling it an honour; you were calling it worth all the land…"

"Yes, I still say, Mir, sir. Let it go; let's forget it. Suppose that I'm not talking about money."

"It's not about the money."

"Yes, sir, that's not the point."

"Then?"

"They say, when two hearts become one, the haystack becomes a sight. Come on, let's get these young people married. Come on, I gave it away!" he said, still waiting.

"I want to hear it from the girl's own mouth. Is her heart content?"

The headman hissed, his belly swaying up and down, "Your youths are already on the job..."

Abrohom nudged him and cast a sideways glance at Muhtar.

"If the young people said yes, it's up to us to give them legendary entertainment."

"Hey, my beloved Mir. My daughter will be a good bride to you. She will wash your laundry, get milk, sweep the house, and do all her duties meticulously... She will never go out of your way."

It was not possible for the girl's father to go to the man's father's house and give his daughter a thousand somersaults. Sileman was afraid that his daughter would start a business on her own. They were going to say, "What should she do when her father doesn't give her permission, she went and committed suicide." It was impossible to prove later. That's why he had Qasim come fall at his feet. It would be put on top of the gold bought for his daughter anyway; it was a sincere bargain. Who knows what the hell was going through his head.

"Come on, good luck," said Muhtar, and he wanted to add sugar to the sweet air.

9

Two women of colour, meeting in the street, stood opposite each other and talked. With one hand on her waist and the other arm ringing her bracelets, she asked:

"Do you agree with the engagement too?"

"It is impossible not to go, neighbour; preparations have already begun. They call the girl a piece of the moon."

"Well, the handsome valiant needs a beautiful chick. His hand is also capable of anything."

"Fatma is very lucky. Do you know how much gold they're going to get?"

"About two kilos. No one's gold has exceeded mine."

"Thank God, we didn't have it at first either; we worked hard and got it." She threw the veil behind her ear and shook it as if to show her Kurdish-made earrings, "thank goodness..."

The weight of the earring almost tore her earlobe. The ear hole seemed to be struggling to carry the earring.

The best cook women of Greenvillage were prepared to stay at the bride's house the day before.

Giant cauldrons were brought, and they gathered the materials to be made for the next day. It was waiting to be loaded with sacks of rice for food. They would also make their livestock for food there. They also took the oil and tomato paste cans. Fully equipped items were loaded into the car without obligation at the bride's house. The season's liveliest, most colourful and juicy fruits were transported in crates.

The groom's family would leave the next day. Leila was also more excited than Mustafa; she couldn't fit in. She would knock herself down at her brother's engagement and dance halay. She would wear the silvery sequined dress she had sewn, and when she passed Yausef, she would twist it and show off. She would take Yausef's eyes, so Leila imagined. But already her mother was not letting her breath. She was getting further and further away from her rush and dreams.

"Go call the twins to load them into the car. Why haven't you washed those dishes yet! Run quickly and polish Mustafa's shoes. Let our groom's shoes shine like the sun!"

Fatma brought the sweets and delight during the feast.

This time, Aziza seemed to have chopped all her roses in the garden. She had prepared rose sherbet. Benjamin and Turabdin carried the desserts and sherbet made by their mothers to the car. Yausef brought the extra tarps that his mother said to bring just in case, and they handed them over. Abdrohom was more hectic and cheerful than Qasim. The Syriac neighbour knew the first day of Mustafa's birth.

Qasim wore clean clothes and continued wearing the same clothes in the village as in Iraq: a white linen shirt, a pure cotton shalwar, and a belt that framed his waist. This time he was also wearing a vest, and his pooch was tied behind his back as usual, softly revealing his sharp features. He was watching everyone around him. He was coughing in between. As the activity increased, his excitement also increased. First eye pride, Mustafa would be engaged and would take a step towards marriage.

Fatma walked confidently, swaying slowly with the charm of a young girl; she closed the house door and headed for the minibus. Her sequined dress swayed as she walked as if she were applauding; it turned the rays reflecting from the sun into a light scene, illuminating its surroundings.

Roses and leaves surrounded Abrohom's minibus.

Mustafa would not go anywhere without his horse Auburn, especially on a day like this; he wanted her to be a witness; he wanted her to see his happiness.

Benjamin handed Mustafa a handkerchief and pinned it to his suit jacket.

"The wife is on you too, Benjamin."

"Thank you, bro."

They embraced each other.

"Watch out, if you ride in cloth pants…"

"Don't worry, that's why I sewed a lot."

Yausef couldn't get enough of watching the brunette beauty. When Leila turned to her side, Fatma pinched her, pushing her around so she wouldn't turn her face.

Villagers surrounded the minibus and struggled for space. Abrohom warned them in his naive voice:

"The groom's family first, please…"

They hardly heard him. The horseless lads did not sit but had to stand until not a single woman remained standing. The bus was stuffed full.

They were having fun and clapping; the women were singing songs for the groom Mustafa and making traditional tongue trilling, ululation. The children's ears would have been almost deaf in their mother's lap, they were covering their ears and looking sarcastically and laughing.

Minibus and Auburn competed with each other. Who could beat the Arabian horse! Mustafa guided the horse, and the brown hair advanced. He had reached the village immediately without dropping the valiant on his waist.

In front of Suheyla's house, on the street, from neighbour to neighbour, lights were connected from pole to pole, and the street was colourfully decorated. All the young girls were as lively as Suheyla; they wore their most beautiful dresses and dazzled.

Conversely, the men eyed the girls discreetly, unnoticed, without lending their weight; They chose what suited them.

Wedding preparations are the most fun way to come together in villages. Weddings were the only common social activity for men and women to sit together and have fun. How else could young girls and boys get the chance to see each other so easily! Weddings were an opportunity for them to socialise.

The cooks got up early in the morning and had already started mixing the dishes in the giant cauldron. As soon as the sun broke, the smell of food covered the whole village, waking everyone with a sweet smile. The kids helped cut and cook the meat. They also cleaned and lifted their heads and feet covered with flies.

Carpets, linoleums and covers were laid on the terrace and the roof. All kinds of sugar, delights and sweets were evenly spaced on the plates so everyone could access them.

The drummer played as if to announce that the groom had come to the village. The groom, Mustafa, entered the village with his horse like a bride, accompanied by drums and horns. His equestrian friends followed him.

Mustafa's armpit got wet; luckily, he was wearing his jacket. He took the sweat of his brow with Benjamin's handkerchief.

In the square, the villagers were waiting for the halay dance, and they were lined up like a rosary, bending their knees simultaneously, shaking their shoulders up and down, and shaking their heads. The women's breasts were also accompanied, bouncing up and down.

Sileman perfectly greeted his guests and showed them the way to sit.

The trillings were repeating each other and their tongues played in their mouths. They sang songs to make room for each other. It even suppressed the clatter of the drum.

It's time to wear engagement rings. Qasim begged Abrohom to put the rings on, and he urged him to his side and brought him to the tray.

"Come Bro, you or me. What does it matter? My children grew up with you more than me."

Abrohom was indeed considered to have fathered them more. Abrohom felt embarrassed and proud at the same time.

Fatma did not stop without saying, "Look at this, look, what he is doing. We have so many relatives, he goes and asks the Christian man. Rings to wear on my son's and my bride's fingers. Damn it!"

Abrohom, with his sparkling eyes, put the rings on the hands of the fresh, excited couple. He cut the ribbon. The flood of applause broke.

The preparations were not complete. As an engagement gift, Suheyla was given a necklace and handcrafted gloves that completely covered her thin fingers.

It was the turn of the kemenche player, who had stuffed his pockets while collecting the tips. He was completely immersed in the energy of the money and was moving his head from side to side with his hand, which made the kemenche scream. The youngsters melted the girls' hearts with their skilful play, and the young girls were looking at them withwith their kohlrabi eyes.

Fatma was doing everything she could so Leila and Yausef did not go hand in hand. While Leila could not even leave the house, she ruined the beautiful dress while serving. She was collecting the dishes and squatting, helping Suheyla's older sister by keeping the leftovers aside. She looked at her mother with pleading eyes, and when there were not many girls from the groom's side, she had fallen into business. So, with Yausef, her dreams were just up in the air. Leila could not find the opportunity to play or have fun while serving. They returned home without expectations. She was sad that she could not make her dreams come true in Mustafa's engagement:

"Anyway, I hope I'll shed all my worms at the wedding," she reassured herself this time. After a while, she sighed from exhaustion and fell asleep in the minibus. As soon as she opened her eyes a bit, she recognised they had reached the house already. Tired entertainers dispersed to their homes with smiles on their faces.

Fatma was again asking for Leila's help to lay the beds. Although she saw no strength in herself, she had to obey the order. She didn't want to cause unrest by bickering with her mother on her brother's happy day. Then, before lying on the bed, she collapsed onto the mat and fell asleep. Mustafa woke his beloved sister up gently, she standed and went to the bed prepared by the twins.

While Fatma was preparing a wool quilt, Qasim's temples throbbed like needles.

"Why are you giving the rings to that Christian? What if it brings bad luck..."

"This nagging of yours will bring bad luck. Know this..."

Qasim went out into the garden, he took out the tobacco from his deep pocket and rolled up one, inhaled the poisonous smoke, coughing more and more, and gasped.

Mustafa came to his side and squatted next to his father. He was happy but didn't know what to say. His father's illness saddened him. Since Qasim stubbornly resisted not going to the hospital, Mustafa had no choice.

"Thank you so much for everything, Dad."

"No need for words, my son, it is my duty as a father…"

"Don't worry about my mother, Dad; she exaggerates some issues. We don't have a separate one. My mother doesn't want anyone else to be better than herself. That's why it's like that."

"I know, son, I know. Let it go. A woman's heart is never satisfied, no matter how much you give, she always wants more. Their hearts are as light and delicate as a feather. They tremble like leaves even from the wave of your voice."

The stars hung like snowflakes in the vast sky. The gin insects, who could not be silent, were making their sounds despite the silence of the night.

"Next time, he will go to military service. Until then, I will raise my bride as I want. Eighteen months, in a month, even a bear will be tamed with training"

She constantly fantasised about her bride. Fatma, who does not see her daughter as close to herself, would love her daughter-in-law if she could. Leila strung the laundry from one shape to another.

"I take all troubles and she'll get the pleasure! That's not fair…" she muttered.

"My bride will cut me some noodles with her thin fingers. Oh, thank God. Aziza's eyes would pop out of their sockets when she sees our bride. I gave forty Yasin readings that if she doesn't desire my bride, at least."

Leila rolled her eyes and shifted in her seat. Her legs were numb. She got up, straightened herself, crouched again and began to brush the laundry.

"Are you looking at that Assyrian's house? Devil's offspring! I'll carve out your eyes..."

Leila didn't know what to do; she thought the minimum of getting rid of him without a word. When the laundry was finished, Fatma acted:

"Give it to me; I'll go and hang it. It's a shame for young girls to hang laundry on the roof! She is looking for a husband, they'll say after you."

"You and these beliefs..."

Mustafa used to gallop with his horse to see the beautiful Suheyla from the village behind the hill. Mustafa wouldn't leave without combing Auburn's mane. One day he took Leila with him so that they would allow them to meet with his fiancee; otherwise, the girl's father would not have allowed her to meet with Mustafa alone. Auburn was also very excited. She had her jet-black and long tail fluffed up, and her golden manes were always waving. As soon as they saw Mustafa, they would start talking, and Mustafa would put his head on the broad forehead of Auburn as if in response to him, and she would smile.

He jumped on his horse like a victorious soldier. As he jumped into his saddle, he pulled Leila's hand in one move and made her sit in front. The brown-haired reared up and galloped through the green, mosaic-coloured soil, the white, shining, stony ground, the rushing stream and the harsh terrains.

She memorised all the hidden corners she went to with her older brother Mustafa and dreamed of coming here with Yausef. In many places, she dreamed of mischief with the dream of her beloved.

With the celebration of the holiday, every square meter of the houses smelled of spring flowers. The smell of washed laundry captured the village.

Women wrapped in silk thread surrounded the peddler who had come to the village. They touched and smelled all they could see. They purchased kilos of sweets for eid.

Before the birds chirped in the morning, the men prayed at the village mosque and returned to their homes. They made house visits individually as if they had not seen each other. Clusters of people were celebrating and greeting in the clean-smelling streets of the village. Men often smelled of the same cologne.

The women cooked bean soup mixed with meat and prepared it for breakfast with rice.

Candies were distributed separately to adults and children. They spreaded out the sweets in front of the children as if they were feeding the chicks. They competed with each other to quickly grab the candies mixed with the soil.

Assyrians also followed the traditions in the village; children would go door to door with their plastic bags.

Qasim visited his neighbour Abrohom first. Mustafa and his twins followed him. Later, as was customary, Abrohom and his sons visited the feast of Qasim.

Leila wore the most beautiful and cleanest outfit of the year. She was wearing the red loafers her father had bought for her, especially from Iraq. She would have walked around in her shoes if she hadn't been afraid of her mother. She served special chocolate candies and musk-scented cologne to the guests who came to the house. She imagined it as if they had come to ask for her hand for their son, Yausef.

Her mother, Fatma, pulled Leila by the arm and said, "Come on, go with your brother Mustafa. Celebrate with their fiance. Stay with them, too," she warned, waking her from her early youth fleeting dreams.

The village mobile coachman came to the village that day and sold the sugary rose water he kept in the freezer as "ice" to the children. The boys had become little men. They looked trusted in their clean clothes.

Children love chewing gums; they would take the wrapped sticky papers and stick them on their arms and bare calves, revealing tattoos. For some, buying chocolate was considered a great luxury.

Single girls also bought crochet and yarn from the peddler, and they would save them for their dowry.

Mustafa used to tell Leila to wait by the horse so she wouldn't witness it when he kissed his fiancé. He promised Leila twenty special chocolates and cash for the secret.

Although Leila took great pleasure in this bribe, from time to time, she would look behind her and try to understand whether they were kissing each other or not. She secretly looked at them with her eyes but made up that she saw nothing. She would imagine Yausef instead of Mustafa and herself instead of Suheyla.

Mustafa placed a kiss on the cheek of his future wife. Their heads were close together.

"Our first holiday..." whispered the beloved.

"She will see us..." Suheyla was pulling her hands from Mustafa's and pushing him away.

"Let her see."

"It's a shame… What if your mother raises it."

"Don't worry," he said, laughing, "she never tells her anything."

He kissed Suheyla on her characteristic arched nose.

When Leila realised, she was noticed, she would turn her head and start talking to Auburn. As if Auburn was her companion too; she was aware of everything around her.

Leila slowly moved her head over her shoulder in that direction, she wanted to see what the kiss was like and dreamed of Yausef kissing her one day.

"I can't breathe without you, my dear, Mustafa."

"Me too, my love. We will reunite soon, darling."

Leila snickered, breaking the romantic mood. Mustafa cleared his throat.

It was an afternoon when the sky was mottled.

"Time to go."

"Yeah, come on."

First, he sat his fiancee behind him then grabbed Leila by the waist and placed her on the horse. Leila was slightly jealous of her brother Mustafa because of Suheyla. According to her, Mustafa should not have loved anyone more than her. Her eldest brother was the one who always took care of her. She glanced forward, proud of being of the same blood.

They left Suheyla at her home, then got on their own horse and returned to their home in Greenvillage.

10

In 1991, about 3 million people settled in the mountains, between Iraq and Turkey. Qasim could not sleep well that night and left the village hastily the next day.

Qasim was such a necessity that he volunteered to present the women's ped to their clothes, secretly arrange for the doctors to supply medicine, and meet the water needs of the masses in the camp with tanks. Moreover, he did this without expecting anything in return. He acted with the love of existence and the instinct to live in better conditions.

He turned back soon; he couldn't stay away because of his bad condition. His cough was getting worse. He was with his family and would support his son Mustafa going to military service.

Yausef approached Leila's house at the exit of the vault. Frightened not to climb the ladder again and knock over the flowers, he threw a small stone at the broken glass. It rang. Leila stuck her head out of the window in anger.

"If my mother sees it, she will think you broke this glass before."

They talked to each other through the window.

"I'll wait for you on the other side of the stream tomorrow."

"Why?"

"There are certain things I will confess to you. Please don't make me wait again," said a young man whose moustache was starting to show.

"I'll think about it," she chuckled.

"Leila, why are you persecuting me like this? Come, I told you."

She complained, "Give me a reason, " there was teasing in her voice. "Why should I come?" She was acting delicately, Fifteen-year-old, Leila.

"Because I'm in love with you…"

Leila could not hear outside voices over the roar of her heart, which was starting to pound. The words "I am in love with you" reached from the young man's heart to his lips, from his lips to Leila's ears, and from there to her heart.

For a moment, the gins had also listened to Yausef. The birds heard him from the branches and were silent. Even the heated earth was no longer buzzing. Leila's lips parted like a cracked pomegranate under the golden sun of autumn. She was about to say something, gasping.

Yausef broke the spell by saying, "You will come, okay? "

"Why should I believe you!" She kept pushing her luck.

"My God, Leila, you—I must have exaggerated my love for you that you were so spoiled!"

"Yeah, tell me why I'd believe that I can't see."

"We have never seen prophets either, but we love and believe in prophets enough to kill another human being for them. And without question at all!"

Before Yausef got mad, Leila said, "My father is here, Yausef, we'll talk later," and cut it off. She stuck her head in. Yausef walked to the village square with his hands in his pockets.

It was a Sunday in October that had its share of earth-scorching heat.

Fatma hastily placed the bowl of fermented dough on her head and caught the tandoor by the square.

"Come right behind me, or they'll take my turn! Oh, my God, this heat is not over!.. I will bake bread for you all under this hellish heat!"

Leila took a bucket full of water with her. When she raised her mother to a tandoor, she left with the excuse of returning home. She spied on her secretly. When the tandoor was out of sight, she turned her way. She rushed to the back of the hill where she had promised to meet Yausef.

Mustafa would go to the stone mill with his father and grind wheat. Wheat would be ground into flour, and Fatma would have to knead the dough and bake bread.

The side of Qasim's house was a large piece of land. The apple tree was no longer but the trunk, its glamour was gone. The children took reference from that tree trunk as a goal; on the other side, they marked two of the stones as a goal.

In the atmosphere painted by the sun, the children had the opportunity to come together and play ball in their pyjamas. Despite all the calls and warnings of the mothers, they did not listen to them and ran to the land and split into two teams: the children of the Christians and the children of the Muslims. The mind of a child did not know about discrimination, but what they learned from their elders shaped them over time.

Children ran screaming across the wasteland between Qasim and Abrohom's houses, bouncing the ball to the goal, one side was winning and the other was losing. Mesut was in front of his home, he was a goalkeeper in his team. Gabriel also bounced the ball as a football striker on the opposite team. When Gabriel thought that he had thrown the ball hard at Mesut, he asked if he was hurt, and Mesut replied back, "I am okay," and put his hand on his shoulder.

With the pass thrown by Alex, one of the Christian neighbour's children, the ball was thrown into the house through the broken window of Qasim's house. It hit the mirror on the wall, the mirror cracked, and some of it fell to the ground. The ball bounced to the ground in front of Lokman.

Lokman was cutting his nails in the house that had released his animals to the pasture. He would take the animals in the evenings, and since it was not yet dark, he would spend time at home. Idris was doing his homework at that time. They were startled by the crackling of the mirror. How the ball got in, how it hit the mirror, they could not understand. Lokman jumped after the still-bouncing ball, caught it, grabbed it and rushed out with fury. He jumped down the back stone stairs after the patio. He ran to the playing area in the back. Idris also rushed after him, accompanying Lokman for no reason.

"Shit, your ancestors… son of a dog!"

He poked the ball with the nail clippers in his hand, but the ball was stubborn and did not burst. He threw his hands on the ground. Gabriel stood starkly in the middle as everyone else scrambled aside. Lokman had grown up to his mother's fill since he was a child, and when he had the opportunity, he would throw a grudge against her. He quickly grabbed Gabriel by the shoulder, shook him, and slapped him. Mesut was stammering to Idris that it was not Gabriel's fault, that the other neighbours had come out of the boy's foot, but Lokman had already started kicking Gabriel down. He bent his knee and kicked it as if he was pulling a halay.

Benjamin was watering his mother's flowers with the water he had drawn from the well on the balcony. He heard children's voices and an adult mingling from the field in front of the houses. The children are playing ball, it sounds like that; then, at one point, he seems to hear his brother's scream. He looked to the side of the field, seeing that Gabriel was covering his face with his hands and Lokman was towring over his feet, he jumped up the stairs one by one, barefoot. Unable to keep his pace, Benjamin attacked Lokman from behind like an angry bull, headbutting and knocking him to the side. Lokman staggered and fell face down on the ground. He saved his brother from Lokman.

Lokman wasted no time on the ground, ignoring the thorn and splinter stuck in his feet, and stood up. As soon as he got up, he attacked Benjamin. They got into a fistfight. Idris also found himself in a fight when he was trying to separate them. Turabdin had also jumped barefoot with lightning speed and kicked and slapped Idris. Benjamin took Lokman's head under his arm, punching him viciously with all the anger he had accumulated inside. Idris also fought with Turabdin; they punched each other like two enemies, spinning on the ground.

Mustafa was going home from the mill, carrying the flour sack on his back. He could make out the commotion from afar, he thought. He narrowed his eyes more carefully, noticing that his brothers were fighting the Syriac brothers in blood and sweat. Mustafa lost himself, and for a while, he ran with the flour sack on his back. At the last moment, he thought of throwing the sack on the ground, grabbed Benjamin by the arm, turned him, and pushed him back. Benjamin sat hard on the ground. Lokman's neck veins swelled. Turabdin got free from Idris; they were out of breath.

Engaged young man waving his hands:

"Stop it right now! How many years have we been neighbours... Aren't you ashamed to fight!"

Mustafa was both built and strong. He grabbed the twins by the arms, shook them, and flung them sideways from the house.

Gabriel's weeping and suffocating in the dust, his older brother Benjamin could not clinch his anger. He threw the large, pointed, sharp stone he had picked up from the ground, and struck one of Qasim's sons in the head. The young man put his hand to his head, felt his head split open, and knelt on the ground. Blood spurted from his head like oil gushing from the ground. The brothers embraced the wounded. It seemed for a moment that he was about to turn around and attack them again, but the Assyrians were already at the house's entrance.

Blood was pouring from the young man's head like he had lost its way. A brother put his hand on his head but couldn't stop the blood gushing between his fingers. The two brothers tried together to stop the bleeding. It was like pressing a hand against the stream to keep the water from flowing.

"Run, tell my father!" said one of them. They grabbed the injured one under his armpits and carried him to the garden. The sack of flour was scattered on the floor. The blood of Qasim's injured son was mixed with the flour.

SESSION 2

A young girl with prominent breasts jumped over the hill and sat next to Yausef. Dust and tiny white stones slid from the floor.

"I would have gone if you had not come. I will never come again."

"I came, but here it is. Do you think it's easy to escape from my despotic mother? I must not be late for the evening; I must be home before that bread comes out of the tandoor. Otherwise, my funeral will be out of the house!"

Yausef had grown into a lanky young man with curly hair, emerald eyes, and thick but well-shaped eyebrows. He snuggled up to Leila, rested his head on her shoulder, said, "The advantage of being full of the flesh is to put my head on your shoulder, fat girl," and inhaled the scent of Leila's sunburned skin. He wrapped his arm around Leila's waist.

"Hold on. Someone will see us!"

"Let them see us if they will. You're going to be my wife next year."

"Hello there, be cool, boy!"

As they struggled, the top button of Yausef's shirt unbuttoned, revealing the gold-chained cross. Leila's eyes landed on it. The cross caught Leila's eyes, shining brightly.

"Do you think we should get married in the church or the mosque?"

"What I know is that the imam will come home and have the wedding ceremony," said Yausef confidently and added, "I only have one condition, fat girl, please lose those kilos. Otherwise, your mother will ask us for each kilo of gold."

"I became like this in order not to look like my mother. In spite of her... I will stop eating bread as soon as the wedding thing gets around the ears, I will lose weight fast!"

Yausef admired Leila's being at peace with herself.

"Where will we live?" she asked.

"I love these places. "

"Is that why you're repeating a grade this year?"

"No, fat one, how could I study, leaving you behind? We will be studying at the same time as you."

"What are we going to do here next? I want to be a doctor and get out of this village."

"No, Leila, even if you are a doctor, you will be with me. Your place will be in my place. You can work in the city hospital here. I'll be your chauffeur, dropping you off at work daily."

"Is that so, what else is there? What do you suppose you'll do?"

"Here, we will have a big fenced-in farm, chickens, goats... We will also buy mulberry trees to feed the goats. Like your father, I would like to read my books while listening to music. And then I can work in vineyards season to season. I will cook for you after I pick you up from the hospital. I'll wash your hair to your toes. Thus, we will be happy together."

Leila poked him with her elbow and changed the subject:

"I'm disappointed now. Who will get the milk from those goats? I don't milk anyway; I am fed up. I'm sick of getting under those animals and milking them."

"You don't worry, my sunshine. Your hand will not touch anything. Leila, I will be very rich, we will afford our assistants and servants."

"Oh, I wish… We could have horses too! I like them as my beloved brother Mustafa does."

"Of course, we will. I'll buy an Arabian horse, for you, for me. Our vineyards will be filled with fruits. We will make the best wine from the most delicious grapes from our vineyards."

Leila was laughing shyly:

"Grover, you dream like that, then why do we go to school in the early morning and stay miserable until the evening? Why don't you deal with animals now and keep saying 'later'?"

"Because I'm dealing with you right now. That's quite a work to do."

"I want to be a doctor," said Leila again, "I don't know about you, but at the end of this year, from now on, I will take the tests and study to get the university. I will do whatever it takes to realise my father's ideal."

"We will go to university together and then travel the world. Then we will come and realise this farm dream."

"Where will we go?"

"Wherever it is, where people do not distinguish society. Then we will come here and instil it in our people."

"It's a little tough, but I got it, curly boy! What will happen to our children? Can we go anywhere with them?"

"Even if there is one…"

"I would like to have my daughters."

"Me too… Let's have a dozen girls if they'll look like you."

"What if I don't pass the exam… Will you still accept me as your wife?"

"You're the most talented and smart girl I've ever met, I'm sure you'll succeed, fat girl."

"What other girl do you know anyway!"

Yausef tried to kiss her on the cheek, Leila turned her face, and their lips reunited. The breath released through his thin lips smelled like fresh peach sweetness, and her heart felt like it would jump. They were startled. She chuckled as if ashamed of what she had done. Oh, if only again! This time, she would never hesitate, would connect their lips and never part again. Leila and Yausef would savor those smooth and fresh lips.

The sun in the west rippled the sky in warm colours. Instead of the sun, which was tired of warming the earth, the wind was blowing in a lemony atmosphere, gently stroking the hair of the lovers.

Time to go back.

The two lovers walked towards the rocks from the place where they met, and from there, they returned to the village. There was an awkward silence. Yausef and Leila had never experienced such a quiet day, no one could be seen in the fields.

Soon they crossed the hill. The old shepherd Zaho walked past them with his limp legs and strength from the long stick in his hand:

"You rascals, the apocalypse is breaking out in the village; you are swarming here. Get out of here!.. You have no idea that your families will be feuding!"

"What do you say Uncle Zaho?" said Yausef as he went up to him, Zaho called out:

"Go home now; your family is waiting for you, kiddo."

"Tell me what you know!" snorted Leila, but the shepherd Zaho was on his way falteringly to fetch his animals from the pasture, and he never turned his back and never left the young people. Leila ran towards the village. Yausef caught up with her, shaking her body. Leila:

"What does he mean, feuding... What is this old man saying!"

"Leila, we don't know anything yet. Please calm down..."

Both were pale and ashen. They did not know who had shot whom or if they were killed. To avoid wasting time, Leila managed to escape from Yausef's arms. She continued to run and cry.

"Leila, stop!"

Leila waited for Yausef:

"What if it's true; what if someone killed someone… What are we going to do?"

"Please, make me a promise. No matter what happens, we're not going to part, are we?"

Leila felt like she would faint but recovered at the last moment. The road was never-ending. He wouldn't let Leila go, stopping and shaking her repeatedly, "Please, listen to me."

She pulled her hands out from Yausef's.

"What if something happened to my father? What if something happened to my brothers?"

"What if something happened to one of mine, huh!?"

Leila sobbed. In the distance, they saw the commotion in front of their house. Two vehicles and a dozen soldiers were visible from the distance where they were.

"Let's not go to the village if you want, let's run away from here, huh? Let's start a new life. Our life, our dreams…"

"Don't be silly Yausef! I would never let my father down. Do you understand me, never!"

That road would never end, her knees were weak, it was as if she was staggering. It was about the sun disappearing in its sadness. Leila continued to run home without looking back. She couldn't even say goodbye to Yausef. Gendarmes in earth-coloured uniforms, with rifles hanging on their shoulders, were waiting for orders from their commanders at the command post, ready.

"I will never leave you, Leila, never... Don't forget that," he said behind her. He wasn't sure if Leila had heard or not. Yausef arrived at the house's entrance with the young gendarmes, there was a rush in front of his house. His mother was crying, and his brother, toddler Samuel, in her arms, was crying with his mother too, as if he knew what had happened around him. He went to his house through the vaulted entrance amid the angry gaze. The commander and soldiers from both sides were there. They were taking him to the police station to take Benjamin's statement. Benjamin's hands were handcuffed. Yausef leaned against the wall on the stairs as they descended, letting them descend. A look of fear and regret appeared on Benjamin's face.

Lamentations were heard from the garden. Leila took her steps in fear. She saw someone lying on the ground, but she was afraid to look, she did not want to know who he was.

The village women gathered around him, weeping over the corpse lying on the ground, tearing their hair and punching their chests.

There she saw her father, whose shoulders were shaking as he wept. Mesut was also crying on his knee. So it wasn't Mesut lying on the ground, it was someone else. One of the twins appeared, trying to understand from his movements whether it was Lokman or Idris. She slipped into the crowd. Her legs were trembling and tangled. On the ground, the head of the lifeless body was covered with blood and a scarf. She looked around with fearful eyes to see where the other of the twins was. There, the other twin, holding his mother's arm, was crying hard on his head. She thought she saw a double, but two of the twins were alive. She had one older brother left. A lump formed in Leila's chest, and her eyes went white. She was looking for her brother Mustafa everywhere.

Fearfully, she shifted her face to the legacy of death, which was lamented over. She looked at the slumped right hand and saw the engagement ring. Her eldest and beloved brother Mustafa, whom she loved very much, had died.

This was the last image that Leila saw.

She stopped breathing. Her eyes darkened, and she fainted. She collapsed to the ground among the women.

Before dawn broke, the burials were prepared. With the first light of the morning, mostly Muslims from the imams and villagers came to bury Mustafa. Most of the Christians could not come because they were scared.

They lowered Mustafa's shrouded body into the pit. They buried the engaged young man. The wounded-hearted father could not hold back his tears as he handed over his son's body to the ground. The thirsty earth absorbed Father's tears and digested them. The drops that flowed from the painful heart became invisible on the ground.

Mustafa's fiancee Suheyla and her family had arrived at the funeral and were devastated. The fresh fiancee's voice was hoarse from crying. Her face was scratched and bled.

Leila was tired of crying and wandering around lifelessly.

She started to cry again, saying, "He fell to the ground that she loved, and passed away from me forever."

Fatma was rocking back and forth, punching her chest, lamenting for her son. Her weak body was about to fall, her eyes darkened by the bondage of crying and lack of sleep.

Nobody had slept. All of Mustafa's friends were also there. While Idris and Lokman were burying their brother, they shovelled soil on him. One by one, the earth enveloped his shrouded body. The shroud disappeared under the ground.

Qasim was very weak, he could hardly stand. He staggered and stumbled, raising his hand to his face as if his eyes were darkening, receiving support from whatever he extended his other hand to. He was dazed, wandering like a spirit.

The condolences were left to pray at home. Everyone was worried about the fate of their neighbours. Assyrians in the village became afraid to leave their homes. They had already planned their preparations to escape from the village immediately.

The gendarme was still waiting at the door of the Abrohoms. They were in a state of being on guard.

If the commander, who was approaching Qasim, were feeling well, they would take his statement too. They talked with Qasim over the drying trunks of apple trees.

"We got Benjamin's statement."

During the ball game, the young people fought, Mustafa fell victim to a stone while separating them... In simple terms, Qasim realised that it was an accident. The children of Abrohom, whom he regarded as loved like his brother, were no different from his own. He knew that it was not a deliberate situation.

"There is intent to injure with no intent to kill, and he will be punished just for that..."

"I have no complaints, sir, don't sue him..."

The commander looked at the brave father in surprise.

"His punishment..."

"I have no complaints... There is no claim from me. Let him go."

"This is out of our decision."

"Sir... They are my heart, my close family... Bro's children are also my children; My children grew up with them. They were all like brothers. It was a sibling rivalry, sir. How can I file a criminal complaint against my brother's son…"

The commander shook his head, tried to console his sadness, and tapped his shoulder to reassure him.

"Thank you again, Mr Qasim. We will do what is necessary."

It was heard before daybreak that Qasim had not filed a complaint. Fatma kept beating her chest and screaming about the pain of losing her son.

Lokman and Idris tried to calm her down but in vain.

"He will be avenged… My son's, my valiant's blood, has not dried up yet. His blood is still wet on the ground… Take my life, my God, take my life…"

Idris:

"Mother, please don't cry anymore… Nothing will bring him back. Do you think he will come back when you cry?"

"This happened because of you; because of you, my valiant fell to the ground."

"How could we have known that this would happen," said Lokman regretfully, "now he is gone, crying will not bring him back, Mother."

"My son is dead. Why didn't he die too, huh, my God? Why me…"

"You're rebelling, Mom," Lokman nudged her.

"Go… Go avenge your brother… What are you waiting for… Go right now!.."

Fatma was choking while shouting, and her chest was growling. The twins stared at each other as if questioning each other.

David, from Syriac, was very sad because the ball from his son Alex's foot hit the window. David was also hesitant to go to Mustafa's condolences. He took his family and left the village before the arrows were directed at them. Worried Assyrians, accompanied by the Gendarme, came out of the village.

The gendarmerie stood in rotation in the village until the next day.

They pacified the villagers, rushed those who had a crisis to the hospital, warned them not to attack the Christians, and became conciliatory among the villagers. The stubborn villagers wouldn't have known their father had he come. They said that if Benjamin, the son of the Christians, returned, he would be stoned.

The Commander warned Abrohom :

"Is there a place to take your family and go?"

"We will go to Mor Gabriel."

Abrohom was paralysed. They released Benjamin after the second day, who had been in custody for twenty-four hours. He was ashamed to look at his father's face.

Qasim had spared his son, breaking Abrohom's heart even more. Abrohom could neither apologise nor ask for forgiveness from Qasim.

Tears welled up in Abrohom's eyes; he wanted to hug his friend's neck and sob. He had to appear as the strong father of the family and watch over them in any situation.

Seeing Benjamin, the villagers tried to attack and booed them. Even though the guards prevented the villagers, they also got their share of spitting and booing. The soldiers joined arms and formed a perimeter.

Abrohom gathered his family, who were waiting in a jogging hall.

"C'mon, pack up! We have to get out of here now!"

Taking her child in her arms, Aziza said, "What has happened to us, my God? Why has this happened? Where is Yausef? Go and find your brother."

Yausef was in his room. He was resisting not going out, not leaving the village and beloved Leila. He was listening to the laments coming from the house next door behind the wall.

"What did you do, huh?" he said and attacked Benjamin as soon as he opened the door.

Benjamin defied Yausef, able to say, "It was an accident."

"Their father separated them, saying, 'Why should I deal with you! Enough already. We need to leave here. Come on, I'm telling you...'"

Aziza, with a frozen face, wanted to make sure about where they were going.

"Where are we going? What will happen to us..."

"We will go to Mor Gabriel. The Metropolitan will surely take care of us. They will protect us. There was no premeditated murder. No intentional situation, it happened by accident. Qasim didn't press charges, but the Muslims won't leave us alone in this village. Hurry up."

"I'm not going anywhere."

Aziza pleaded with Yausef, "Please, my son, we have no other choice... Don't you see the crowd outside the door?!"

As darkness painted the earth in its colour, the crowd continued to sit in the mourning house. Imam Salih had also arrived and was murmuring quietly enough to be heard:

"I tried to tell you, but you didn't listen to me."

The village headman gestured with his eyebrows and eyes as if saying, "Now is the time."

The gendarmerie created a corridor for the Syrians. Abrohom and his young family packed their belongings and placed them in the minibus.

Yausef looked inside through the broken window of the house, agonizing with the desire to see Leila.

They had to leave the village with the soldiers, the gendarmerie retreated to the police station, and the Assyrians went to the church.

One of the condolences reported that his next-door neighbours were on their way with the gendarmerie. The news reached Fatma immediately, and without wasting much time, she took the twins to the kitchen and lamented to them.

Fatma was still having inexhaustible nervous breakdowns and fainting and sobbing.

"My son's, Mustafa's blood has not dried yet. I just buried him… This revenge will be taken before his soil dries up. There will be justice for him. It should be done immediately, immediately!.."

Idris and Lokman could not calm their mother any longer. Idris looked into his mother's eyes.

"Mother please, the guests will hear!"

"I'm going to die, I can't live anymore. This revenge must be taken before Mustafa's blood dries up!"

"If I kill someone, will you shut up now, mother? Will you calm down?..." said Lokman provocatively.

Lokman turned to Idris and said, "You go get the rifle and the horse. Quick! Before it's too late… I won't leave my mother alone." He left the task to Idris in a sneaky way.

Idris grabbed his father's hunting rifle, cleaned it and loaded the cartridges. He even brought spare cartridges with him.

Auburn was not at peace in the barn. She felt everything, as if she knew. She was neighing, stomping, making a clatter, as if she was crying non-stop.

Leila covered her ears so she wouldn't hear Auburn. She wanted to cry, but her tear ducts were dry. Leila's eyes shifted to the twins. Idris rushed down to the stable in quick steps. Sensing his activity, Leila followed after him.

He saddled Mustafa's horse and mounted it, adjusting the rifle on his shoulder. Leila stood by the door, arms outstretched:

"Brother, please don't do this... Let there be no more deaths... Don't listen to our mother, brother, please give up..."

"Step aside!" he said, placing his foot in the stirrup and spurring Auburn. He charged toward Leila. Leila had to step aside.

Leila's voice grew hoarse, "Please, don't shoot Yausef, brother, he knows nothing!.."

Her pleading was no longer effective, even if she screamed, Idris wouldn't hear her. He wouldn't listen... Leila pinched herself, thinking that everything she had experienced since the previous day was a nightmare. Her fearful eyes turned bloodshot from crying.

Idris spurred the horse at a gallop, and before reaching the fork in the road, he caught the red-coloured minibus. He accelerated Auburn a little more and blocked the way of the minibus. Abrohom could no longer step on the gas. The speed of the minibus was considerably lower than the speed of the horse. Idris rode the horse in front of the minibus. Helplessly, Abrohom swerved to the right, skidded over the loaded pebbles, and stopped.

"Nobody gets out of the car. I'll talk to him."

Yausef acted but had to listen to his father.

Abrohom got out of the vehicle, came to the front of the minibus, and showed his surrender with his hands in the air.

"My son Lokman, please listen to me. It was by accident. You know it too. We are a family. Our separation was not our own."

"I am not Lokman..."

Abrohom's tearful, trembling lips and all his naivety could not soften Idris's steely face. He looked at him in surprise, as Benjamin, who was sitting next to the driver, got off the bus. The passenger door opened behind him, and Turabdin got off. Yausef immediately jumped after him.

Aziza couldn't hold back her tears, shaking her toddler Samuel in her arms.

"Sons, please don't get off."

Benjamin rushed forward, and Turabdin hugged his brother in advance, pulling him back. Gabriel watched his elder brothers and father with fearful eyes. Yausef jumped forward:

"Idris, stop! Don't do anything wrong!"

Benjamin went ahead of his father:

"Idris, you know how much I love you and Mustafa. I became a victim of my anger, it happened by accident. How could I have known he was going to die!"

Turabdin "What will you get, Idris!" said. Idris panicked against the crowd and immediately fired his rifle. He aimed the rifle at the crowd and shot over the horse. The horse was startled by the sound of bullets and reared up. Idris was almost falling off the horse, at the last moment he caught the halter and held onto the horse. The horse, on the back of Idris, immediately ran away from there like crazy.

Turabdin, who had collapsed to the ground, had been shot while Benjamin was targeted. The shot had hit him in the back where his heart was. Turabdin died right there.

Idris rested with Auburn in the cemetery near the village until the morning. He knew that the gendarmerie would immediately go to his family without waiting.

Even if he returned home, he would not be able to tell his mother the gospel, and he would be ashamed of his father. Idris had broken his father's promise.

Wasn't Qasim who had already forgiven Benjamin... How did he get gassed by his mother all of a sudden? For a while, he could not realise whether his action was a mistake or not. He touched the soil of his brother Mustafa's grave. They had placed a large stone upright on Mustafa's grave, and Idris caressed the tombstone:

"I got your revenge, brother Mustafa! Rest in peace…"

Auburn was constantly restless.

The weather was getting cold. The sky was on the alert as if it was about to spill its waters.

Idris didn't have any idea if it was from the cold, but he started to tremble and could not bear to wait there any longer.

Qasim lay on the ground; He was supporting his head with one hand and hitting his knee like a darbuka with the other. He was watching the rug on the floor indifferently. The villagers who came to offer their condolences were sitting next to Qasim close to each other.

Mesut was crying softly in the corner of the room. Fatma was lying on a mattress in the next room. Neighbour women came to help, serving and washing the dishes without stopping.

Lokman was waiting impatiently for Idris's return. He was standing on the patio in front of the door, watching the people coming and going. Those who came out of the condolence were saying goodbye to Lokman and asking for patience.

Idris turned around in a sweat, dragged Auburn to the barn, and went out to the house.

When Qasim saw him with the ruffle he rushed to his side, caught Idris and shouted, "What have you done?" His weak hand trembled in the air, shaking Idris's cheek with a 'crack' sound. He slapped a child for the first time. The villagers sitting in the hall for condolences were confused and sad. The death of two young people in one night was the heaviest mourning this village could experience in history. The villagers dispersed to their homes.

Qasim felt that he was having a heart attack with a sudden feeling of pain and tightness in his heart. He staggered to his feet, his eyes closed, his jaw clenched. Leila and Lokman put him on the mat and put two pillows under his head. Mesut had brought water in a metal cup for a run. Qasim drank the water pouring down his face like a baby.

The gendarmerie had come to the village, and they detained the first twin, Lokman, who came to the door.

"I didn't kill anyone. I am innocent…"

Idris rushed forward with mad courage. He surrendered himself.

"I killed him. Take me."

The gendarmes were looking at the twin in one hand and the other in front of them. They also had difficulty distinguishing between identical twins.

"Then take him too. We will investigate the two of them," said the commander solemnly.

Qasim knelt down and opened his mouth. He was having a nightmare as if his voice was not stuck in his throat. He couldn't even cry from exhaustion and lack of sleep. His eyes looked sickly. He was seeing everyone blurry. He felt the need to get up and stumble, clinging to the walls, and when he entered the house, he would lie on the cushions again. He was smoking cigarettes now. It was the only way to numb his brain.

Idris testified in detail that he committed the crime himself and how he committed it. His twin Lokman was released.

Not long after, they took Idris to court.

"According to Article 428 of the Turkish Penal Code… for the crime of intentional murder… life imprisonment…"

He swallowed every word of the judge's decision, staring into the mouths of serious, unfamiliar men. Now Idris was aware that he had done wrong, he was helpless, and he regretted and cursed himself. Young wrists were handcuffed and taken to Midyat M Type Closed Prison. He would be sentenced to a total of eighteen years in prison with good behaviour.

Qasim no longer had the strength to resist, to utter a word. He was deaf to what was being said, closing his eyes like a little owl and swaying slightly. He had become a sick old man waiting to die.

The sky was covered with dark clouds. Obviously, it was going to empty its tears down, without a single drop of rain, however, lightning was falling on the ground from place to place. Lightning flashed briefly, the village rumbled with occasional thunder, and the ground split open.

The autumn rain did not stop for days. After the rain, nature had lost its colours and faded. The earth was encircled as red as tile dust.

Leila was building her whole future on Yausef, all her dreams were ruined with a simple stone, a worthless stone. Would she be able to recover and stand up? Spending a day without Yausef terrified her. Now she would spend every day without Yausef.

Fatma didn't forgive anyone that blamed her. And finally:

"This is all because of your father. He did not go to the mosque on a Friday and pray. If he had been a religious person, God would not have brought them to me. Oh, I'm going to die."

The woman's nagging drowned out even the thunder. It was more comforting than listening to the woman's angry words while watching the rain pour down in anger outside. Leila was in the back room, watching the dark house of the Yausef's through the window covered with nylon. It was as if he was going to light the lamp soon and greet Leila with a smile.

He was getting weaker day by day, deflating like a balloon before his eyes. Qasim's sharp gaze could not maintain its influence over Fatma's nagging. Steel-piercing eyes were like the eyes of a sad and begging helpless person.

"It happens all the time… One side is dominant and the other side is the oppressed… When the time changes, the roles also change. When the oppressed dominate, they begin to oppress others at the first opportunity. It's in one's blood…" These thoughts were giving him a headache. Sometimes he thought he was in Iraq and dressed as if he was preparing for a meeting, sometimes when he realized that he was in the village, he continued to mourn more fiercely from where he left off.

Qasim faced Lokman, burdened by the weight of his feeble body carrying his spirit, he took a stance.

"My son, I am dying now. As the elder of this family, I will leave you behind. Please, my son, make every effort for your sister Leila and little brother Mesut's education. If the animals become a burden, you can sell them and open a shop in the town to run. But for the others…" coughing interrupted his speech, splitting through his lungs, "do not make any decisions regarding the land and the house without the approval of your siblings. You can still cultivate the fields; I believe you can manage by paying a few labourers. The family will depend on you. You will be both a father and a brother to them."

He couldn't continue speaking as he coughed, almost choking. Despite the echo in his lungs, he smoked another cigarette on top of it. Qasim was willingly committing suicide. Life had lost its meaning for him.

Trees shed their withered leaves. Streets were muddy, moulded by the footsteps of animals. Grey smoke rose from the chimneys of houses. The village had an unsettling silence. The villagers no longer gathered together as they used to, drinking tea and joking around. Fatma had buried one of her sons and sent another to prison. Despite tearing her hair out every day, she didn't go bald. Leila sometimes even thought that she was putting on a show. She would collapse next to her father, trying to talk to him. Qasim couldn't see anyone anymore, not even sensing Leila's presence. He had lost his appetite for food and drink.

Leila realized that her father would never come back.

"Daddy, please talk to me," she said, sobbing, "I can't handle it..."

Qasim's steely face turned into an expression of pain within a few days. "Wouldn't you say, 'You are no different from my sons'? Why are you indifferent now towards me?"

Qasim turned his head slowly to that side, staring at her pointlessly. She heard the wheezing of his nose, his heavy eyes not blinking. He was saying to himself:

"We couldn't establish the revolution in Iraq, and we couldn't find peace here either."

Qasim has turned into that carefree stone that had existed in front of the door for years, of no importance. On Qasim's slumped face, his eyes closed, and his breathing became more and more difficult.

Mustafa's death and Idris's imprisonment were a fire jacket for Qasim, he could not stand it any longer.

Qasim passed away.

His partridges fluttered wildly between the wooden bars. They felt the death of their owner. Just like Auburn, the partridges were beating from side to side, singing a song as if they were lamenting.

Never had spring been so blurry and muffled.

The condolence was only on its twelfth day. While the villagers were at the gathering, they sought something to discuss. Imam Saleh broke the silence and cleared his throat, expressing his opinion:

"I told you, two different religions cannot coexist. Brother is killing brother, how can religions not shoot each other? Muslims should always be one."

"Oh Imam Saleh, you should keep your sermons to yourself. At least shut up in his condolences."

Imam Saleh got up, offended, and went home.

"You offended the imam."

"He's all the way to hell."

"He is an imam, it is a sin. Don't talk like that, you'll burn in hell."

"Is he going to decide where I go... We are all human."

"Qasim's spirit has been revived," one man murmured to another.

"If you use your mind, you don't need to hear his rambling ideas. I have full faith, and I don't want parasites to get in the way," the guy continued.

"Yes, thank God. I also perform my five daily prayers and keep my faith."

Clasping his hands on his cane, the elder wiped the moisture from his eyes and joined the conversation:

"There are elections soon. What do you think, will the state give us farmer support this time?"

"God knows," said the villagers in unison.

People from other villages and cities came to offer condolences. Qasim had many admirers and acquaintances. Those who came to condolence attributed a lot to his passing away at this young age to many things.

Saying "There is no age for death", they also remembered the fiancee Mustafa, who died before him. They recited Fatiha for both.

Relatives who came from other cities for condolences cried out with their hands on both thighs from the gate of the garden and cried with cries that pierced the sky.

"My valiant Mustafa... my valiant Qasim... death does not suit you at all..."

Among the women, there were Behiye, Muhtar's wife, and Latife besides his mother.

Latife got up and helped the dull-faced Leila, who was distributing lemon cologne. Leila's hands were shaking, she couldn't mourn around her guests, she had become an indifferent stone among a room full of crying women. Latife filled the teas and handed them out to the women one by one.

The villager women who were cooking for Mustafa's engagement were cooking for the late Mustafa and his father Qasim this time, in cauldrons in the garden.

Latife also brought tea to the women. At the first opportunity she caught Lokman, they talked in a whisper in the corner of the house.

"Are you crazy, Latife? My father's condolences are on the ground!"

"Shall my father sell me like my older sisters? He intends to remarry soon so that he can have a son... From what I heard, he will give me to the next village and take a girl from there. He has found himself a young woman, and he will give me to his father. Then you'll see!"

Those who saw Latife crying, thought that she was crying for Mustafa or Qasim, joined in with "oh wow" cries. However, as soon as the condolences were over, Latife was crying at the prospect of her father giving her to an old man. She imagined her own death and Lokman would give his condolences for her as well.

"This condolence will not end. If he weds me too, I will strangle myself on that wedding night with my veil."

"We'll think of a way, Latife, come on in now, they'll hear us."

Lokman handed them the empty tea glasses and told them to pour the tea again. He returned to the condolence tent. Latife's chest went up and down, and she went inside to pour the tea.

Since her older sister's wedding, Latife had never shut up and put pressure on her. Latife did not come to offer her condolences the next day. For a moment, Lokman thought he had lost her, but Muhtar was sprawled on the chair, quite in the mood among his condolence visitors. Lokman opened the barn door and placed the leather saddle on the horse. Fatma was distracted by the tumult of Auburn, but still weak, she went out and poked her head into the barn.

"What is going on there?"

"Mother, it is me. I'm going to the back road."

"Well, not now. You have to go and sit with the guests. The man of my house..." While she was prolonging her words, Lokman immediately interrupted:

"I will go to meet the guests. They might be lost, they still haven't arrived. I'll go and show them the way," he said, leaving the house behind, and blending into the village from the side without showing his condolences.

Fatma did not understand, she was still lamenting and fainting for her sons and husband. Leila didn't even have time to mourn. Meals were eaten, dishes were washed, and tea was brewed on top of tea. Mirra was cooked and served to villagers many times. Her hand was trembling; she remembered the days when she and her father drank together, tears flowing softly. Mesut was left alone and hosted the condolences until late hours.

Lokman had not yet returned. The headman got up and went home. Leila and Mesut put the chairs on top of each other and collected them. Leila was looking at the Yausef's house from time to time. She thought about the possibility that he might still be there. She seemed to see his shadow in every corner of the courtyard. But having Yausef there wouldn't change a thing, she thought. So she bent down again and swept the floor as if she was collecting her emotions with a broom, and the drops from Leila's eyes mingled with the ground.

Together with Mesut, they would not return home until evening, staying by the grave of Mustafa and their father Qasim, who lay beside his son's grave. Leila had reached the verge of madness. She had become pale-faced from crying.

12

he foam was coming out of Muhtar's mouth. Even his oversized pants squeaked between his legs. Patent leather shoes had sunk in the mud and lost their shine. He was walking with difficulty under his weight, panting. Since Qasim could not jump over the wall of the house, he walked around it for a long time and attacked the door of the house.

"Fatma... You know the customs. All these guys look at my one word" he mentioned the servants behind him, "with a word, they go and bring your son's body."

"For God's sake, Muhtar... Did I tell him to go and kidnap the girl? Please don't do it. I beg you, let me kiss your feet."

The poor woman clung to his shoes, which were covered in dust.

"My mourning continues, Muhtar. Don't you have any conscience... I'm begging you..." she pleaded.

"Just look at Qasim's wife... Stand up, woman!" Muhtar said, freeing himself from Fatma's grasp.

"I have buried one son, my other son is in prison, I just recently buried my husband. I implore you, Muhtar, don't oppress us. Don't harm my boy Lokman, I'll be your servant, your slave," Fatma uttered her words rapidly.

Leila, standing at the threshold of the house, saw her face darken and held onto her brother Mesut, observing her mother's helplessness. Muhtar glanced at Leila and twisted his moustache.

"Death is not a necessity, of course..."

"No, it's not necessary. Allah gives life and Allah takes it away."

Muhtar looked at his servants and grinned slightly.

"As if your son, Idris, hasn't buried someone else's child, woman."

"My son Idris made a mistake, he couldn't bear his brother's death, Muhtar. Please forgive us!"

"I told you to stand up! I will make another offer..."

Fatma shook her dress from behind with her hand and said, "Whatever you want, Muhtar, whatever you want..."

Muhtar hesitated at first, feeling that this attitude was beneath him, then quickly dismissed it. He straightened himself up again and whispered sharply: "Your daughter in exchange for your son..."

Fatma was about to say, "You don't even have a son," but she bit her tongue. She realized that he wanted Leila for himself.

Fatma only said, "Okay, when she comes back from the cemetery of her father, I will bring her with my hands."

"My servants will be after you Fatma, don't do anything wrong."

Fatma hadn't even prepared a dowry for Leila. It had never crossed her mind to set up a dowry for her daughter. Her father had said to Fatma, "My daughter will study, don't cloud her mind with dowries and trousseaus!"

She said to the headman of the village "Our daughter was going to study. She was a high school student, after all... That's why we never prepared a dowry for her." She demanded the dowry money and snatched a substantial amount from the Muhtar.

When Leila returned from the cemetery with Mesut, she thought the strangers standing in front of the door might have come to offer their condolences. Mesut stood by their side as the man of the house. Mesut felt sorry; these men neither recited the Fatiha nor spoke a word. Leila was about to go inside and wash her hands and face.

Fatma said, "Go wash up and change your clothes... The labourers will take you to the Muhtar."

"Why?" Leila asked.

"The Muhtar wants you in exchange for his brother."

Leila thought she had misheard. Her mother had submitted to wed her to the Muhtar.

Leila didn't trust her mother; she felt that she was now all alone. Mesut was still too young to comprehend what was happening. Nevertheless, Mesut held onto her sister and said, "Don't leave me, sister," Mesut cried.

Her senses were clouded with anger, and she couldn't think clearly. If only she knew where Yausef was, she would definitely run to him. Neither her father, whom she could vehemently reject, nor her beloved brother Mustafa would oppose. Leila sought a solution for the dilemma.

She felt as if boiling water had been poured over her brain. She raised her hands in the air, dropped to her knees, and screamed, "Father! Please help me. This woman will ruin my life and do as she pleases in the end. Why did you leave me alone and defenseless?"

"Stop begging. They're dead and gone. They abandoned us."

Mesut clung to his sister's waist, saying, "I won't leave my sister."

"Even if you kill me, I won't go to that hairy sack of fat! I will study, and so will my brother... What will my brother do? Aren't you afraid at all?" cried out Leila to Fatma.

"What is there to fear? Besides death, what else is there to fear? Lokman kidnapped his daughter and now I have only Mesut left. Should I lose him too, because of you?"

Mesut's arms went limp; he had never thought that he could die. Fatma fired her words with full force:

"My valiant son is dead. One of my twins went inside and the other one kidnapped the daughter of a rich man in the village. Your father left us. I have only one son, Mesut, and should I surrender him to the bullets of Muhtar's captives for your sake!"

"I must read!"

She was trying to choke on sobs. Leila couldn't understand what she was saying. Her eyes were dry and no tears were flowing from her eyes anymore.

"What are you going to do when you read? Will school feed us?"

"Kill me but don't send me Mom… I beg you; please don't end my life …"

Those who served with Muhtar until late that evening had stayed in Fatma's house. They aimed to take Leila away, even if by force. The headman was fat, and it was hard for him to move. Fatma left the door open, and while Leila hadn't changed yet, they grabbed her by the hair and pulled her under the protection of Muhtar.

Imam Saleh was also in Muhtar's house. While the Imam was performing the marriage, they received acceptance from Fatma's mouth as a proxy. She would have objected if he had asked Leila if she was like her father. Imam addressed hers mother directly.

He gave a bag full of gold as gifts to the Imam and Fatma, the mother of his new wife. Leila was now Muhtar's wife, unwillingly, Behiye's second wife.

Leila cried out for the whole village to hear, but no one answered her pleas for help. They beat her until she fainted and was locked in the shed till the morning.

Behiye had prepared a white dress like a tulle curtain. Leila was struggling tossing the dress, refusing to wear it. She was removing off makeup. Behiye, who was also Muhtar's cousin, was in tears. On the one hand, she was sad about her daughter's abduction; on the other hand, she was happy that Muhtar would get rid of her trouble. The price of Lokman's selfish behaviour cost the life of Qasim's only beloved daughter.

According to Qasim, Leila would be a great person, and all the villagers knew that. But Leila is now here in Muhtar's house, no different than a slave.

Leila was forced to dress. They put makeup on his face and she tried wipe it off.

There was no wedding; he did not want to attract the attention of those who loved Qasim by having a wedding after the village's funerals, but the village men ate the wedding dinner until their stomachs burst. Dozens of dishes went round and round.

The day held no joyous moments. Only the Muhtar had prepared himself like a young groom, taking a bath and shaving. He wore a clean suit that reeked of strong soap, the buttons on his shirt threatening to burst. It was evident that the suit was too small for him, as even the sleeves of his jacket strained against his movements. Desperate to rid himself of the attire, he barged into the bride's room, instructing Leila to close the door behind him as he secured it from his side. Any chance of escape had now vanished for Leila.

He pounced on her without a shred of mercy, rendering the young girl unable to move an inch. Her breath became shallow, forced to inhale the odour of onions the man had consumed for lunch. She pleaded, "Help me..." hoping her calls would summon Yausef back. Three times she cried out in vain, left utterly helpless.

"Uncle Muhtar, please don't..."

"I am your husband now! You spawn of the bitch!" he spat, brushing aside her pleas. He ripped off Leyla's dress like a curtain, revealing her vulnerable body. The Muhtar, with the voracity of a famished wild animal, attacked the fair-skinned girl. Leila fought against his touch, but her efforts were futile, her strength was powerless. She turned her head from side to side, struggling to free herself from his grasp. She pushed him with delicate arms, but it was as feeble as pushing against a wall. Her tears flowed unabated, and along with the losses her family had endured, she had grown weak from days without nourishment.

It was painful for Muhtar to touch her. Her milky white skin was bare in an instant, and she shuddered. The old fat man drooled all over her milky white skin. She tried to grab something to get rid of this putrid tyrant, but she couldn't get anywhere; the mass on her was too heavy, and his lips and saliva already soiled her delicate body.

"I want to die! Oh my God, please take my life!"

The headman could hear the girl's cries as a groan. He enjoyed the way his rabid body roamed the fragile ground.

After the cry of "Father!.. Save me...", Muhtar stopped, backed up a little, and twisted the girl with a strong slap.

Leila groaned, begged and cried, but Muhtar did not notice anything. She continued to breathe through her bloody nose, not giving up, still pushing him, but this move made it more attractive for Muhtar to have her. Muhtar slid off his own clothes with a movement of his feet and remained naked on the girl. Leila felt nauseous when her skin touched his, her whole body trembled. There was no escape. Her father's rosy-cheeked daughter was pale under the lips of a rascal. Muhtar was biting her, sucking and slapping her with his instinctive, primal gesture. Tired of struggling, having no solution, and being unable to move, Leila also took off her simple cotton underwear and threw it away. The headman snuggled into the girl, who was lying like a statue. Leila let out a bitter cry, her untouched breasts heaving up and down. Her body was severed. She gritted her teeth, tears welling in her eyes for the last time. She was very ashamed. There was no one to turn to for help. Yausef's shadow disappeared like the others. Even though they came, they couldn't rescue her, she was no longer the old Leila. Her cries were unsuccessful; no one came to her aid. Was everyone in this world this cruel? Were all the women waiting at the door enjoying it, or were they just as helpless as Leila?

Muhtar pressed his hairy body against her smooth skin. He bit her newly defined breasts and rounded shoulders, leaving them bruised. He let his stinking sweat run down on her. Not only was the nauseating bad breath enough, but also, because of the leather shoes he was wearing in the middle of the heat, his feet made the room stink.

Leila was sick of every object in this bridal chamber. She took the opportunity and looked for a weapon that would be enough to kill herself. She was blind, she didn't want to close her eyes and see anything. Her fists were clenched, and she felt reluctantly at the body soaked by the spit of the man who was her enemy. She could no longer make a sound or cry as if iron had been poured into her throat. Leila felt nauseous, her face turned pale, and she fainted on the floor.

When she opened her eyes, she realised that a woman who looked like her mother was sitting beside her and caressing her hair.

"Mom, why did you hurt me? Please take me away from here, kill me, but don't bring me back Mom…" she muttered.

"Oh my baby girl, oh my unfortunate beautiful girl. Ah, the only daughter of valiant Qasim…"

She cleared her eyes, looked at the lamenting woman, and saw Muhtar's first wife Behiye. Next to her, the woman was crying like a mother and stroking Leila's hair. She felt ashamed, and she cried, apologising.

"Behiye sister…"

"Don't cry my girl, it's not your fault. This is how your destiny is written…"

Leila had been unconscious since the previous night. She was still bleeding after the forced reunion. She was not taken to the hospital because she was underage. A doctor was brought to the house. She was given medicine to stop the blood. If the doctor complained about her, Muhtar would be in trouble. But unfortunately, the swelling of the doctor's pocket had taken him away from his conscience.

"You know how to wash your body, right?" said Behiye, "I suppose you know what ghusl means. Didn't they teach it at school, my beautiful girl, my unfortunate girl…"

Leila looked meaninglessly; no sound came out.

"Your mother didn't teach you anything, of course."

Hatred and anger dripped from his mouth.

For the first time, Leila found her father's teachings empty. The Epic of Gilgamesh did not matter here, the meaning of Omer Khayyam's poems was lost, and Dengbej's words had no meaning anymore. She had memorised the story Mem and Zin in vain; the literature of Cegerxwin and Mehmet Uzun was insufficient here. What women did in history was no longer essential. She flew away before any of them could save her.

There was a young woman alone, lonely, helpless, tired and powerless. She was far from all the rules of being a woman. All that history, philosophy, mathematics, and geography had not worked anymore.

Behiye took Leila to the hamam by pinching, tugging, and stripping her. She washed her and had her memorise how many times to pour water and which suras to recite... Leila was no different from a dead person. She could not understand whether Behiye treated her like a mother or cowife.

Plagued by a throbbing pain in her belly, Leila had found a way to sneak out of the house unnoticed. The following day, she managed to escape, but Fatma refused to take her back in:

"You are not welcome here anymore. You have a husband and a home. Be a decent woman!"

"I am not his wife! You sold me like a slave!"

Fatma burst into tears, sobbing uncontrollably. She turned to Mesut and pleaded:

"Mesut, take this wretched woman to her husband's home, or they will come and kill you. Must I lose another son?"

Leila looked at Mesut, who remained motionless and silent.

"You ruined all our lives! I won't stay in this house for even a second longer! My father left us, and I don't care if this house burns to the ground!"

Fatma briefly considered the possibility of burning down the house but was relieved when Leila disappeared into the night. Leila thought of Yusuf and went to his home. She headed to the swing where they used to play together. The ropes of the swing were tangled, dirty, and abandoned. She fixed it and swung for a while. Night had fallen. The village headman and the labourers made their way to the garden where the swing was moving. Leila swung and cried.

The villagers gossiped for a long time about Leila, saying she had gone mad. The headman feared sleeping in the same room with her, thinking she might harm him. After waiting for an opportunity to relax his frenzied body, he left Leila alone in the room and locked the door out of fear.

Rumours had been circulating among the villagers about good news regarding the Syriacs. It was said that the Christians had migrated to Europe. Oh, Europe! Which country, which city, which street... Leila wished she could teleport herself there. She longed to become invisible and simply observe Yausef from afar... But ruthless despair shattered her dreams, bringing Leila back to harsh reality.

In Muhtar's room, Leila stared at the plastic dresser, the old wardrobe, a trunk filled with dowries, the worn-out steam carpet, and the soft double bedspread imported from Saudi Arabia. She didn't feel like she belonged here; she felt more like an uninvited guest.

Leila hadn't eaten anything, nor had she looked in the mirror. Now, she had become a thin, slender young girl, just like her mother. Though Behiye kept her distance from her daughter, she felt deeply sorry for Leila's condition. If she were to talk to Leila, she would start crying herself.

Leila had taken a water canister and went to her brother's grave. If she didn't water those flowers in the scorching sun, they would wither away immediately. Muhtar was furious even about Leila's unauthorised visits to the cemetery.

Muhtar was restless at home. He found faults in Behiye's cooking and meddled with the housekeeping. It was too easy for him to find an excuse to show his violence towards the family. All he needed was the birds hitting the windows to terrorise the household. He would beat all of his daughters individually, starting with Behiye.

Leila was amazed that Behiye, who was the same age as her mother, didn't make a sound while being beaten by Muhtar. Leila attacked Muhtar and began punching his thick belly. Muhtar looked like a fool. Leila warned him not to lay a finger on her co-wife ever again. Leila's natural disposition, her cunning, and her quick-wittedness had returned.

"Ha-ha... so you're not crazy after all. You sneaky snake! Where do you think you're going without telling me, huh? I'll give you your punishment. Wait!"

The labourers dragged Leila by force to the garden. Though she resisted, she couldn't overpower the two tough men. Muhtar swung his long, serrated stick in the air as a lesson to his co-wives and daughters. The stick whistled as it flew through the air, mercilessly striking Leila's delicate, cotton-like body.

"I am the head of this village! Even government officials straighten their jackets before me. You will obey me! You will be respectful towards me! No one can ever humiliate me in my own home... You won't even go to the bathroom without my permission..." he blabbered.

Behiye's heart couldn't take it anymore; she turned her back and cried softly. She pitied Leila and couldn't summon the strength to stand up against Muhtar.

"God forbid nothing happens to her face," she prayed silently while Muhtar's servants were beating Leila.

Surprisingly, Leila didn't feel pain; she felt like she had been reborn. She looked up at the sky and laughed. "Oh, life, how beautiful you are!"

The labourers stared at Leila and stopped beating her. Muhtar cursed at them for stopping and not continuing.

The sun beat down mercilessly upon the parched earth as Leila trudged through the fields, a small wicker basket hanging from her arm. Her once-plump figure had become gaunt and listless, a shadow of its former self. She had aged beyond her years, burdened by a heavy weight she could not shake. The absence of Yausef, her former love, had left her reeling and heartbroken, and the passing of time had only deepened her pain.

But amidst her sorrow, Leila had found solace in a simple pleasure: the act of drawing intricate designs in the soft, red soil. She had cut her hair and used the tresses as makeshift brushes, carefully crafting patterns that danced across the earth like delicate lace.

One day, as she made her way through the fields, Leila came upon the local overseer, Muhtar, who was busy barking orders at the field hands. In a fit of rage, Muhtar seized the cane from one of the labourers and began to flail it wildly in the air, striking the workers and even landing a blow upon Leila's delicate frame.

But despite the violence that surrounded her, Leila remained resilient, finding comfort in the small moments of beauty she could carve out for herself. She brought a simple lunch of bread, a casserole, and bulgur to Muhtar, along with a cold pitcher of ayran, and settled down nearby to draw in the soil. And in her private moments, she turned to the forgotten art supplies she had discovered in the storage shed, painting vivid images of the village and the people who inhabited it.

Though others may have viewed her as a mere teenager, Leila had an inner strength and a tenacity that belied her youth. She persevered, finding beauty in the everyday moments others may have overlooked. And in doing so, she crafted a life for herself that was uniquely her own.

Eve ventured into the granary and retrieved the picture books her stepdaughters had long since abandoned. Among the toy dolls lay shrunken or unused paint brushes, which she, too, collected and stored away in her own cellar. To save time, she resolved to paint. She would depict the village, the people who vexed her, and those who brought her joy. Through her art, she could express the emotions she dared not share with anyone.

She cut a tuft of hair and, with the deftness of a painter, stroked the white paper with watercolours. The paper soaked up the paint, swelling in response. Leila found solace in this engaging activity. Behiye and Rukiye whispered about her, saying, "She's still undeveloped in mind; she's still a child..."

The paint quickly ran out, so she sought help from nature to find the colours she needed. She used turmeric, radish, spinach, orange peel, tomato paste, coffee, and all sorts of garden flowers, even using the kohl applied to her eyes. She climbed the mulberry tree in the courtyard, gathering purple berries to crush and transform into pure paint. She took tufts of hair from various animals and fixed them to the ends of sticks with string. These organic bristles painted the paper more effectively with her natural pigments than other brushes.

She drew figures and applied diluted paints to them. Rukiye complained about Leila, who had not left her room all day.

"She paints pictures like a nursery kid... She doesn't do any work. We do everything for her. Who knows what she's doing inside?"

Muhtar breathed heavily like an angry bull. His face was swollen like a tomato, and he turned bright red. With Rukiye's encouragement, he called Leila, whom he believed was wasting her time and not doing housework. Imam Salih also criticised Leila's paintings, saying, "These are the devil's creations!" which further fueled Muhtar's anger.

Muhtar caught Leila off guard as she was painting, grabbed her by the hair and dragged her head until his hand cramped from hitting her repeatedly. Behiye tried to stop him, but she received a slap too.

The little girls, Nuriye and Bese, tried to pull their father away from Leila's hair and legs, but they couldn't push him with one fist. Leila's nose bled, and a drop of blood fell on one of her papers. Muhtar couldn't calm down his anger and tore the papers into pieces.

"Is this your father's house, you bitch! You act like a disobedient child! If you don't know how to be a wife, I can teach you forcefully!.."

At first, Leila started painting to pass the time, but she had grown to love it passionately. She didn't care about the beatings anymore; she would never give up this hobby that made her happy. On the days she didn't paint, she felt empty inside.

Recently, Behiye's hands had started to tremble. She would spill a full glass of water without realising it, and she couldn't even hold a plate steadily due to her shaking hands. Muhtar would beat her until she couldn't take it anymore because of her mistake. He would feel uneasy if he didn't beat one of his wives.

"Clumsy woman! May your hand break..." He shouted and attacked her.

"I can't help it; please don't hit me, Muhtar..." Leila couldn't stand Behiye's screams and rushed out of her room. She found Behiye lying motionless beneath Muhtar, who was as wide as he was tall. She jumped on him like a ninja and pushed him aside. Muhtar rolled over like a watermelon. He would have continued rolling if the ground friction hadn't slowed him down.

"You dare raise your hand to me! You son of a bitch! Even your father can't save you from my wrath now..."

When Leila opened her eyes, she saw the village midwife and a few other women. She was pregnant. She didn't even know it. She had a miscarriage.

Muhtar didn't seem to regret what he had done at all. On the contrary, he blamed Leila again:

"Perhaps it could have been my son! You intentionally caused him to be unborn, you offspring of a bastard!"

The headman's eyes clouded, and he began treating Leila with even greater violence than before. The cruelty intensified. Except for Rukiye, the other stepdaughters also came to Leila's aid, allying with her. Rukiye, on the other hand, enjoyed watching Leila get beaten, rubbing her chest and saying, "Oh, oh!" every time she was hit.

Since that day, they had always been in alliance with each other. If the headman tried to beat one of the girls, the others would support her, and this time the girls had also gathered the courage to stand up to their father. Angry and uncontrollable, the headman turned red like a tomato when he became upset, and it seemed like he was about to explode. He breathed from his nose, which covered half of his face. He bit his tongue and foamed at the mouth like he was suffering from rabies, and his bulging eyes shot flames.

After Latife ran away with Lokman, Rukiye became the next stepdaughter to struggle with Leila, "Because of you, my mother is suffering. Get out of here, we don't want you!" she said.

"I tried to leave, but I have nowhere to go," Leila said calmly, accepting her situation helplessly. "Besides, if it weren't for me, your father would have married someone else."

"Because of your brother, my sister went down the wrong path."

"What wrong path? It was a decision they made together. And yes, I'm in this situation because of my brother and your sister! None of this would have happened if she hadn't seduced stupid Lokman. Your father would have given her away in exchange if she hadn't run away. She was right in her own way..."

They fought bitterly, and Behiye had trouble separating them. "Shame on you! Now you'll both get a sackful of beatings from the headman..."

Huriye, the headman's fifth daughter, was taken out of school when she came of age and never sent back. Like Rukiye, she worked on embroidery at home and began preparing her dowry. Only Nuriye and Bese were left, attending the village school... There was a two-year age difference between them.

Leila loved Bese and Nuriye because they both listened to her and studied together. Leila helped them with their homework, and they had their pictures drawn by Leila and showed them to their teachers.

A fresh young teacher with curly hair arrived at the Greenvillage school. When the villagers heard that he had come from the big city, Istanbul, they crowded around the school window as if they had seen an alien. The young teacher, a tall and slim young man with a moustache, had a cheerful face and looked proud and noble, just like Qasim. He had a Nubian nose, and his well-aligned teeth shone brightly when he smiled.

The villagers, especially Muhtar, went to show the new teacher how important he was to them. They provided him with all his needs, including food and drink. The mothers of the children brought eggs, butter, cheese, and milk to the young teacher's house behind the school to ensure their children were treated well.

"Ahmet Teacher, he treats our children well, doesn't he?" They hesitated and flattered the Ahmet teacher.

Ahmet Teacher was from Istanbul. This was his first appointment. After coming to this village, his entire perspective changed. He embraced the village with all his being.

As the sun slowly rose, first darkening and then illuminating the sky, Ahmet Teacher took a deep breath, gazing at the endless sea of land beneath the azure sky as if he were watching the Bosphorus in Istanbul.

When the roosters announced the sunrise to the villagers, Ahmet Teacher shaved his stubble, revealing his baby face. He combed his hair to the side, ran a comb through his moustache, put on his blue short-sleeved striped shirt, tied his wide and long tie over it, put on his dark brown pants, and checked his schoolbooks and notes in his black single-strap document bag. He went to the front of the school, just five steps away from his house. Atatürk's bust also smiled at the sea of land like Ahmet Teacher.

He would open and lock the school door himself every day.

Ahmet Teacher had an uncontrollable excitement and an unending enthusiasm for teaching.

At first, Ahmet Teacher had difficulty communicating. He laughed and felt sad when encountering a rough accent compared to his smooth Turkish. Some new students still needed to learn the language. During the first five years, students were in the same classroom, separated into clusters of desks. There were four dozen rows in front of the blackboard. Like their mothers, the children gathered around the garbage can, the tandoor, and the corners of the class, sharpening their pencils with razor blades. Finally, they checked the sharpness of the tip with their fingers before returning to their seats.

Ahmet Teacher used a section of the blackboard for each class.

The first-grade students stood by the teacher, wearing colourful shalwars under their aprons, asking to go to the bathroom. He wrote "Ali, look" on the board, referring to the row designated for the first grade.

From second grade, Ali didn't know where to look when he stood up, and the older students laughed at him. When the teacher realised his name was Ali, he loved him from the start. Then, from the last row, a voice was heard:

"Teacher, if only our other teachers behaved like you."

Ahmet realised that these children needed to receive more education and love. At first, he felt like a "Çalıkuşu" (a character in Turkish literature by Reşat Nuri Güntekin), but as time passed, he became addicted to the village that he initially found strange, daunting, and challenging. He had become accustomed to the village's atmosphere and had finally stepped into the natural life he had dreamed of.

The teacher didn't like the way she emphasised her name, "Bese…" Bese stood up sharply and made him to approve it, "Bese, Bese…" she repeated, "meaning 'enough'."

When the children had fun, the teacher still didn't know why he was greeted with such an attitude. "Hikmet and Bese, are you siblings?"

"Bese is my sister," Nuriye said, standing up from the pillar near the door.

"Most of you have the same surname… Let's learn your names over time."

Ahmet, who taught five different classes in one day, tried to teach different lessons and give assignments to each row of desks in the same classroom. It was as complex and exhausting as teaching in five separate classes in one day. However, Ahmet's smile and politeness never diminished.

"Do you not know the multiplication table, children?" The last-grade students didn't even understand what the multiplication table was. "Our previous teacher was a soldier. He didn't come to our classes much, teacher."

"But Nuriye knows multiplication and division very well, teacher!" Ahmet was surprised. Nuriye's urban look also gave her a slightly shrewd expression, like her father, Muhtar.

"Well, Muhtar's daughter, come and tell us. Explain to your friends what you owe your success to, so they can study and be successful like you."

"Teacher, she's cheating."

"Yes, her young mother is helping her."

"Her mother? How did her mother learn it?"

"She's not my mother, teacher. Later, she became my mother. Her name is Leila."

Teacher Ahmet became increasingly curious about the identity of Leila, who was frequently heard from other children.

One day he was going to hold a parents' meeting and make an evaluation for the children. He encouraged the children by saying, "If your parents come, I will give you a high grade".

The women whose husbands did not come were predominant. He turned to the oldest man:

"Do you have any children still in school, sir?"

"I have a grandson. His mother is raising the children; his father is a lorry driver. I am here as his parent."

"What was his name?" he was going to look for his student's name in the roll call.

"Shepherd Zahir, the same name as mine."

"Yes, but he doesn't come to school often; why?"

"I send him to my place when I am absent, teacher. He's my rookie, my hand and foot. Without him, who would I send, my wife?"

The villagers snickered at Zaho as the women sat on the desks with difficulty, straining, covering their mouths with cheesecloths.

"Your children, your grandchildren... Please, please let them pay more attention to school."

They looked at the teacher without understanding.

The women shyly covered half of their faces with their cheesecloths. There was a young woman sitting confidently, her green chintz cheesecloth wrapped in a row under her hair; she tied the two ends of the cheesecloth together and let it hang from her shoulders. The teacher thought she might be 'Leila', but looking at her age, he thought this might be impossible. She was a young woman with an expression that still carried the innocence of a child and eyes that penetrated deeply into one's soul. Her fingers looked dirty, and even if she washed her hands, the traces of the paint did not disappear. The young woman had her eyes on her hands and her ears on the new young teacher.

Teacher Ahmet got to know the parents of the children and introduced himself. He talked about his purpose for coming to the village, his ideals, and his goals. Leila raised her eyes to Teacher Ahmet, looking desperate.

"Mrs Leila, isn't that so?" the other parents giggled mischievously.

"Mrs, yes. She is Muhtar's wife, so she is a lady" said the other.

Teacher Ahmet cleared his throat:

"Your daughters Nuriye and Bese are very successful children; well done. You were behind their success. How do you know how to teach them? Nuriye can solve maths questions that would be difficult even for a high school student; her interest and participation in lessons are high, especially in Bese's paintings... Her paintings are even more beautiful than many paintings I have seen!"

Everyone was silent; they looked at Leila and poured out their faces. Leila said nothing as if Teacher Ahmet's pure Istanbul accent was coming out of a radio. She bowed her head. Leila's hands were calloused from milking and colourfully stained with paint. She was trying to make sense of the patterns of her hands. She was leaning against the bench as if about to get up. Her lips were an inverted crescent; she kept looking with a sullen expression. She had been a great Leila in her childhood, and now she was speechless.

When teacher Ahmet noticed the parents getting bored, he told them that was it for the day and that they should pay more attention to school instead of their children becoming labourers.

Rukiye didn't get along with Leyla, who was her peer, and she had a strong dislike for her. Falling into the gossip of the village women, she added slander to Leyla's name and presented it to her father. Confronting the Muhtar, she said, "Your wife has set her eyes on the new teacher, and you have no idea!"

The Muhtar brutally beat Leyla. Leyla couldn't bear it any longer and cried out, "I swear, I'm leaving with Bese and Nuriye, Muhtar. If you have no mercy for me, have mercy for your child in my womb!" Her voice echoed shrilly. The Muhtar paused, instantly regretting his actions.

"Hopefully, this time there won't be another child," he murmured to himself.

Leyla's hair was dishevelled, and her nose was bleeding once again.

Leyla had become pregnant for the second time, only a few months along.

She wondered about Yausef with a strange foreboding, "I wonder if he thinks of me in the same way."

Leila noticed a red and black cover book in Huriye's hand. She snatched it out of her hand in a huff:

"Give it to me!"

She shuffled the pages of the book. Most of the pages were missing, and the rest were burnt. She saw her father's handwriting on the back cover; some faint letters remained. After reading Qasim's books, he used to write down his evaluations on the back pages of the book. Leila's eyes shieled. She couldn't speak; she swallowed. She looked at Huriye angrily. She waved the book in her hand, "Where did you find this..."

"Why are you angry with me?" Huriye huffed, "I found it by the tandoor... Let me read it. The pages are all burnt anyway..."

She felt bitterly from the bottom of her lungs.

Her thin, flower-printed scarf was slipping from her hair; she went to her father's house with tears in her eyes and her belly protruding.

Soggy footsteps on the muddy road shared his anger.

Sheep were sheared at the beginning of April, and the wool was washed in the stream. The wool was beaten in water by a spindle. Some washed the laundry by hitting the stones with water. The voices of the women by the stream could be heard from afar. The water in the stream was gurgling.

Fatma spread a white sheet before the door and spun the wool she had washed by the stream. She had softened the wool by beating it with a kindred. When she saw Leila entering the garden gate, she stopped. There were pieces of yarn on her head, and dust was flying in the air. She fixed her eyes on Leila, who came angrily from the door:

"What now! What are you coming here for? Does your husband know that you are coming here all the time?"

"Where are they!"

"What are they, what do you want again..."

"My father's books... We used to hide them in the carriage. They were mine, my father's..." she cried bitterly.

"The village burns down, and the idiot tries to save the hay... You don't want the field share, but you want the books. You are such a smart girl..." said Fatma.

Leila waved the burnt book in her hand in the air and shouted with all her might without letting her speak further:

"Where are the other books!..." She tried to go inside, but her mother hit her leg with the spindle.

"I won't care that you are pregnant; I'll beat you. What do you want from us? Get out of here, the seed of the devil..."

"The books were my only inheritance from my father; they were mine. I never go anywhere without them..."

"I burnt it all, oh well..."

"What?!"

She sat on the stone as if she was going to fall. She covered her face with her hands and sobbed; she had never cried like this, even at her father's and beloved brother's grave.

"Go away from here; I swear I will go and call Muhtar. Go cry at your home!..."

Leila felt helpless and deprived, stumbling back home, as her mother called it.

"I told you and your father, those Christians are useless to us... They bring us bad luck... You didn't listen to me..."

As she left the house, she looked back; the stone seemed to be crying for her; the stone spoke:

"Why couldn't you keep your promise to your father? Why didn't you take those books when you left this home..."

Leila felt embarrassed when the stone talked like that. She had kept her father's books and the cassettes she listened to a lot under that stone for a while, but she had not been as good as the stone. She could not fulfill her promise to her father.

She had not taken the books because they would be safer at this home; she wished she had... To avoid hearing Muhtar's "these are the devil's inventions, " she had left them in the cargo hold and thought she was hiding them. She was holding the half-burnt book in her hand. She did not feel the presence of any organ in her abdomen.

"Dear Sister,

We found a way to get rid of boredom. To avoid getting tired of laziness and unemployment and listening to the same stories, we started doing handicrafts. We make rosaries, wallets, key rings, and car ornaments from beads. It is incredibly tiring, but we also earn money while selling them out.

At this rate, I won't be interested in my mother's neglect of me. I don't mind if she doesn't send money anymore. She and Mesut used to come often initially, but they cut ties and stopped coming around. Good luck to them anyway...

Some of our friends make models: houses, cars, and ships. I admire them for making a ship they've never seen.

I guess I'm not very skillful at this handicraft, either. My mind keeps going to books. Even when I stop momentarily and look out of the grilled window at the horizon, I feel bad. I want to read, just read, be alone with myself... I was supposed to study and become a professional man, but whatever...

Maybe I'll get a job in a library; then I'll read books all day.

The other day there was a misunderstanding here. When they realised I wasn't eating the food, they thought I was on a hunger strike and forced me to eat the tasteless, saltless food. It was like torture! When I shouted that the food was bland, this time, they mistreated me because I wouldn't say I liked the food. It was hilarious...

The ward guard is charming; sometimes, he is merciful to me and understands what I say. He likes to read books too! I make him memorise poems so he can say something fancy to his girlfriend.

I'm also sending you a handicraft keychain I made clumsily, maybe you can make it into a keychain.

I greet you with longing."

Nuriye handed the letter to Leila. Leila took the embroidered and beaded key ring, coloured to look like a rose, and put it to her nose, inflating her lungs so much that she couldn't inhale any more breath. She felt as if she could smell the odour of Idris's hand on the key ring. Her heart ached. She took the letter, wearing and tearing at her eyes. Her throat was knotted. She read the lines repeatedly, profoundly feeling the meaning of each word one by one. Sometimes she was sceptical, wondering if her brother might be tortured, but she could not find any clues. She wrote a letter to reply to him back.

"My dear elder brother Idris,

What I experienced in the village and what you share inside are almost identical. So, to not drown in boredom, I've developed a talent: I found myself; I paint now, and I'm sending you one of my folded paintings. It's not as beautiful as our village, but I guess it isn't as beautiful as it used to be. I want to send you books, but the woman who would be our mother burnt all my father's books without my knowledge. Before she baked bread in the tandoor... If she had choked on that bread... I don't want to upset you, but I can't give

*you any other good news. I'll get the books for you as soon
as possible. Take care of your health.*

Your beloved sister, Leila, who loves you very much."

Leila pushed and pushed for a long time.

With Muhtar's impatience, the day came, and Leila gave birth to a baby girl. When the midwife handed the baby to Leila, Leila did not take it. She thought she couldn't love her. Behiye came and whispered in her ear:

"Are you going to treat this girl the way your mother treated you? What is wrong with this baby?"

Leila's eyes sparkled as if possessed, and she swore she would never treat her baby like her mother.

Muhtar was furious. He did not recognise her as a child, but he owed the increase in his wealth to his daughters. Because he thought that when he married each of them, he would get twice as much; if it was a son, he would give just as much. He twisted his moustache and laughed sincerely.

The baby became restless, waving and making the sound it made before crying: "Eh, eh, eh..." Swaddled and kicked the air. Soon she would sing a powerful lament. Leila took her in her arms again, cuddled her and sang lullabies in her ear. Until the baby stopped stirring and softly fell into a sweet sleep. With a soft moan, she carefully put the baby back in her bed.

Rukiye was going to Midyat M-type prison with Leila. She was going with a sour face and coming back with honey dripping from her face. While Leila was in a meeting with her brother, she was looking at Leila's daughter, but more than that, she was flirting with the soldier on guard outside.

Sooner or later, one of the villagers had already told Muhtar. Muhtar was furious. He tormented Rukiye between his hands, shouting at her. He warned Leila not to get up from her seat. Otherwise, he would put her and her baby under his feet. Behiye couldn't stand her mother's heart; she intervened, and Muhtar's plump flesh landed on Behiye's weak face with a violent snap. She had also received her share of the beating. After the assault, no one made a sound.

Muhtar could no longer contain his anger and locked Rukiye in the barn. He also warned his other daughters:

"If you come near her, I will break your feet!" and shouted at Leila, "You will not go to see her again!"

Leila took a plate of their eaten food and waited to go to Rukiye. Muhtar ate and drank tea immediately afterwards. He only took a few sips from his second cup when he fell asleep with a snore. He slept like a log all night.

Leila opened the door and came to Rukiye, where she gently put the food in front of her, and Rukiye attacked the food and water like she had not eaten for days.

"I swear I didn't say anything."

"Who else would say anything!"

"How should I know? He banned me, too, so I can't see my brother from now on."

Rukiye cried with emotion.

"We must stick together. If we don't stick together, your father will persecute us separately. But if we are united, he won't be able to use violence against us." Leila was looking for a solution to go to her brother again with Rukiye.

"What about those worthless men? They all look at his mouth."

"If we become one, Muhtar will not be able to voice our disobedience to him... Even he will be afraid of us."

Rukiye ate and handed the empty plates to Leila.

"You always bring discord into our family. My father has never beaten me until now because of you..."

Leila said, "What is this? I have talked so much; I have wasted my breath!"

Leaving this bulletproof-headed girl to her own devices, she returned home empty-handed and unhappy.

Lokman and Latife had squandered the money from the sale of Auburn and were broke.

They continued to insist on returning to the village. They had sent a letter saying that they would grovel at the feet of Muhtar and obey him. Leila was as unresponsive as a stone. Muhtar did not say a word.

"Those bastards will not enter this village! Only their funerals will return!"

Lokman had also written a letter to his mother. Mesut took it and read it shakily. He noted that they couldn't last long in the region and were going to Istanbul. Fatma's eyes widened. Even the word Istanbul excited her.

"We will sell the remaining field and send the money to them. It's empty anyway; we don't plant anything. We will even sell this house. As long as my Lokman is not in trouble."

There was silence in the house, and Mesut started eating the meat dish before him.

"I thought you always cook meat when a guest comes, Mum."

"Well, I guess we will cook it for ourselves. We won't stay here anymore anyway."

Mesut was very hungry; he was eating the meat with an appetite; on the other hand, he was wondering why the house was silent.

"How is it, son? Is it delicious?"

"Yes, Mum. What meat is this?"

"Your father's treacherous partridges."

As soon as he heard it, he froze, and blood rushed to his brain. His whole body trembled. He threw away his hand away in disgust. With the remaining morsel in his mouth, his stomach swelled with terrific nausea. He ran to the courtyard. He started vomiting while he was still on the patio. Mesut vomited all the contents until he vomited blood. He was hurling and crying at the same time.

"What have you done, mum? Why did you do this?"

"Why, what did I do? No one was buying them. They told me to cook the meat deliciously. So I did."

"They were my birds. They were my father's heirlooms..."

Mesut was vomiting from his mouth, and tears flowed from his eyes. He had no choice but to submit to his mother. He had no one around him.

Mesut had been ill for a long time, and Fatma had already found an excuse to go to Istanbul as soon as possible... She would be able to treat Mesut there.

A boy of about eight years old, wearing corduroy trousers with tattered knees and a T-shirt he couldn't remember how many holidays ago, knocked on the door of Ahmet Teacher's house. He must have knocked slowly and timidly because the door did not open at the first knock. Ahmet Teacher opened the door, saw the boy and compassion appeared in his face. He was always dressed in a suit, he knew that the villagers would always knock on his door, and he would walk around the house in his trousers, short shirt and tie until nightfall.

"Yes, Ali?"

"Teacher, my brother is sick."

"What's wrong? What happened?"

"He played too much by the lake. He got sick. Have a look."

Teacher Ahmet was both puzzled and was raising questions to his student. He put his shoes on his feet like slippers.

"Why don't you take him to the centre, to the hospital?"

"Teacher, come here; my father will only listen to you then."

They passed by the school and headed towards Ali's house. They met Leila on the street; he couldn't take his eyes off her. Muhtar came out of the door just then:

"What's the hurry, teacher?"

"The child is sick; I'll take a look, we'll call a doctor, or I'll have to convince them to take him to the hospital."

"Let me come with you. Why don't they tell me? We are the Muhtar of this village for a reason."

Muhtar could hardly keep up with Ahmet Teacher because of his weight. He was running after him like a penguin.

Day by day, mud-brick houses were changing form. The cement-floored, perforated briquette-framed houses, which made the sweltering summer heat more bearable, had taken the architectural road.

The agricultural engineer, urban planner, transport engineer, topographer and Muhtar talked among themselves. The villagers were too far away to read their mouths. They were making guesses. The old shepherd, who slowed down as he passed them, first greeted them and then came to the villagers with his mouth close to their ears.

"I will finally get rid of shepherding; I will not be a shepherd for the rest of my life."

All the old villagers started to speak in unison:

"What do these officials want?"

"Good news, my neighbours, a road is coming to this village."

"There are already so many roads; why are they going to build another one?"

"It is a village on an important axis, they say. It will be shorter and wider. Double pairs of cars will be able to pass."

"God forbid… What the hell are we going to do then?"

"Don't worry. Everyone will get their share, and we will settle in the city. They'll give us a house there."

"They'll give us a house in the city?"

"What will happen to this land?"

"Zaho, you didn't stay with them for five minutes; how did you learn so much?"

"You are kidding us, Zaho. What if I don't want to give up my land…"

"Then you will continue to live in this barn."

The old shepherd whistled with trembling lips, called his animals, and led them towards the house.

"I will get rid of this job, this village. I will live a modern life."

The villagers looked after Zaho, who was moving slowly.

"Look at Zaho. What he's saying. How many years does he got to live?"

"They shouldn't have built the road over where our dead lie."

"What if they trick us? We'll be left in the middle like arseholes…"

"So this is what will happen to this beautiful village, God damn it!"

The elders of the village worried among themselves.

Some had become city enthusiasts, while others said they would live in their villages until their last breath. Like before a war, they were all putting their heads together and making a defence plan.

Those who had once thoughtlessly shot each other and fought for the land had to leave the village for the sake of common interest.

Imam Salih was the first who left the village immediately. He realised that the few remaining households could not meet his needs. The village was mostly empty when he left with his three wives and children. Although he said he lacked the strength to call for prayer for a few households, his intention differed. He planned to move to a richer and more populous village. Imam Salih would spread his superstitions there, too and continue his reign.

The Assyrians had emigrated to Europe. They told Muhtar that one day they would return and repair their houses. Muhtar sent word to the European Assyrians that they could agree with the state if they wanted to sell their houses. If not, they would propose a solution so their houses would not be touched. In return, they would be given a sum of money.

In the project, the road passed through Greenvillage. The houses with the talismanic appearance would be demolished one by one.

Fatma had sold the land, animals and the house left to them by her husband to the state. Leila had fallen at the feet of Muhtar for the first time to prevent this, begging and pleading to at least get her father's house back. She made an offer to Muhtar so the road would not pass through there. If she got the house back, she would sleep with him again, and this time she would get pregnant with a boy. Muhtar twisted his moustache. There could not have been a more pleasurable offer. But Leila knew, too, that it was the man who would give the male or female sex gene. She did this on purpose; her only concern was to return the house and garden where she had spent her childhood. It was not difficult for Muhtar; he persuaded the officials to attend a meeting and got the title deed back.

While her husband made animal growls over Leila, she had the title deed in her dreams, even though she was unhappy with the union. She had heard of peasant girls who had been with soldiers in exchange for money, and now she understood them better. A man was a man. While he surrendered, he dreamt of returning the deed to the house where he had spent his childhood.

Within two months, Leila realised she was pregnant. The headman gave the deed to Leila as a gift. He did not refrain from saying that if she gave birth to a boy, he would give her the village.

Not long afterwards, Huriye, one of her stepdaughters, reported that Fatma had packed her household goods and loaded them into a strange car.

Leila was about to faint from anger. She didn't care if Muhtar beheaded her anymore. She couldn't take her speed; she tied Benazir to her back with the shawl in her hand and ran out of the house. She crossed the only asphalt street in the village in her slippers. One hand supported her baby under her back, and the other went back and forth at the elbow to run fast. She ran like this with her daughter on her back until the corner. Finally, she caught up with her mother, who was trying to escape. Mesut had packed enough stuff in a special car.

"Where are you going?" Leila cried out.

"Sister, it's not my fault. Mum is using my studying for university as an excuse; we are going to Istanbul to Lokman."

Leila wailed:

"Fatma!"

Fatma was pulling and locking the door of the adobe house.

"So you are leaving now! You're leaving the village too, huh?"

"What was I supposed to do here? What's left..."

"Yes, you're right! Who else is left whose hearth you haven't extinguished!"

Fatma took the bag in her hand without looking at her face and headed towards the village minibus.

"God damn you! You ruined all our lives! You killed Mustafa! You got Turabdin shot! You ended my life! Idris is wasting his young life in prison because of you! You don't even visit him! Lokman is living in exile because of you! What about my father? You buried my father in the ground because of land disputes! Then you sold that land. Don't worry, I have the deed to this house now!"

She couldn't take her anger, "give me that key..." her mother threw the key. The people in the minibus were watching what was happening with curious eyes glued to the minibus window.

Leila continued to wail with bloodshot eyes despite the cries of her baby, who was squeezed by a shawl on her back. Leila bent down and took a handful of soil in her hand:

"Look what you did to us for the love of a handful of soil? Here, can you take this soil with you?"

Fatma went to the car without looking at her. Mesut was sullenly looking at his mother; his complexion was pale. He knew they were going to Istanbul because of the jaundice on her skin.

"Look at me, Fatma, look at me! Our family fell apart because of your greed. We have become like this because of you. Don't ever forget that..."

Fatma pulled Mesut into the car, then sat down and pulled the door. The car moved. Leila, who was under the exhaust, screamed as if she was tearing her throat:

"Mum! I will never forgive you. This land will not even accept your death."

Leila returned to the gate of her father's house and sat on the big, carefree stone; the way to calm her crying daughter was to breastfeed her. She untied the sash wrapped from her back to her waist, took her baby in her lap, and put the tip of her breast into her baby's mouth with two fingers. She looked at her father's house and looked at the trees with their waist cut. She wiped her eyes with her writing. She sniffled. She cried secretly.

The sun had set dysphorically towards the evening hours with all its vibrancy. With the wind blowing gently, she took her father's house behind her and escaped that loneliness.

"Dear Leila,

Please ignore our mother. Suppose we lost her in childbirth. We're only related by blood, that's all. You don't need to go to that house again. Look, I'll quote you from what I've read from Dostoyevsky... He says, 'Man is a creature that gets used to everything. I think that's his best quality.'

My dear sister, please don't mind. Man gets used to everything. Say, 'This too shall pass,' and just move on. Don't look back; nothing is worth being sad about.

I kiss your eyes.

Your brother Idris."

Just what she needed at this time was to receive news and linger over that news. Leila first embraced each letter from Idris, smelled it and then read it as if she had memorised every letter. She was going to write about the unpleasantness of the village; she did not want to write; she was going to write that Muhtar was persecuting her; there was no point in upsetting her brother within closed walls. He found the solution by writing a few lines; he was both crying and writing. The flood of water flowing from her eyes soaked the writing on the letter and dispersed the ink. The letter became fluffy; Leila folded it and put it in an envelope. Rukiye could no longer go to the Midyat bazaar to sell her embroidery by herself. Leila went with her; delivering the envelope to the post office was an incredible opportunity. She would even be able to visit her brother İdris in prison. Midyat Type M prison was between the village and the post office. Nevertheless, the letter would first stop by the post office and then pass through the hands of the guards before reaching Idris.

> *"Dear brother Idris,*
>
> *I didn't know what to write to you. I'm so sad… Before one problem ends, another one begins. I haven't even mourned my father or my brother Mustafa yet. However, time is very cruel, it thinks we will forget, but it is not. Our pain does not melt away; on the contrary, it is petrified and made visible.*
>
> *According to the news I received, they say they will soon build a road through the village, and Greenvillage will become even more beautiful. I am not so sure about this. I hope they won't uproot us.*
>
> *I have bad news for you, I will tell you face to face, but I still want you to be prepared for the bad news.*
>
> *Maybe I can make it to the interview before you read this letter. I will arrange it somehow.*

Dear brother, I'm afraid I'll do something bad to myself
if I don't see you this week.
I can't breathe.
Your only sister Leila."

Idris read and read and choked and cleared his throat. What more bad news was going to happen? He was looking forward to Leila's arrival. He could no longer sleep at night; he was overwhelmed. He brought all kinds of bad news to his mind. Did something happen to his other siblings? Were they going to evacuate the village? That must have happened because they say a road will pass through the village. But since the village will become even more beautiful, they shouldn't evacuate it. I wonder what this bad news is...

Leila loathed visiting the prison, despite the permission she barely got from the headman. She hated going through the deep search checkpoint, let alone seeing her brother through the wire mesh. It was horrible to be searched in a way that made her ashamed of herself, pinching and pushing her up to her crotch. Once a week or once a month, she made sure not to miss the open visit and to see Idris from behind a pair of grill wires. She went with her mother Fatma at different times to avoid going nose-to-nose with her. Now that Fatma was gone, Leila would visit Idris without hesitation. This time she would have to endure a thousand pains to get permission from Muhtar.

"Please don't cry, dear sister, don't persecute me... I can't do anything here; I can't do anything."

Leila was in a closed area visible through a double-wire grid. She looked like a tingling image behind the grating wire. Leila's face was red from crying, and she looked very different from her age with the traditional cheesecloth on her head. She could not look at Idris' pale face; it hurt. Idris was wearing a striped T-shirt; he looked like a relic in it and had lost much weight. His palms had collapsed, and his shoulders had fallen. He had a ragged appearance. He was looking with empty eyes, trying to comfort his sister. He tried to wipe the tears from his sister's face by running his fingers through the wire, but he couldn't touch her.

"Our mother sold everything and went to Istanbul to be with Lokman."

"Our mother sold everything and went to Istanbul to be with Lokman."

"Our mother sold everything and went to Istanbul to be with Lokman."

These words echoed in his head repeatedly, and Leila's sobs made it even more dramatic. The bad news kept playing in his mind. Idris also wanted to cry, but Leila was crying so much like a madwoman that he didn't need to cry. Leila was trying to talk in a choked voice, but Idris couldn't understand her.

"Please don't cry, Leila... Look, I can't cry, and that's harder for me..." Idris said, gritting his teeth.

"Why did this happen to us..." Leila could only say, sobbing heavily. "That woman did this. I hate her."

"No matter what, she's still our mother."

"What kind of mother does this to her child? I also became a mother at this age..."

Leila couldn't continue; her face crumpled. "We were supposed to go to school, become educated. That woman played with our lives."

"This too shall pass. I know it will pass. Nothing stays forever." Nothing he said would be effective. He found the solution by sending her away.

"I don't have any more time. Go, please don't come back crying. I'll await your mischievous, sneaky looks, my dear sister."

Leila immediately followed her tearful brother's warning, composing herself and wiping her eyes.

"The village is being evacuated... But I will continue to stay with Behiye's sister.

They say if a road passes through our village, it will develop even more. They say it will become a city. It will be directly connected to the city Midyat. Then I will be able to come and go more often."

Idris felt sad, struggling to control the tears welling up in his eyes.

"Don't worry, brother; I returned the title deed to our father's house." Leila grinned, remembering how she had taken back the title deed thanks to Muhtar.

"Even if our mother tried to sell it, I was able to get it back, one way or another. I put the key under the stone in the keychain you gave me as a gift. I know you will come out one day, and that house will be yours..."

"Our house..." he cleared his throat and stopped.

"These pictures are amazing. They're like surrealist works."

"Sureyya? Like a woman's work?" Leila's eyes lit up, feeling proud that she was following a woman's movement.

Ahmet teacher laughed:

"Surrealism... we can say it's an artistic example of Sigmund Freud's work on neurology and psychoanalysis. The famous painter Salvador Dali is quite prominent in this movement. He is the most famous painter in this field. Its theme is based on emotions..."

"Yes, I always express my emotions; that's why it turns out like this. Sometimes it seems silly to me, but you like it a lot, teacher."

Ahmet Teacher tried to be serious, but he couldn't help laughing.

"What are you doing with these surreal works of yours? You're hiding them, aren't you? Don't forget our painting exhibition target in Istanbul."

"What can I do with them, teacher? Muhtar gets mad when he sees them and beats me."

"Why is that?"

"He says it's an invention of the devil. School is an invention of the devil; art is an invention of the devil... According to him, everything is an invention of the devil..."

Leila averted her eyes when she mentioned the headman.

"Mrs. Leila, you may not realise it, but your paintings are as magnificent as those of a famous painter."

Famous painter... The words beamed into Leila's brain like an epiphany. Even hearing these words excited her.

"Forget about the devil; if you can't hide them from Muhtar, you can entrust them to me. I can even send them to Istanbul on your behalf if you want..."

"Let the headman kill me too..."

Teacher Ahmet could not convince her. Nevertheless, he tried to persuade Leila not to give up on her homework. Leila needed to give a few compliments to disperse the clouds of discouragement.

"Sometimes I am afraid that you are teaching me a lot of information like my father, teacher because most of the time it is useless to me. I think I have learnt in vain."

"Nothing is in vain, Mrs Leila; you can never doubt that. One day you will definitely reveal all of what you have learnt. You are now brewing what you have learnt. It is up to you to mould and present it, especially to turn them into art and thus become immortal."

"Brewing, huh? Don't let it go stale."

"It is neither too early nor too soon for anything. When the time comes..."

"You know, teacher, the day I lost my father, I thought I was dead too. After he left, I was dying every day while I was alive. But this painting assignment seemed to bring me back to life. I can't thank you enough. You are the only people in this village who have supported me. And my little stepdaughters..."

"Shall I tell you a secret, Mrs Leila? I was also interested in painting. But I was assigned here as a village teacher. At first, I was very hesitant to come, but now I am glad I did. Teaching something to those bright-eyed children keeps me connected to life. Of course, there is a reason to be attached to something in this life."

Teacher Ahmet became her best friend in this village. However, the village interpreted male-female friendship differently, and they were stigmatised forever. If Muhtar's wife laughed at the teacher, they would say she was a loose woman. Leila didn't care, but when she was beaten, her brain was shaken, and it took time for her to recover from her injuries. Thus, her drawing assignments were delayed. She knew she had to be more careful because she used time properly.

"I have to go, teacher. I have to go in first before the headman gets home."

The picturesque nature outside the school window resembled a painting. It was just time for Leila to sit and paint. She had to go home. Otherwise, she was terrified that someone would overhear her and bring her to Muhtar. She would feel embarrassed; she wouldn't go to school after being beaten up; fortunately, she would be exempt from beatings when she is pregnant.

"There are good things about being in prison. You have plenty of time, and you read the books all the time. I had the opportunity to read a lot of books here. My friends and I lend books to each other. Since resources are limited, this is how we manage for now. But if I get out of here alive, I will definitely build a library at home, and just like our father, I will dive into deep dreams and find peace among books. There is no place more beautiful and happier than being alone with oneself.

I recently picked up one of my bunkmate's books. I wonder why I hadn't read Epicurus all this time. He says, 'God either wants to prevent evil but cannot; either he can but does not want to prevent it; either he neither can nor wants to; or he wants to and can. He is powerless if he wants to and does not prevent it; if he can and does not want to, he is morally corrupt. He is weak and immoral if he does not want to and cannot. If he wants and can, why does he not prevent evil?" Dear brother, these words have been gnawing at my brain for days. Epicurus has put his finger on a subject that I have been thinking about non-stop. I constantly think about God, wondering where He is and what He is doing... Is He content to watch us? Who makes these decisions, and why do we suffer the punishment if our fate is predetermined?

Which religion is more merciful, and whose god is more compassionate and just? Whichever one takes me under his wing, I swear I will only believe in and obey him. I will do nothing but sacrifice myself to him. I will think of nothing and no one but him. I will never harm anyone. I promise I will dedicate every breath and step I take to Him; I will only beg and pray to Him... I will also beg him to rewrite my destiny, but this time to ask me. As long as I first find out which religion's god is better...

> *My dear sister Leila, I'm going crazy. Please, write back to me back."*

Muhtar received the letter. He read the lines with a strangled snarl.

"Both Epicurus and you..." he tore the letter into pieces, "the spawn of the devil..." he spat, "these are all sinners in the family!.."

He never mentioned this letter to Leila and never mentioned the letters from Idris.

"My dear sister Leila,

> *Our father was very famous, did you know that? The head of our ward was a friend of my father's from Iraq. He's been travelling around the prisons since the 80s. He got me a job as a tea boy. On certain days of the week, I look after our library. There are very few books and the ones there are often taken away and never brought back by book thieves.*

> *I make tea, drink it and read books all day long. I even earn three to five liras as pocket money. I created a circle of friends thanks to this tea-making job. Our ward master loves me very much, sometimes we chat for hours, but when we start discussing politics, our conversation stops there. Politics is a bad thing, especially in prisons. There is nothing as ridiculous as discussing it. Even if I know I'm right, I bite my tongue and don't comment; otherwise, he might think I'm disrespectful to him and stop me from being a tea seller.*

On the other hand, a few other prisoners read books with me. There are people in our ward, some of whom became murderers unintentionally, like me, and some of whom became murderers willingly. We have all become 'so-called literate murderers' here. This is the bitter reality of prison life.

Dear sister, I haven't received a reply to the last few letters I wrote to you. Is it me, or am I in too much of a hurry, or are my letters not reaching you?

Please, write me back. Your silence fills my heart with anxiety.

Your brother Idris."

Leila's belly had grown to the point of bursting; she was much bigger than before. Muhtar would get hopeful, "This time it will definitely be a boy".

Leila gave birth. Muhtar was waiting in the courtyard, sweating blood. He was very sure it would be a boy. The midwife came and broke the news to Muhtar in a huff. Muhtar stormed in, howling with rage.

"Not one, but two girls!..." Muhtar shouted, raising hell.

Leila was cradling one baby in one arm and the other in the other; she had given birth to twin girls. The babies' delicate fingers were stuffed into their mouths. Now she had what felt like a dozen girls who looked like herself. She dreamt about Yausef's saying. She always was thinking of him as if she was still with Yausef. There was no moment when she did not think about Yausef. She was constantly dreaming of him, talking about him. She had never given up on him, always dreaming of him even in labour. It was as if she was pregnant with him and would give him a child.

The house had become a house of mourning. Muhtar could not have a son. He used to swear at women and beat them until he got tired.

"You sons of bitches… Is it so hard to give me a son huh? I will remarry; you all will see."

Muhtar had distanced himself from Leila after that day. He was afraid she would give birth to triplets next time, so he gave up getting her pregnant. Leila would never smell his bad breath again.

Since Muhtar did not visit her, she painted Yausef, the beloved, she was hiding inside, and spoke to the picture.

"Darling, I have daughters just as I wanted. And they look like me…" she said in a whisper.

She kissed Yausef from her drawing and smelled him; she could not smell anything but paint. She brushed over the painting again so it would not be recognisable and then tore it up.

Unfortunately, she could not register her daughters in her name because they had no official documents with Muhtar. Muhtar legally married Behiye, his uncle's daughter, and registered Leila's daughters in Behiye's name. It was how the law is working.

"My dear sister Leila,

When you don't answer me, I feel terribly depressed. But I can't stop writing. It's a different feeling, a kind of relief. Are you all right? Everything all right?

I'm the same, as you know…

I'm looking forward to spending time in the library, although I was recently reprimanded. Why? I'll tell you. To pass the time, I arranged the books one week by type, one week by size, one week by colour, and one week by alphabetical order. Finally, I sorted them by colour. The guard got angry that the book he was looking for kept changing its place and swore at me. I didn't misbehave again, but what could I do? When someone asked me where the book was, I would find it myself and hand it to them. Helping someone gave me great happiness. I liked that they were coming to me to ask me about the book. It was an enchanted feeling to be loved, admired, appreciated... I felt useful.

That's how I filled this page, Leila; I hope you will answer me. I'm more worried and concerned about your health than anything else. Please, don't keep me in suspense any longer.

Your brother Idris who loves you very much."

It was in the same corridor as the Eye and Paediatrics clinics. While Leila was standing with her twin babies, she sat down when she was given a seat on the bench opposite the Eye Clinic. There were two other women next to her on the triple bench. Two gendarmes in brownish uniforms were waiting in front of the Eye Clinic. They stood like dull statues with their mouldy green caps on their heads. Their rifles were slung over their shoulders. The woman next to Leila sighed.

"Alas, alas... Who knows whose heart has been extinguished."

"Pity the parents... Who knows whose son is inside."

"A rapist or a thief... Who knows."

"Maybe it's political..."

"What difference does it make? He's a convicted criminal, after all!"

Leila couldn't help but shake her babies and overhear the conversation.

The clinic door opened, the gendarmes took their position, and Idris appeared at the door. Two gendarmes were holding his arms. His hands were handcuffed. Leila's eyes widened when she saw Idris, and she let out a cry:

"Brother!"

She jumped up from her seat and chased after the gendarmes.

"What's wrong with you, brother? Why are you here? What happened to you?"

The gendarmes tried to stop the woman with two babies. They pushed Leila back with their hands.

"It is forbidden to talk to the criminal. Please go away."

"Leila! It's nothing, my dear! It's all because of those books. I've ruined my eyes from reading," Idris' voice sounded positive, "they will give me glasses; maybe it will add some air... Why are you here?"

Leila was defying time and soldiers. Leila was simultaneously bouncing her twins in separate arms, lifting them into the air. Taking advantage of the opportunity, she quickly summarised her situation:

"Look, I had twins too. I'm here to check on these little ones. I hope they will both be drawn to your beautiful heart!"

"I said forbidden; stay away!" the soldier continued to warn Leila.

"Please give me two minutes; let me talk to him. The bastard who will be the father of these little ones won't let me go to my brother's meeting, commander..."

"It is forbidden to talk to the convict!"

"He is my brother!" Leila cried, "Please give me two minutes, commander."

"Why don't you answer my letters to you, Leila? How many times have I written to you..."

Leila paused her brain throbbing. She realised her brother always wrote to her, but those letters got lost. Or someone hiding them from her. With this thought in her mind for a few seconds, she followed the soldiers without losing track of them. He immediately called out to Idris, who was hurriedly taken into the prisoner vehicle:

"Send it to the village school, brother, to teacher Ahmet... I will definitely get it from there and write you an answer."

Leila followed them outside. She followed her brother Idris until he got into the blue prison car with a red stripe down the middle. She bounced her twins in her arms so that the crying babies would stop.

Leila watched without blinking her eyes until the prison vehicle moved off. She could not control her tears in the excitement of this accidental encounter.

Perhaps Yausef hadn't forgotten her either, he was definitely writing to her, and those letters were not being delivered to her.

15

She named her first daughter after Benazir Bhutto, whom Qasim mentioned in his list of powerful women. Benazir Bhutto was the first and only Muslim woman Prime Minister of Pakistan. Leila named her first daughter 'Benazir' because she believed people were drawn to their names. She wished her to be a successful and strong woman like her. She gave similar names to her other twins: Arin and Narin.

As her twins grew up, she followed them closely, wondering whether they would take after their uncle Idris or uncle Lokman… Her daughters were very naive and affectionate. Leila was relieved. Her daughter Benazir was very hardworking and intelligent, like her mother.

Teacher Ahmet:

"Although your daughter is very young, she is much more successful than the older children. Mrs. Leila, you should definitely educate your daughters."

"Of course, teacher. The woman who will be my mother did not send me to school, but I will not do that. I am willing to burn in hell for my daughters, don't worry."

"I advise you to get an education for your paintings, if you get the chance."

"But Teacher Ahmet, after this age… If you come from within, you don't really need school, because school is the person themselves."

With Teacher Ahmet's help, Leila packed the books in parcels for the prison. Among them were primary school stories. She took them in her hand, and after shuffling the pages, she made sure:

"A line is a line. Reading makes time more quality."

Teacher Ahmet admired Leila's every move. Parcels waited in the corner to be sent. Teacher Ahmet handed the letters to Leila one after the other.

She opened one and read it:

"Dear sister, I hope you are much better than I thought.

I was very touched when I saw you and the twins the other day, but I couldn't show how happy I was. I wish I could have loved them and stroked their little heads.

Now I am writing these lines to you with a pair of framed glasses. Idris the Wise, they call me. It's not that I don't like it. These glasses gave me a little self-confidence.

Sometimes I wish I never read books and just sit around dreaming. I wish I had lived without learning, researching, and having knowledge. I'm sure I would be happier that way. But I can't; I get bored like that… I feel like my brain is being harassed when I sit and talk to people with perverted mindsets. I hope they read books too and their mindsets are cleaned. Books come to my rescue when I can't find anything to do.

I haven't solved this equation yet, whether the more I read, the more often I encounter people who don't understand or the more I encounter people who don't understand, the more I cling to books.

Just as a Muslim wishes to go to Paradise instead of Hell, I would rather be a mad sage than a straw brain who does not read books. The more I read and learn, the more my soul bleeds, but I've come to enjoy it for some reason. I'm happier this way. I think I will take after my father; completely…

Tell me about yourself and your sweet twins… How many children do you have now?

I send you my love and greetings.

Your brother Idris."

Teacher Ahmet was checking the children's homework while trying to understand Leila's facial expression:

"What did she write, your brother?"

"Nothing. Just Khayyamite verses…"

As Leila sat down with a pen in her hand, she wrote in response to Idris's letter:

"My dear brother, I kiss your heart full of pain.

Believe me; I cannot help you in this matter. Unfortunately, it does not seem possible for us to rewrite our destiny. The intervention of others shapes our lives. I wish we could struggle and have the luxury to say, 'No, I don't want to take it'. Because of our mother… I hate that woman. I hate the god she believed in as much as I remember. All I know is that there is only one faith. God is one, and he is always on the side of man.

Please, hold on a little longer. This will all pass as you always keep saying…"

She attached it to one of the pictures she had coloured and tucked it into the envelope. After writing the prison address, she handed it to Teacher Ahmet to deliver to the post office.

"I wish I knew Yausef's address; I would have written to him too: How much I miss him, how I will forget all my troubles as soon as I see him..." Leila's eyes filled with tears, and to avoid showing it to the teacher, she immediately excused herself and left the school.

Teacher Ahmet called out to his students waiting in the garden:

"Come on, children, go home... Remember, work hard on your homework. I will check tomorrow. No sweets and biscuits for those who don't do their homework! Is that clear?!"

"Y-yes!"

The students responded in chorus and left the school like rats fleeing from a barn on fire.

Teacher Ahmet received another letter from Idris. He had the urge to open that letter and read it; he was very curious. He knew that the letters sent from prison contained emotion-laden verses. He preferred to wait for Leila. He couldn't do this shame to her anyway, but this time he would ask her to read the letter to him if she didn't mind.

Leila did not refuse Ahmet Teacher's request and read Idris' letter aloud:

> *"My dearest sister Leila,*
>
> *We can go out to the garden twice a day. When I go out to the garden, I feel like primary school children running out of the classroom at the recess bell. I feel happy and joyful like them."*

Teacher Ahmet could not hide his smile. Leila continued to read slowly.

> *"...If the God of all religions is one - and Allah is undoubtedly one - then why are these people separate? Why do they need to carry different labels?*

Anyway, dear sister, please don't take this as rebellion. While I was afraid to confess these words even to myself, here I am writing to you.

By the way, the books you sent me in parcels have barely arrived. All of them were read and approved by the guards. But these storybooks are very good. Did we have these books in our childhood? And where were we?

Many greetings to Teacher Ahmet…

I kiss your heart, your brother Idris…"

She folded the letter and put it back in the envelope, "He said hello to you too, Teacher."

Teacher Ahmet's eyes were moist. He realised that Idris was trying to talk to Leila about everything. Some questions haunted him; he could not hide them in his mind any longer:

"I am very impressed… Is your brother a thought criminal?"

"Teacher, what do you mean by a thought criminal?"

"Is he in prison for political reasons?"

"No, why did you say that?"

"Because a person who reads books cannot commit a crime… He would be a thought criminal."

"You're wrong, Teacher; my brother is a murderer! But he wasn't reading books back then; he was preparing for the university exam; we were both going to study at university…" Leila paused when she remembered the incident.

"That's not possible!" said Teacher Ahmet, still mesmerised. "How is it possible?"

"It is possible, Teacher, if a mischievous woman has a child in such a simple life, he will be a murderer or a fascist…"

Whenever Teacher Ahmet saw one of his students barefoot and playing in the soggy mud, he felt ashamed of himself. He blamed himself for not being a good teacher.

He didn't even cook at home; he ate and drank every day with the help of the villagers in Greenvillage. Even if he didn't want to or didn't accept it, the villagers were very insistent and wouldn't leave his side until he had eaten.

He did not spend money anyway, he had everything he needed. Therefore, he took out the few months' salary he had saved from the bundle and went to Midyat. He bought children's shoes of various sizes in the bazaar, put them in the back of a lorry and brought them to Greenvillage. He wanted to leave good memories before leaving this beautiful village and his pupils.

When he arrived at the village square, all the village children and their mothers were waiting there as if they had heard about it beforehand and had camped there. They surrounded the lorry, pushing and shoving each other to the point of crushing each other. More women than children were competing for the children's shoes...

Teacher Ahmet called out to the women causing a stampede:

"Stop. Slowly, please don't push each other!"

For the first time, they were not listening to the teacher and ignoring him.

The woman next to him teased the woman who bought shoes in pairs, saying, "They will wear this next year too."

She was clinging to the side of the lorry even though she was covered with jewellery, "Get out of here, that's for my son... Give it to me quickly..."

"You thief! That's my daughter's shoe!"

Ahmet Teacher was looking from side to side in a dazed state, not knowing what to do. The jazzy peasant women went head-to-head, knocking each other to the ground and tearing the cheesecloth and dress of whoever was on top.

Teacher Ahmet was bent over the boxes, shoeboxes in his hand, and he froze. Should he intervene, should he give the shoes to the children who were staring at him...

He stepped between them with his clean and ironed shirt and tried to separate them. As soon as he did this, he regretted it, but it was too late. While the women were pushing each other, Ahmet Teacher was being pushed and pulled along with them. He thought for the first time that these innocent and sad-faced women could be so strong. Ahmet Teacher was also slapped in the face as if he was the cause of all this stampede, not the women. His beautiful shirt was torn like a simple fabric.

Muhtar waddled over. He could hardly separate the fighting labourers and women from each other.

Ahmet Teacher's face was also attacked and scratched by women.

They carried the shoes from the car's crate to Muhtar's warehouse. The shoes would be stored there.

Ahmet Teacher still could not realise whether what he had done was a mistake or not. He took the tea handed to him with embarrassment. Muhtar put sugar in his tea and stirred it noisily.

According to Muhtar, Teacher Ahmet was causing mischief in the village. Muhtar was the first to speak, with a red face and a mocking expression:

"Well, did you see? It doesn't work like that, Ahmet Teacher..."

"But I thought those children were in need, did I do wrong, Mr Muhtar?"

"You made an eyebrow while trying to make an eyebrow, teacher! What else... Do these women even need shoes?"

"What do you mean? The children are barefoot..."

Muhtar chirped:

"Don't you see their gold, their husbands have many animals, vineyards, land... They have houses. Do you? Look at yourself first Mr. Ahmet!"

"I... How could I know? I thought they had nothing."

"They don't?! They are used to it and happy to be integrated with the soil. They are children... I beg you, Mr Ahmet... If there is a need, the villagers come to me first. You are entrusted to us by our state. You are the crown of honour. But you, please... You, please, don't interfere in anything except education," he said angrily, "and nothing at all."

In the village, fights would break out for trivial reasons and could result in death. Because of this responsibility, Muhtar would not come out at first in any disturbance, but after the warning from the police station, he was more cautious. The first person he reprimanded was the poor teacher of Greenvillage.

"The village will be evacuated anyway... You have a short life left here, Ahmet Teacher," said Muhtar, slurping his tea.

Muhtar planned to distribute the shoes from the warehouse for his own charity in the coming days.

Muhtar's neighbour was a lorry driver going back and forth to Iraq. The village mourned the news of the accident. He and his wife Cemile had been married for ten years. They had one son, and Cemile had not had any more children in the years since. After forty days of condolence, Cemile's eyes were always on Muhtar's house. Muhtar had carried out many procedures for her. From certifying the property left by her husband to Cemile's kitchen utensils, everything was taken care of by Muhtar himself. Leila, who did not miss Cemile's behaviour, was quite enjoying the situation.

Cemile had married very late and there was no one in the village who did not know that she was a horny woman. She did the laundry especially when Muhtar was at home. She gathered her skirts and exposed her thighs while doing the laundry she kept in the basin in the courtyard of her house. During the washing, she shook her breasts as if she was suffering from epilepsy. Muhtar easily saw Cemile from the balcony of his house. He twirled his moustache in greeting, and Cemile tugged at her skirt as if embarrassed. She lowered her chin and blinked her eyes like a young girl and looked at Muhtar.

"Should I take this wife for myself? Besides, she has a son; maybe she will give me a son too," Muhtar twisted his moustache.

Leila visited the school more often because of her brother's letters. Because of the rumours between Leila and Ahmet Teacher, the young woman was beaten to death by the headman. Nevertheless, she did not give up going to school and did not refrain from asking Ahmet Teacher about the letters from her brother Idris.

When the village started to empty, the first thing that happened was that the schools were moved to the district.

Leila knitted a washcloth and a scarf for Teacher Ahmet by hand. She had also brought other necessities in a bag. She also put the local pure *bıttım* soap in the bag in case it would suit Ahmet Teacher, whose forehead had receeded a lot. His yellow-coloured eyes were smiling.

Leila no longer hid her purple eye; she had nothing to be ashamed of. She looked at Teacher Ahmet as her brother. She kept his pictures in her other hand so they wouldn't wrinkle.

"Ah, it's you, you came..."

"Of course, I came, teacher. Neither she comes nor allows me to attend meetings. I thought I would attend school anyway, even if I get beaten."

He carefully handed over his bag and pictures:

"Ahmet Teacher, I especially thank you for being a postman between my brother and me. You supported my daughters and me and enlightened me. These pictures are for you too... You can hang them on the wall of your new home." Ahmet Teacher's eyes filled with tears. "Are you crying? Does it suit you to cry, Ahmet Teacher? Did I say something that would upset you?" "The sight of a gracious, charming, and intelligent woman like you living in such circumstances makes me very sad, Mrs. Leila."

"See, you still call me 'Mrs'," she said, puffing and laughing.

"I wish I could do something and take you to Istanbul with me. We could open a course there for your pictures."

"You never know, Ahmet Teacher. My only hope is my daughters. If my Benazir wins Istanbul, we will come riding too."

Ahmet just showed his support by touching her shoulder. The thought that those beautiful bodies would rot underground made him feel helpless and miserable. He handed her the paints he had wrapped. He provided a bunch of watercolours and oil paints again. Leila would make pictures with watercolour and oil paints on the remaining pages and show them to the teacher. Ahmet Teacher would sometimes criticise and sometimes add comments. He could not find anyone to comment on his pictures anymore.

"Please, Mrs Leila. Never give up on your dreams. Call me if anything happens; I'm always at your service."

Leila was thrilled to see the unopened paint package in her hand. She was as happy as newly enrolled children at school.

"Thank you, teacher. My paints were running out again…"

"I'll always help you." He was writing something on the paper.

"As much as I can from now on… I didn't choose this life. I didn't choose my mother or my husband. But my daughters won't be like me; I'll support them to choose their own lives if that's meant to be."

"It's my misfortune too. Just when I had gotten used to being here with you…"

Ahmet Teacher wanted to say goodbye.

"Do not be sad, Ahmet Teacher; it will be someone who sees and hears again. They will misunderstand us. If you go, what happens will happen to me."

Ahmet Teacher laughed involuntarily. Ahmet Teacher handed Leila the paper on which he wrote his phone number and address in Istanbul.

"You can reach me here whenever you want."

Leila read the paper, then crumpled it and gave it back.

"Thank you. Don't worry; I memorised the address. If the headman sees this in me, it will not be nice; he will interpret it badly. I have nothing to defend. Either I will kill him, or he will kill me, teacher," she laughed herself. Ahmet Teacher could not stop the tears from flowing.

"Good luck, teacher; I hope we meet again someday."

"You didn't let us read; at least let those little puppies read!"

Rukiye was now more mature and more conscious. She resisted not marrying like an old wife, and with the income she earned by making and selling her lace, she was covering the expenses of her half-brothers. Muhtar challenged Leila's daughters to continue their education in Midyat.

"I see these girls studying, avoiding the lesson, meeting with boys in a corner and talking loudly. The endings of the games are not good at all; they are all bitches."

Leila stood up to Muhtar and started to fight with him again, but Rukiye rushed forward and sacrificed herself and was beaten by her father. Nuriye was also thrown at her, and her father beat her. In this house, where the population of women was high, it was customary not to raise a hand to the man. If they were all united, the headman would fart out of fear, but the women did not fail to respect their fathers even when they were beaten.

Leila, who found a way to educate her stepdaughters until the last year of secondary school, was beaten until the donkey came out of the water when her secret was revealed. Leila wouldn't care, the day she wouldn't be beaten, her body would itch like she had scabies. Now it was her daughters' turn; she would get them educated at any cost.

"These are devil inventions! As you say, the girl sits at home, and when her fortune comes, she goes on her way!"

The headman did not resonate at all.

Cemile especially overheard the shouting. Leila suddenly made a move to scare Cemile. "How is it, good news?"

"Oh, neighbour, you scared me!" Cemile, holding her heart, looked as if a demon had struck her.

"And I was going to say..."

"Yeah, what would you say?"

"If no man is home in the afternoon, let me come. Having a man in the house is not suitable for me. As you know, rumours spread quickly in the village. They don't leave out what they don't tell me because I'm a widower."

"Yes, being a woman is hard. Especially if you are stuck in the village, it is very difficult. Moreover, it is much more difficult if you are a widower."

Cemile still looked at Leila as if seeking an answer.

"Come, of course, neighbour. The headman will be out soon. You already know better than uswhen he came and when he left... Come on... Tell me what's wrong with you, Cemile."

Cemile told Muhtar that she had a burn. He had a hard time not laughing at her.

"The man is all guts... What did you fall in love with about the frog-like man?"

Leila remembered Muhtar's hissing laugh. It reminded her of his childhood fear of snakes. Even Muhtar's smile was annoying. She itched as if a strand of hair remained in her undershirt. Especially because of that garlic that he could not give up - God bless him, who said that garlic is useful - not for its smell, but because forty days, forty years would not pass from the house. Tooth brushing did not exist in the headman anyway. Moreover, it was considered a luxury in the villages. Leila's heart rose, she was still waiting for an answer from Cemile.

Even if she didn't get an answer, the answer was clear: Muhtar knew how to talk and say something that would make women happy, and he had a lot of money. Muhtar was the richest Muslim in the village.

"Okay, come and be with us," said Leila, "but on one condition."

"I will do whatever you say, Leila," said Cemile, her breasts bouncing.

"You will help me educate my daughters, and the other girls will marry the boys they want and leave. There will be no bride price. You will respect Behiye sister like your mother. You can have Muhtar as many times as you want. Understood?"

She listed his only condition at length, and although Cemile was confused, she accepted the offer without hesitation.

"I have a son from my first husband. I can give Muhtar a son too."

Leila snickered.

They agreed to it as a secret deal.

The headman was hopeful; he worked day and night for Cemile's son and didn't care anymore what his previous wives and daughters were doing. It would come to fruition.

Muhtar reserved an apartment for his third wife, Cemile, in a cement-plastered two-storey building in the city centre and reserved the ground floor for his first two wives. However, Behiye was one of those who did not want to leave the village. The headman did not force him; he did not care because he was already old.

With his new wife, Muhtar's lustful feelings were heightened, and they made love here and there, regardless of who saw or heard. Cemile had not been with anyone for five years since her husband's early death, and the fire of those five years was burning within Muhtar. In the newly built bathroom of the concrete house, in the kitchen without cabinets, on the floor bed that could not be lifted from the floor… Leila, who saw them in the kitchen, said "Bismillah" and made a U-turn, determined not to go up again. They took Cemile's son with their stepdaughter, turned on the television for them and turned the volume up to the highest level. Despite this, Cemile's groans still could still be heard. The fire had burned Cemile's head. It was as if they were making love in the living room. While shouts were heard from one corner of the ceiling, groans rose from the other corner. Two old people could hear them making passionate love.

Leila would often return to the village, and after visiting her father's house, she would stop by Behiye and stay with her that night.

"Oh girl, I'm glad you came to me."

"What? I don't understand you, Sister Behiye."

"If it weren't for you, that devil would have married someone else. I don't know if you were a blessing or a sin to me, but my daughter, you are my angel of goodness. If it weren't for you…"

"Please don't say that, Behiye Sister."

"I know this is selfish, but I am lucky because you are here, and my daughters are lucky too. I pray for you constantly. My heart is crazy and unlucky, my beautiful girl."

Despite all the troubles caused by Muhtar, he sent his stepdaughters to the handicraft course at the Public Education Centre in the district and did everything to make them happy whenever they wanted. Although he was saddened by not being able to send his stepdaughters to university, he managed to send his own daughters to school with a thousand lies and tricks. Well, it was also thanks to Cemile, Leila, who somehow caused the elderly woman to distract Muhtar with lies. Now she could write letters to her brother İdris as much as she wanted and even go to see him.

"My dearest sister, Leila, entrusted to me by my father,

    I have good and bad news for you.

    Due to Rahşan's amnesty (Rahşan was the prime minister's wife of the time), my sentence has been slightly reduced. I could have been released last year, but the process was prolonged, and I will be back this year. I am eager to hug you and my nieces. I was very saddened by the fact that the village was empty. I already miss Mr. Ahmet the teacher.

Teacher, whom I connected with without even meeting. I wish we could have met... The bad news is that I won't be able to return to the village as soon as I get out of prison because they will draft me into the army. But there is also a good side to this, of course. I will serve for fifteen months instead of eighteen! My dearest sister, I will also write to you during my military service. Don't worry about me.

I am waiting for news about you. You can write to this address until I go to my new address.

I kiss you from your eyes."

The process of meeting with her brother was short-lived. Idris would be acquitted by taking advantage of the amnesty, but he would first complete his military service. During his military service, correspondence continued. Leila was the first to read the letters before anyone could get them.

She sent the letters to which she wrote the answer by going to the post office with Rukiye. Then she waited until noon in the yoghurt market to sell butter and milk.

Those fifteen months passed like any other long and gruelling life. As a matter of fact, days chased days; months followed each other...

All the residents of the house ate at Leila's house. Cemile always looked like she had just come out of the bath; she never had her hair dry. Leila used to cook in the kitchen and invite the children to the table. Everyone was lined up around the round table like necklaces. They did not favour Cemile's son either and insisted that he eat. He always acted shyly, as if he were responsible for his mother.

Rukiye met a clerk at the post office that year. The headman was most pleased with the news that aroused great excitement for a woman stuck at home. The fact that the grooming candidate was a civil servant was more than enough for Muhtar. The request happened immediately. He gave his daughter away without getting anything in return.

A civil servant meant a regular salary, meaning the state and father were behind it. For the first time, Muhtar even performed play at Rukiye's wedding. His obesity was troublesome, and since he could not bend his knee and swing his shoulders, he was making it difficult for those in the halay, who were lined up like beads. He was disrupting the flow of the dance, but despite his sweaty face, the headman was mindful of not being hostile to a civil servant. The officer was going to be his father-in-law, now the headman. Rukiye jumped three times in her wedding dress, which looked like a relic. Rukiye finally got rid of being old who stayed at home. She finally found someone she wanted, and got married.

"Did you see how Rukiye looked at me when she left the house? As if I was not his father, but a treacherous enemy… No bride had ever been happier when leaving the house. She officially came out of this house celebrating goodbye," said the headman, his moustache waving up and down.

With resentment, he dipped the spoon into the food and brought it to his mouth, chewing it with a smack. He continued to speak even when the food was in his mouth.

"I always wanted the best for my daughters. I did my best so that they could reach their good fortune. I have always tried to make them live a comfortable life. But they acted like I was an enemy, not a father."

"Have you ever asked your daughters if they consented? You didn't treat them as individuals. You sold them like animals" Leila was so confident she wasn't aware of what she was saying.

Muhtar's eyes turned, and he threw the iron glass at the head of Leila, who was sitting in front of him. Leila professionally avoided these attacks from her childhood; she reflexively lowered her head. Had he not tilted her head then, the glass would have crashed directly into her forehead. The glass hit the wall, and the metallic sound reverberated and bounced to the floor. It rattled continuously all the way to the edge of the carpet.

"Am I going to consult them for advice? Are they my father, or am I their father!"

"Girls should get married before they melt... When they get smart, they start a business. Didn't you always say, 'They embarrass us,'" said Leila. She moved Cemile to action with his gaze.

Muhtar blushed and shifted uncomfortably, Cemile's breasts rose before him.

"Leila says this out of goodwill, my dear husband. You have to be happy that the girls are lucky. Never mind, don't worry about useless things..." she said, and the headman's face softened as he looked at her breasts. Cemile took the headman's hand like a little child and led him to his room.

16

The air was cut thinly. Despite all its radiance, the weary Sun could not find the strength to warm the cold air. In a bright city, people breathing the frosty cold breathed like a stove chimney.

Leila was thinking about him again with her hand on her chin. Her dreams were still in her childhood; she could not escape them. They would go to college and school together in this city. She remembered them getting off the minibus, crushing each other, to go to school.

She watched the passers-by as she waited by the sidewalk. She noticed women who dressed neatly and elegantly in private vehicles. Their education was reflected even in their walks. She also wanted to study and become a doctor, but life had condemned him to sell butter here. When she became a doctor, she would come and make this butter again, but she never dreamed of having it under these conditions. She knew those who were educated bought the butter in the colourful packaging sold in the markets. "I wonder how they paint those packages," Leila thought.

In front of him stood a man as a pole. He wore men's long flared trousers.

She rolled her eyes upwards. A bald young man was looking at Leila with his emerald eyes:

"Hello, Leila," he said, his voice full as if it were coming out of the throat of a mature and enlightened person. By the smoothness of his voice, it was immediately clear that he was an educated man.

Leila remained crouched for a while; she thought she was dreaming. The man held out his hand, waiting for her to take it and lift it up. Leila got up herself; her legs were numb. Her face tensed; she rubbed her eyes. The man was smiling at her with his green eyes.

Yausef did not hesitate to introduce himself by name.

His eyes and smile were the only expressions that did not change on his face. Leila felt the need to wipe her teary eyes. Her eyes burned with the need to blink, and her lungs cried out for air. Her tongue felt like it was stuck, and her heart pounded in her mouth while her stomach clenched. Her turned upside-down life played like a filmstrip before her eyes. Her eyes filled with tears, and she wiped them with her scarf before looking at him again. What she saw must have been a dream. One of those dreams she never wanted to wake up from...

The sound of people passing by brought Leila back to reality. She felt embarrassed in front of this handsome, clean, well-dressed man for a moment. She didn't know what to say or do. Her scarf was disheveled, and her henna-dyed hair fell on her face. Her white chiffon dress with large rose prints had faded, and the seams were frayed. She always wore a knitted vest that covered her hips, making her look older than she was. Her eyes were rimmed with kohl, but she didn't know how to do any other makeup. Her dry skin made her look even older and wrinkled. Perhaps there was still the smell of sweat and barn on her clothes; she felt ashamed. The scent of Yausef's perfume made her head spin. She filled her lungs with the fragrance, trying to memorise it. She had never smelled this scent before. The oriental scent of amber and sandalwood spread throughout Leila's body.

She wanted to embrace him, but she was afraid of her thoughts and turned away. She reminded the seller beside her to keep an eye on her belongings and left immediately. The well-dressed man was still following her. At that moment, she only wanted to escape from him. She walked away quickly. Her nausea increased, and her heart felt like it was about to jump out of her chest. Her eyes blurred, but she wanted to cry out loud. She had never thought of meeting him like this.

Yausef did not leave her behind and caught up with her.

"Leila, don't you recognise me?"

Leila's brain was paralysed; she couldn't think or act maturely. Yausef grabbed her by the arm, and the snap on her chiffon dress came off.

She couldn't hold back any longer: "Where were you? Where have you been all this time?" This question came out of her mouth like a scream. She started crying like a child, and Yausef felt a lump in his throat. He knew that he couldn't turn back time by apologising.

Leila freed her arm and walked through the streets, crying. Yausef stood still like a statue until she disappeared. His longing, loving gaze hardened and shattered on his face. He had caught her but let her go like a bird. When he heard that the village was empty, Yausef went to the village. He had taken responsibility for Leila, the only family member who migrated to Berlin.

He couldn't find Leila in the village, so he went to the headman's house to ask. Behiye, the old woman, couldn't recognise him with her tired eyes:

"Welcome son; get well soon. Leila is either at her city house or the yoghurt market..."

He thanked her and left immediately.

"Idris son, if you need anything, let me know," said Behiye, thinking he might be Idris.

Yausef hadn't even heard Behiye's weak voice as he had immediately left.

Since he could not know the address of Leila's house, the first thing to do was to wander around the bazaar. Yausef had wandered around Midyat. He breathed in the hope of meeting Leila once more.

Yausef's desperate attempt to see him, his dreams were shattered. He dreamed of Leila all night. She longed to be in another life and soon awoke to reality again. Leila was avoiding him; she didn't want him.

Every night Leila wondered where with whom and how. Why did she run away from him now that he was before her? What would anyone else say? Was it because of the fear or the pain of what he had lost... She shouldn't have been reminded of the nightmare she lived through. She cried until her eyelids grew heavy, thinking about whether she fell in love again, got married, or had a child. She calmed down and fell asleep.

"Why did Yausef appear before me? Why did I act so thoughtlessly? Why didn't I tell him how much I miss and hug him... Ah, Leila, how stupid I am."

As Leila sat in silence, dinner untouched, her mind was consumed with questions.

"What was Yusuf going to say to me? That I should leave my beautiful daughters and run away with him? Was he trying to create chaos when everything was already turned upside down?"

Clearly, Leila's feelings for Yusuf were not something the village leader, Muhtar, paid much attention to, as she rarely displayed her emotions. She was disciplined regarding her daughters' studies, but

Leila stayed up all night when everyone had gone to bed, lost in thought. Her first and only love was now right before her, and she couldn't help but wonder why she didn't tell him how much she missed him and embraced him when she first saw him. "Ah, how foolish I am," she thought.

Her solitary contemplation consumed her mind with a never-ending sense of unease. "I froze when I saw him, but I should have hugged him, kissed him... I wish I had the courage to say what I was feeling. I acted like a cowardly chicken. Yusuf was braver than me; he came out and faced me." Leila knew she could never be with Yusuf now, not after years of mistreatment from her mother-in-law, and she didn't think Yusuf would want to be with her in her current state. Who knows, he might even be married? She wondered why he didn't look at his hands; perhaps he was wearing a ring. Even if he wasn't married, what difference would it make? She was already married to someone else, even if it was just an Imam Nikah marriage to Muhtar.

Yausef looked rich and polished, and when she looked at herself, she felt poor and unattractive... Leila was overwhelmed with self-doubt. That curly-haired boy from her past was now a handsome and heart-wrenching man. Memories flooded her mind, and tears streamed down her face. Her father's tenderness and longing mixed with everything she had tried to forget. Strong women, politics, painting, music, literature... The bards and the picturesque life of the village... Her mother's beatings and her escape... Meeting Yusuf in secret on the shore, their meetings filled with reverence...

If the children hadn't played that day, if the ball hadn't broken the window... If Lokman hadn't been at home, if the fight had never started... Leila drowned in her "if only" thoughts. There was a strange taste in her mouth. She took a deep breath and whispered aloud, "I

wish my brother Mustafa had not returned from the mill that day,"
and continued to weep until dawn.

She washed her face, went to the kitchen, and prepared breakfast
for the children.

17

The sky was adorned with clusters of clouds; the ground was tinged with shades of green here and there. Greenvillage, like a framed embroidery hung on a wall, was losing its charm with each passing day.

The trees, which could have concealed the ugliness of the dilapidated stone houses, were no longer swaying. Feeble, dry branches, tree skeletons abandoned by birds, and clusters of rocks of varying sizes were all that remained around the trees.

The village had emptied out, but a few households still clung to their homes, continuing to live in their small but peaceful havens. Water had been drawn to every house, and women no longer had to trek to the creek. Every twenty meters, an electricity pole had been erected. Even telephone poles had been connected to the village. However, most of the villagers still yearned to move to the city, to concrete structures. As long as the stubborn villagers who refused to abandon their village were still there, geese and ducks would continue to roam the streets.

Idris had completed his military service and returned home. He had spent the most beautiful years of his youth in prison. Starting anew seemed quite challenging for him. The impudent sun, shining bright enough to blind, had completely warmed Idris.

He paused for a moment and looked around. He closed his eyes and took a deep breath.

The single-story white houses of his childhood had gradually turned to the colour of hay under the summer sun. The Christian neighbours' house had cracks in the walls, and some parts were swollen. Birds had made nests in the vaulted entrances, and as soon as they saw Idris, they took off from under the embroidered beams of the house.

Idris went to look specifically at the side window. He went back to the day when children played soccer. The children were happy. Mesut was the goalkeeper, and Gabriel was the striker... The children were having fun, shouting and screaming, but they were still quite happy. They calculated the mischievous ball's impact on the mirror on the wall. His lips trembled; his eyes became moist.

The window was still the same, unrepaired. What would happen if it were repaired? Wouldn't the ball still shatter the glass and come crashing inside? Covered with thick transparent nylon, it looked worn-out, battered by the heat of summer and the cold of winter. It had become like torture. Like the other windows, it was draped in spider webs. Idris was about to cry behind his intense emotions; he got angry at his helplessness and clenched his fist. He could never bring those days back.

Feeling regretful, he turned to the fence of the house. The stones in the garden had disappeared, lost among the wildflowers sprouting around them. He hesitantly entered through the open garden gate. This house was a completely different place from the house of his childhood.

The barn was covered with useless weeds from inside to outside, articulating its loneliness to the world. The roof was sagging, and wild weeds had taken over every inch of the place. His father's adobe home was also overrun with wild plants. It had been half a century since humans passed these two houses. The doorknob had rusted from lack of use.

He made his way towards the door, struggling to open it. The heat had caused the door to expand, making it difficult to open. It was as if the door did not want to let Idris in. He turned around and looked at the garden once more. He dropped his bag on the ground and clasped his hands behind his back. Lizards and centipedes were crawling on the wall. When they noticed the stranger, they started running in all directions. Idris hesitated to enter the house.

He thought the stone under the stairs had been moved. Leila had told him in her letter that the key might be hidden under a stone, but he wasn't sure if this was the right one. He turned the stone over. The key to the house was hidden there. He had attached it to an embroidered, beaded keychain that resembled a rose and hung it on his father's house key ring. He took the key, put it in the lock, and turned it. He pushed against the steel blue door, struggling to open it. Suddenly, it squeaked open on its hinges, with dust and bug nests falling on top of him. He stepped back and waited for the dust to settle on the threshold. The rooms were filled with the sound of Idris' footsteps. The walls were crying from their longing. The moth-eaten curtains reminded him of the times he used to play hide-and-seek, hiding behind them as a child. Young Idris had no idea that his feet could be seen. Idris smiled.

He walked around the dust-covered rug, not wanting to dirty his feet. He leaned against the door of the adjacent room and pushed it open with his help, then entered. Idris took off his worn-out shirt and tore it in two to use as cleaning rags. He started by wiping the windows and surfaces clean of dirt and bugs. He had to get rid of the spider webs in the corners and told them, "This is not your place. Get out!" as he shooed them out of the house.

He carefully unfolded and shook out the bedding in the niche on the wall, airing it out in the sun. He took a significant number of dishes in the kitchen and washed them again. Next, he moved on to the garden, mowing down the wild weeds, sweeping up all the corners of the chicken coop, and piling up the trash in a corner. He was sweating profusely, and the sun was still overhead, refusing to leave. He washed thoroughly in the old-fashioned bathroom with the stone floor. He washed his clothes with soap, rinsed them, and hung them on the garden wire to dry in the stubborn sun.

He brewed tea, sat on the stone stairs, and watched the clothes dance in the gentle breeze. He poured the remaining tea onto the stone. He got up and made another cup of tea, realising that time had passed quickly.

Idris went out into the streets to rediscover his village. All the streets of the village had transformed. At the top of the street was Muhtar's house, which had managed to maintain its old appearance. As it was regularly painted every year, it looked clean and well-maintained.

Feeling anxious about getting lost in the streets, Idris hurriedly ran back to his house. After thinking about what to do, he took action and rolled up his pants to his knees and rolled up his sleeves. He tried to repair the toilet in the garden. He opened a hole in the pile of cement, poured water into it, diluted it, made it into a mortar, and carried it to the toilet with a three-wheeled cart. He plastered the wall. Just behind him was the Syriacs' house. It seemed to be shouting at him with its embroidered arches, vaults, and ornamented windows...

"Didn't you have any sense, boy? Why did you act recklessly and burn not only your own life but also the lives of others? Don't you have any shame, boy? Now you're staying next to us as if nothing happened."

Idris tried to avoid looking in that direction and continued with the repair. The creaking of the garden gate saved him from his inner turmoil. Idris turned around and saw Leila enter the garden, out of breath and sweating.

"Brother!" Leila's scream pierced Idris's heart like a sharp knife.

She tossed the bags she was carrying to the side and hugged Idris around the waist with her frail body as if taking revenge for years of separation. She hugged her brother tightly and shed tears of joy. It was as if she was also hugging Mustafa and Qasim. She would hug him like this if she ever saw Yausef again. They hugged each other over and over again, swaying from side to side. Idris kissed Leila's head, ignoring the cement stuck to him, and embraced her with longing.

"Oh, how wonderful it is to embrace each other freely!" he said, wiping away the tears from his cheeks and collecting the scattered vegetables back into the bags.

"What are these, Leila?" he asked.

"Oh, don't even ask, brother. I heard you were coming and ran to the bazaar for toilet supplies. I also brought my art supplies. Whenever I can, I'll come here and paint with you. Muhtar doesn't let me paint at home. He says, 'If you want to paint so badly, then paint the house.' Ignorant fool, what can you do!"

Idris laughed and helped her carry the easel and other boxes. He had cement on him.

"What are you doing, brother?"

Idris remained silent for a while and couldn't say, "I've been searching for a bit of peace all day inside the house." Instead, he said, "I was busy fixing the unfinished toilet. It's an urgent matter..."

"If you want, I can help. I can paint it for you. But don't tell anyone; rumours will spread throughout the town that I'm a painter."

Leila first cleaned and swept the house. Then she took vegetables and meat from her bag and prepared the meal. They set the table on the floor in the house's entrance hall. Idris and Leila, two siblings, sat cross-legged, watching outside while enjoying their refreshed meal. Spoons were raised to their mouths with the mixture on the plates, and the tip of the spoon disappeared in their mouths. Their eyes were gazing into the distance, and the chirping of the insects broke the silence like background music. They rested and satisfied their hunger.

The sun was rolling like a woollen ball above their heads.

Leila looked at the stone in front of the house's stairs, sat down and caught her breath. She opened her headscarf and started again.

"No one around here gives me a job. Once you're marked, why would they bother to give you work? I wish I had never been released from prison. At least there, even though it was bad, I had a routine," she said hopelessly.

"Why do you say that, brother? Of course, everything will be alright one day," she sighed. "The blooming rose will one day wilt and the weeping person will one day laugh."

The chirping of insects outside broke their silence, brother and sister listening.

Leila took off her bracelet from her wrist and handed it to Idris.

"What is this, Leila? How can I accept this?"

"For God's sake, brother, what am I going to do with it, take it to the grave?"

"You're already struggling to educate your daughters; spend it on them."

"If you don't accept it, you'll see my death. Please take it."

Idris pretended as if he wasn't there and looked to the side, furrowing his eyebrows.

"Come on, take the bracelet. It's already weighing me down; I can't even paint," said Leila, offering her bracelet to Idris to sell.

If the matter was about her being unable to paint, he should take the bracelet. Idris slowly took the gold bracelet and said, "If I go to the jeweller to sell this, won't they think I stole it, Leila?" He put the bracelet back on his sister's wrist.

"Okay then, I'll go and sell it. I'll bring you the money next time I come and you can take care of yourself for a while with that money. Whenever you need anything, I'll bring it to you whenever Behiye sister is here or whenever you need it."

"All right, Leila, I got it... But still, don't let that grump touch you. If he drives me crazy, I'll come and hit him."

Leila giggled and felt proud.

Idris went in, made tea, and brought thin-waisted glasses for himself and Leila.

"They gave me the job of making tea in the army and in prison, I got along well with everyone, so time passed nicely from that perspective." Idris took a sip of his tea.

"Do you know, brother, the first painting location is ready?" Idris looked at her brother curiously.

"Oh, this impudent rock..." she said, pointing to the stone underneath, "what secrets are hidden in it now. The name of the painting will be 'If only the stone could speak,' brother."

She stood at the door, adjusted the position of the painting, fixed the canvas legs on the ground, and delicately drew the outline of the stone. Leila seemed patient. She drew the lines of the stone, then mixed the colours together and thinned them with water. After taking a little on the brush and making sure of the palette, she painted the picture. After completing the stone's size, texture, and colours, she created waves as if her father's house was shaking in an earthquake. The stone was still, but everything around it shook in the earthquake.

Leila seemed to have made her peace, took a deep breath, and wiped the sweat from her forehead. Leila had such exciting and enthusiastic feelings that the villagers who heard her were coming to greet Idris and ask about his well-being. No one knew when the road would be finished.

They said it would be soon. While painting, construction on the road ahead was still ongoing. Leila was so focused on her paintings that the construction noise didn't bother her at all. She hummed long songs and painted her pictures. She took her painting and left it to dry next to her other canvases in the inner courtyard. Without knowing the source of her enthusiasm, Leila wanted to draw Idris sitting on the stone steps with a cup of tea in his hand. Leila started drawing Idris with his cup of tea. Idris had drunk more than half of the cup, but he grumbled as he waited a long time. Idris took a deep breath, got excited, turned his face to the sun, which was about to set, and continued to stay still.

Leila had painted another head next to Idris's head on the painting. One was bright and cheerful, while the other was dark, grumpy, and filled with hatred. Idris impatiently came to the front of Leila's painting, and disappointment poured over his face:

"This doesn't look like me at all." Idris was upset and restless, waiting for Leila to explain.

"I don't draw someone exactly the same; a few figures are enough for me. Teacher Ahmet has said 'surrealism' once. I translate the soul more than the human landscape in my paintings," she said, speaking as if answering an interview.

Idris entered the house, declaring, "I'm going to heat up some tea."

Lost in thought, he began working on a new painting - this time of Mustafa on his horse, Auburn, with sharp and dignified features. Like in real life, he painted the horse in a velvet-like light brown colour.

"Let's take a break and have some tea together," he said, interrupting his work.

He planned to continue painting Mustafa and Auburn the next day. Looking at the painting of himself and Mustafa, he felt an inexplicable sense of envy.

"I wish you had painted me with Mustafa instead of Lokman," he mused.

"Your twin is Lokman. Don't worry; it's just a painting. I'll paint you many more times."

They agreed on this and Leila returned to her concrete home in the city on the last bus. Her hands and dress hem were covered in cement and paint.

Meanwhile, Cemile and Muhtar visited every hospital and doctor they could find, but it seemed that having a child was becoming increasingly impossible for them. They even consulted with sheikhs, spiritual leaders, and sorcerers, but nothing worked. Due to her weight gain, Cemile's ovaries had become too fatty, and her age made it even more difficult to conceive. Muhtar had lost all hope. Cemile knew how to keep her composure and always tried to please Muhtar, saying sweet things and being playful.

Leila stopped by Behiye's house in the village and sent someone to the market to buy butter. She then hurried to her childhood home, setting up her painting equipment. With a slender and elegant brush in her hand, she fearlessly moved it over the canvas. She painted the memory of Auburn's first day in their garden - a moment that had stayed with her since childhood. Mustafa held the horse's reins and

Auburn's young sister. Leila felt his heart pounding as he held onto the reins, and she felt safer in his warmth. Their father stood behind them, leaning on the saddle with a smile.

Now, none of them was there except for Leila. She was alone and helpless. But now she had Idris by her side and promised never to let him go.

When Idris entered the garden gate, he was taken aback. His feet scraped against the ground. He caught Leila painting in the garden.

"You're up early today," he said, kissing her forehead.

"Where were you? You're covered in white dust," he observed.

"Yes, they opened a quarry ahead of our village. I go there and sometimes they give me work. I do labour work, and sometimes I polish stones. I earn pocket money by working daily."

"Wow, so you're working now."

"It's temporary... But the good thing is I've also made friends by going back and forth to the quarry."

"I go there when you're not around. The masters carve the stones so beautifully, like sculptors! They shape them like dough and turn them into sculptures. Just like I varnish my paintings, I polish their stones. That's why my clothes are covered in dust."

The older brother and sister laughed.

Leila continued the painting of Mustafa and Auburn. It was as if Mustafa's unfinished life would be relived the next day. She drew his fiancée Suheyla on his shoulder like a winged pigeon.

She painted Auburn with such a velvety hazelnut colour that the horse seemed like it would come out of the painting. It was as if Mustafa would reach out from the painting, grab Leila's hand, and put Auburn in front of them. Leila didn't let go of her control to avoid crying. She clenched her teeth and kissed her brother's lips on the painting with longing.

Being with her brother made her a more productive person. She prepared another painting without being satisfied.

She painted Gabriel and Mesut in that painting: they held each other's hands on their shoulders, put their feet forward, and posed with laughter. Gabriel also had a checkered ball under his arm.

All the paint tubes were crushed and used up to the last drop. Leila didn't neglect to use the remaining paint by cutting the tubes with scissors. Only one black paint tube was left. She wanted to make her mother's painting, so she painted the entire canvas with black oil paint and made a stain with a brush stroke from the red oil paint tube. At that moment, birds passed over Leila and dirtied the painting.

"I ran out of paint; you did me a favour," she grumbled to İdris.

"What's wrong with you? Are you also going crazy like me? Why are you talking to yourself?"

"I understand that even the birds don't like my mother. Anyway, I won't waste this painting, let it dry on the side."

The paintings she left in the sun looked like an open-air museum. After Leila painted them with oil paint in the garden, İdris would be responsible for varnishing them. They had to protect the paintings from the birds flying in the dazzling sky. They pulled the plastic over them and fixed it on the stone wall with large rocks. Just in case, they made a tent out of the plastic over the paintings so that the birds wouldn't dirty them again. They wouldn't take too long to dry anyway, as the weather was dry and sunny.

Leila was using her brushes more boldly as time went on. She was almost as talented and productive as a professional painter without formal training. The weather was partly cloudy. She painted the same pattern as the robe she was wearing that day. This was a sort of warm-up. Then, she painted a single weak-looking eye on another canvas. This portrait had no mouth, only a big eye and a big ear. Idris approached her and recoiled:

"What's wrong with you Leila? This looks like a 'cyclops'. It's as if it's going to eat me." Leila burst into laughter.

"Did you say 'Kikilo'?"

"Yeah. Cyclops. A type of creature. It looks like this."

Leila continued to laugh uncontrollably. "It doesn't even have a mouth; it's even scarier."

"Yeah, so it won't talk," she laughed. "Kikilo."

Idris examined the painting like the thoughtful art lovers in the museum.

"They look so scary. Please take them down before I see them in the bathroom; I'll wet my pants before I get there."

While Leila laughed, her brush created patterns on the canvas.

"Who would pay for this, for God's sake?" continued Idris.

"I'm not doing it to sell, brother. Could you please leave here now? Leave me alone with my creation."

Idris withdrew to the stairs, watching Leila from behind. He refrained from making any comments.

"A one-eyed monster."

Idris had bought a small television to avoid talking to himself. He turned on the television and realised something serious happened. He turned up the volume a little bit more. The news was about Saddam Husein. As soon as Leila heard the news, she ran into the room beside Idris. She rushed, still holding her painting brush in her hand. She was looking surprised and terrified. Saddam's execution was buried on television news. The footage was repeatedly shown on the ants-sized screen.

"I wish our father had seen you bleed, you bloodsucker!"

Idris furrowed his brow as he looked at his sister's wounds. A bit later he brewed tea and brought it to Leila too. They were looking satisfied with the news and could drink their tea cheerfully.

"So, you tell me. Why do you allow him to beat you? Why don't you defend yourself?"

"I am strong, resilient, and used to being beaten," Leila laughed, but Idris remained serious.

"I can defend myself; yes, I have that power. But I know he will be hurt if I hit him back, so I don't resist. Once I pushed him lightly, he rolled like a Diyarbakir watermelon, almost cracking."

Idris didn't enjoy his sister's humour and couldn't agree with her.

"Look at me, Leila. If he ever raises his hand to you again, I'll come and cut that leather ball of his in half from the middle. I already have a record! It wouldn't be much of a surprise!"

"Calm down, brother, don't worry. That's just his way of relieving stress; what can he do? At least he's not interfering with my daughters' education anymore. Even if Benazir gets into university this year and leaves. Allah is great for the others too…"

Trying to change the subject, but İdris seemed quite uneasy.

"Let me come over to Muhtar's house for dinner one evening. After all, he's our brother-in-law, isn't he?"

Leila felt terrible nausea inside. She was about to throw up. "I'll show him what it means to lay a hand on my sister…"

Leila's pride was stroked. İdris hugged her sister from the waist and rested her head on his chest. "Forget it. Is it worth going back to prison for an undeserving fatso like him?"

"You're right; he's worthless. Who's worth imprisoning yourself behind four black walls for anyway?"

Leila went to the kitchen to see if there were any unwashed dishes, but İdris had become more organised and tidier. He was doing the housework himself. But she noticed the same food had been in the big pot for days. She took it and put it in front of the neighbour's chickens. "You don't have to cook all the pasta in one package. Please cook only as much as you can eat. Then it won't be left over and it go stale. Besides, don't you know any other food except pasta, brother?"

Leila had also made cakes and sweets for her brother. İdris, who couldn't hear Leila's voice over the fridge noise, carefully placed the sweets on the fridge shelf. "Did you say something?"

"I'm saying not to eat the same food repeatedly. Anyway... You're doing your own thing as always."

After washing, he plucked and sliced the turkey that Behiye had brought and put it in the pot. He placed the pot on the single gas stove and cooked the turkey. He plugged in the single electric stove and poured the bulgur water on top. He quickly cooked the meal and went down to the garden to set up the table.

Apparently drawn by the headman, a round mass was painted, and feeble arms and legs protruded from it. The point between its legs was vaguely visible, and he muttered, "Addicted to his desires, just a stomach."

Idris burst into laughter, his childlike laughter echoing throughout the village. "You're painting science fiction! But Leila, you look very happy. I'm very glad about that."

"What can I do? Should I beat myself up and postpone my dreams? Right now is important, right now... I am here and in my own space of freedom. I am doing the work I love. Right now, there is only me in my mind; I am not thinking of any responsibilities; it's just me and myself. There is no time outside right now. It's all about right now."

"After this conversation, I thought you would make a happy painting, Leila." He came over and looked at the painting, seeing the skinny arms and legs of the round mass, the point between them, and the hairy head that looked like a head and continued to laugh with the same smoothness. "This is the best I've seen..." Idris' stomach started to hurt. "Yes, this is the best until I make a better one." In her head, Leila constantly imagined that Benazir had won the law exam. If she wins, especially if she chooses Istanbul, she will take her paintings to the address she has memorised and deliver them to Ahmet Teacher with her hands. Ahmet Teacher will also open an exhibition for her. Leila was burning with dreams of this. "I hope my Benazir will be successful in her exam. Let my daughters' study, have a profession, and not be crushed like me... I really want it."

In the summer of that year, she was painting her final painting here, at the feet of her older brother. She wouldn't leave this job unfinished without painting her father's portrait. She started to sketch her magnificent, powerful, deep-eyed, proud, but arrogant father with a pencil, carefully marking the lines. When she swept the brush over it, those pencil lines disappeared. In one hand, he held a snake's head, which he had squeezed tightly, crushing its head in his palm. On the other hand, there was a tiny hand, the chubby hand of Leila from her childhood. They seemed to be going somewhere with her father, with her father looking happy and Leila not afraid of anything, jumping and playing in the painting. She diluted the paint with poppy seed oil so it wouldn't be too thick and used bright colours to make them more vivid.

The pleasure she felt while the painting was equivalent to that of a village child with a mouthful of chocolate. She dipped the fan brush in the water, shook it a few times, and put it aside. Then she took the angled brush and painted the details on the painting.

The figures in the painting were moving. Leila's cheerful laughter was grating on her brother's ears. The path was filled with flowers, and the leaves of the flowers resembled book pages. Leila used bright and vivid colours, with the sun and twinkling stars in the painting. Idris had sliced up the watermelon and constantly examined the painting with curious eyes.

"How talented you are, Leila. By the time I slice up a watermelon…"

"Well, the materials are ready, the dreams are in my head, and with talent, it's not difficult to present them." She shook the brushes in the water to remove the excess paint, washed them with soap, dipped them in olive-green oil, and placed them in the sun to dry on the ground. She took a deep breath, straightened her writing, sat next to her brother, and took a painted fork in her dirty hand, skewering a slice of watermelon.

"Your face and nails are also dirty," said Idris, smacking his lips.

"This isn't called getting dirty; it's called effort. Unfortunately, I have to clean up and leave for home. Muhtar might realise that I'm still running away here to paint." Leila was so determined and diligent that not even the beatings she received from Muhtar could make her give up her dreams. However, she never lagged behind when it came to being cautious.

"My father used to say people resemble their names," Leila thought, thinking of her siblings. Although they all had the same parents, the paintings of their lives were different, with brush strokes, colours, shapes, and descriptions unique to each one. She looked at her brother Idris's bruised eye and noticed the bruising on both eyelids this time.

"Did that piece of shit hit you again?"

"No, no… It's from before… It wasn't obvious at first, but the bruising showed up later. I painted the other one too, with red and blue mixed together, to make them equal. It looks like makeup. So, the villagers won't say anything if they see it, and I won't have to deal with them."

Idris clicked his tongue and furrowed his brows, unable to control his anger. Leila gave him the news she thought would make him happy.

"I have something to tell you. I'm really upset about it."

"What?"

"When you truly want something and work for it, it really happens. Benazir got accepted into Istanbul University Law School."

Idris's tongue stumbled.

"Well, why aren't you happy about it? This is something you really wanted!"

"The problem is that Muhtar is against the girls attending university…"

Idris gritted his teeth and took a deep breath as he spoke the words:

"I'm coming tonight. Don't stop me this time."

Leila's heart fluttered with joy. She prayed for her daughter day and night, and Benazir focused on her exam and succeeded. But Leila didn't feel as happy as she thought she would after receiving this good news. Despite Leila's fear, Idris and Leila jumped on the last minibus to the city and headed towards the concrete jungle.

Muhtar was constantly lying down, and during his waking hours, he would fool around with Cemile. They had no real responsibilities left; their only goal was to have a son.

Idris stormed into the living room and grabbed Muhtar by the collar.

"May I have permission? I haven't even said 'in the name of God' and 'welcome brother-in-law' yet."

"You son of a bitch… You sack of shit… You've tormented my sister enough!"

"Wait, brother-in-law, let's talk this out. Please don't hit me for the love of God…"

Idris slapped Muhtar. As he had aged, Muhtar had gained more weight and was slipping through Idris' hands, unable to avoid the blows.

"I'll tear you to pieces, damn you!" he said, delivering two more slaps, "I already have a record…"

"Okay, okay, I'm yours to sacrifice, your servant. Don't hit me, especially not in front of my children. Take your sister and her descendants if you want. I won't say anything. I'm yours to sacrifice!"

That night, the suitcases were packed with excitement. Leila couldn't contain her volcanic sense of triumph. Joy sparks flew from her face, and her eyes shone crystal-clear. She never imagined she would welcome her dream of going to Istanbul to a new city with such happiness, let alone with her brother's support.

Leila pulled Cemile aside and made her promise to look after Behiye's unmarried daughters.

After locking up their village home, Leila took all three of her girls and set off for Istanbul with Idris.

Benazir's enrollment was completed. With Idris's insistence, they visited Istanbul University and the Darülfünun Library. Its cracked concrete exterior filled the building with old, coffee-scented books.

There was neither the sound of a bird chirping nor the sight of any greenery in the neighbourhood. Leila had already begun to feel bored from the first month. She sometimes thought she saw Yausef, but he disappeared like a figment of her imagination. She dreamed of her village, the one she had not felt peaceful in when she was there but longed to see when she was outside it.

As she took out the garbage, she ran into her neighbour, who happened to be from the same hometown. Her eyes shone with a longing for the soil. Thinking that she would immediately become acquainted with her neighbour, Leila opened all the curtains of her heart to her.

"Is that bespectacled man your husband? Mashallah…"

"He is my brother! When my eldest daughter was accepted to university, we all came here together."

"What is your daughter studying?"

"Law."

"Mashallah, mashallah," the neighbour said enviously, her eyes bulging.

"Where is your husband?"

Leila didn't respond.

"We're supposed to be siblings, but we're actually up to no good," the neighbour said.

"What impertinence! You shouldn't meddle in matters that don't concern you. Please… Even in the village, there was never this much malice. Oh, my goodness…"

A few days later, the neighbour knocked on the door again, just for the sake of chatting, and brought up the topic:

"There is a smell, a paint smell…"

"Yes, I am painting. Does it bother you?"

"Yes, other neighbours are bothered as well. But since we are from the same hometown, we should look out for each other, right?"

She thought of her mother and didn't want to be a pessimistic neighbour like her. Leila made amends with her neighbour and brewed her some coffee. They chatted for a while. Every time Leila entered and exited her room, the neighbour would look up and peer inside with curiosity. When Leila said she didn't want to show her work to anyone, the neighbour didn't insist and left.

Leila was disappointed that she couldn't freely paint in the big city, which made her sad. She remembered how happy she was in the village. She wanted to return to her old habits but couldn't leave her daughters behind in this chaotic city. This city frightened Leila. She felt even more sorrowful when she thought of what her neighbour had said. She felt nauseous as she looked out the window and watched the passers-by. The building was tall, and the street was narrow. When she turned her head to the sky, she tied her hands together and thought of nature. Was this city, which was often talked about, just about these narrow streets and chaos?

The migrant community, who never left the textile workshops, truly thought they were living in Istanbul. They didn't even venture beyond their own neighbourhood. However, they had become slaves to money in underground, foul-smelling dens, spending all their time serving demanding bosses and dreaming of going home after earning a few pennies in harsh conditions...

Leila enjoyed listening to her migrant neighbours and had become accustomed to them. Observing was her indispensable duty. They had rented one of the small nests close to Kumkapı, where two people could barely pass by each other without touching. She had taken the largest room and turned her observations of the knights she had hung opposite her into compositions on the bed. Leila found solace in this way.

They introduced themselves as Istanbulites who left their land and their homes behind. They refused to accept being villagers and would even get offended, thinking they were being insulted when someone asked them which village they came from. Leila was taken aback when she asked the neighbour woman, "Which village are you from?" and received a strong reaction.

The neighbour Zeynep had spoken clearly and slowly with her mouth full, "We've been living here for fifteen years. We are city people, Istanbulites."

Leila found it strange that someone with such a distorted dress and tone of voice could neither be a villager nor a city person.

"We are not villagers or anything. Thank God we've been in Istanbul for years. We earn our bread here. We are practically Istanbulites. Of course, it's not where you were born, but where you live that is your homeland..." she said.

She remembered her father's story about the partridges: "A friend to others, an enemy to oneself..." for the partridges, "just like us..."

Idris was calling from below, but Leila noticed his voice after a while: "The doorbell must not be working. Open the door for me!" Idris appeared at the door with a sad face and a loaf of bread.

"What's wrong, sister?"

"Nothing..."

"There is; tell me so it doesn't stay in you."

"When I was in the village, I painted a painting daily. I've been here for a month and have heard complaints from the neighbours. The smell is bothering them..."

"It's a different smell, that's why. They are used to their own smell and react when it's different, of course."

"I have to get used to it for my daughters. I promised to do everything to educate them. I'll get over this, too."

She was absent-minded and unhappy. She regretted bringing her brother along but couldn't say it aloud. If it wasn't for him, they wouldn't have been able to come here in any other way...

He put his shoes back on. "Come on, Leila, let's go to the beach and take a walk. We'll order food from outside tonight. That's what everyone does here, from what I've seen."

"At this rate, we'll run out of money. Besides, I can't sell my paintings."

"I think you told me once that you didn't paint them to sell them. Besides, I'll take care of you now. I'll find a job here soon. I won't let anyone sell your beautiful paintings for a few coins."

Benazir attended university, and the twins attended a high school near their home. Idris went to the coffeehouse in the neighbourhood, drank a few teas, and talked to his fellow citizens. He told them he had come here to educate his three nieces and find a job.

The elderly man in the coffeehouse, his moustache yellowed from smoking, was obviously a manager, asked in a deep voice, "What experience do you have, son?"

"I am an avid reader. I can read to visually impaired people without tiring all day long. Additionally, I can teach mathematics, which I have never forgotten since high school. I can teach math to children."

They looked at his glasses and laughed, "Obviously, but books are rarely read here, and no one is interested in math," said the café owner. They had given him glasses to help his tired eyes. The glasses keep sliding down his nose, and he would push them back up with a finger gesture.

"I was also a tea boy in prison. As a child, I always made tea. My father loved rabbit blood tea, especially the one he brought from Iraq, and we always drank smuggled tea."

Idris's honesty must have caught the man's attention, for he immediately gave him the job that day. He spent his entire day making tea and washing cups until late at night. He did not mind this and was very pleased to have found the job, but his hands started to develop calluses from the constant contact with water. It had been the same in prison.

He looked at his hands and said to himself, "These are the hands of a worker," and he loved himself.

hen Leila opened the door, she faced a young man and a beautiful young woman holding hands whom she did not recognise.

"Welcome, whom were you looking for?"

"Sister, don't you recognise me? It's me, Mesut!"

Leila hesitated, but then she burst into tears, hugged her brother tightly, and held him close with longing.

"Oh, my brother, who smells like father! How did you find this place? Come on in, don't stand there…"

Leila stepped aside from the door, invited the young couple inside, and said, "Is this your wife?"

"She's my girlfriend, my partner," Mesut said, laughing, as he hugged his niece Benazir. It was clear they had made a deal. Leila couldn't hide her surprise:

"Well, well, well! Look at Leila's daughter… What else have you been up to behind my back?"

"There's something called the internet, Mother. When you enter the name and surname, you find it immediately."

"Oh, really? How ignorant I am."

Arin and Narin also hugged their uncle Mesut.

"I heard that my brother Idris also came. I couldn't sleep tonight if I didn't see you."

Leila checked the clock on the wall.

"He won't be here for another two hours. Let me cook for you right away."

Although the young woman insisted that they had eaten, Leila didn't listen and went to the kitchen.

"You can't convince my mother. When she decides to do something, she does it. Even if you're not hungry, take a bite or two."

As Leila checked the meat in the freezer, she murmured, "This should be enough for us."

"Mom!" Benazir called from the living room, "Uncle doesn't eat meat, don't insist for no reason."

Leila looked up, "What do you mean he doesn't eat meat? Oh my god... how can a villager not eat meat?"

"Sister, I'm a vegetarian. I can't eat meat."

"What does that mean now? Old village, a new habit," Leila muttered. "All right, I'll cook some vegetables for you. Will you be full with that?"

"I'm not even hungry, sister, believe me... If I could have a cup of tea, that would be enough."

When Mesut thought of quail, he got sick again...

Just in time Idris opened the door and came in. When he saw Mesut they hugged each other freely, comfortably, taking away the pain of years. There was a short silence after the hug. Mesut opened his mouth and continued to talk a bit more.

"There's something I need to tell you, Leila sister. I feel so ashamed for keeping it hidden for so many years."

"What is it, Mesut? Is it about your partner? Are you going to get married?"

The girls were used to their mother's jokes and laughed. The young woman blushed.

"No, it's not that... It's about Yausef."

Leila's cheeks sank and her forehead creased.

"Yausef never forgot about you; he never gave up on you."

"Where are you getting this from, especially in front of my daughters?"

"Sister, he always wrote to you, always asked about you. Even after you got married..."

"I didn't get married; the woman who is my mother sold me!"

"Yes, when you left that house... She forbade me from telling you. I was just a child; how could I have known... If Yausef had returned to the village, then my mother would have said that she herself would have shot him."

"Or she would have made you do it."

Idris hung his head, leaned out the window, and lit a cigarette. "Yausef stayed away to protect you from harm. He was so helpless."

"Where are those letters then?"

"My mother burned them or used them on the stove to start a fire."

"And you ate those meals with pleasure, didn't you!"

"Sister, I'm so sorry."

"Don't blame Leila; it's done. What are you after?" Idris tensed.

"So where is that woman?"

"She's probably staying at Lokman's house; where else!" Smoke shaped from his cigarette.

"No, brother Idris... Latife never wanted her there. Except for the first days after we arrived, we couldn't stay there. No one could tolerate my mother. Lokman put us in a dilapidated house before a year passed."

"Where is she? I'm going to hold her accountable for our lives!" Leila shouted.

Mesut swallowed hard; his eyes filled with tears. After a while of silence, he responded to the angry looks directed at him:

"Our mother died, sister."

"How did she die?" Idris was startled; he and Leila had sworn never to visit her, but her death still surprised and saddened him. Leila listened to Mesut with a frozen expression.

"It was last summer. I stayed at my girlfriend's home to take a break from my mother. When I returned home after two days, the entire building had a strong smell. As I approached the door, a heavy smell made my nostrils hurt. I rang the bell, but no one answered. I went inside with my key and heard voices from the TV; I thought my mother was sleeping there. But when I got closer, I saw her body was swollen and purple. According to the autopsy, our mother had a sudden heart attack... She had gained too much weight recently."

Leila's facial expression froze. After Mesut finished speaking, she burst out laughing. Everyone in the room looked at her in shock, not knowing what to do. She went to her room and continued laughing. Her frightening laughter turned into crying sobs.

Idris and Mesut couldn't take it anymore and burst into Leila's room. The room smelled of paint and thinner, which could make an unaccustomed person dizzy.

As Mesut looked at his sister's pictures, he felt a sense of admiration. He knelt down in front of her and said, "Sister, please don't be upset. We couldn't bring him to the village. As you said, the soil would not accept him."

"Ah, you did the right thing! Am I mourning that woman's death? I'm upset that she died without suffering!"

"Now that you've found your Uncle Mesut on the internet," said the mother, and her daughters looked at her with curious eyes, wondering what she would ask.

"There was a teacher in the village who encouraged me to paint. Benazir, you remember him, right?"

"Yes, Mom, Ahmet Teacher."

"I'm calling his phone, but it says the number is no longer used. He wasn't at his home address either. He moved, and no one knows where. It's like he vanished into thin air. It's like he never existed. I thought maybe we could find him on the internet, just like you found Uncle Mesut..."

"Mom, hundreds of thousands of people with that name are in the country. We can't find him."

"Can't we find him through the switchboard?"

The girls burst out laughing.

"If we search for 'Ahmet Teacher with a moustache' in profile pictures, we might find him."

"Unfortunately, Mom, that's very difficult," said Benazir.

Leila drifted off into the distance, her eyes fixed on a point.

"He said to me, 'We'll put my pictures on display whenever you want. I'll be with you.' The teacher enabled me to paint; he became my muse. It seems his life was only that long in my life..."

Benazir had always been a travelling companion for her mother and had even learned most things with her. She had chosen her as a role model. In return for Leila's sacrifices, she prepared a little surprise. The twins took photos of the paintings; one held the light, and the other edited the images in the digital environment. They selected a few from the thousands of pictures taken and emailed them to art galleries. Benazir continued to send emails to different places until she achieved her goal without waiting for a reply to her mail.

Not long after, they received a response from Tate Modern in London in a hay-paper envelope. Benazir embraced the envelope, waiting for her mother, Leila, who would return from the market soon. Leila, wearing a long-sleeved woollen cardigan from the village and a patterned dress, entered through the door. The twins screamed in unison, taking the bags from their mother's hand and carrying them to the kitchen.

"Mom, we have great news."

Leila looked at them inquisitively as they handed her the envelope.

"What is this?"

She carefully tore the envelope at the edge and opened the high-quality triple-layered paper. She looked at it for a long time, her face unclear.

"Well, this is probably in English; I don't understand it..."

Arin and Narin snatched the paper and raced to their mother to translate it, both excitedly brimming. "All right, I'll tell you what it says, girls. Don't worry about it," said the eldest daughter Benazir.

"What does it say, Benazir? What are you keeping from me again?" asked their mother, curious.

"They're inviting you to London, Mom. To an art exhibition... They loved all your paintings! Especially the 'Stone' painting..." Benazir read from the email that had been sent to her.

The invitation card indicated that Leila was invited to London, and the twins jumped up and down joyfully. They had also mentioned that they would cover everything, including Leila's expenses, daily allowance, and accommodation, for her upcoming exhibition at Tate Modern.

"What? How did my paintings end up there? In the Queen's country... I... Benazir, what have you done to me, my child? What am I going to do, Arin, Narin? I think I'm going to be sick," Leila said, unravelling the message. Benazir rushed to get her a glass of water while the twins fanned their mother.

Overcome with excitement, Leila's words jumbled together as she kneeled on the ground, covering her face with her hands, crying like a child. The twins hugged their mother tightly, one after the other.

"Your dream has come true, Mother. You will now have an art exhibition and be introduced as an artist!" they exclaimed, showing their happiness.

Their teeth were visible as they shared their joy on this special night.

"England... My father always talked about England. He had memorised its history and legal system like the back of his hand. As if he had been there before, God bless him," Leila said, squinting and looking into the distance. The twins listened intently, like schoolchildren.

"But how will I speak there now? I don't know the language!" Leila panicked, remembering that she didn't speak English.

"You won't have to say anything, Mother. You'll have a translator with you," Narin reassured her.

"How can I leave you now?" Leila asked as Arin stroked her arm gently.

"We won't be alone, Mother. Our uncle will be with us," said Arin.

"I'm now an adult woman and mother, and I'll study hard and focus on my lessons. After my internship, I'll finally become a lawyer and earn money," said Benazir.

"My paintings will be your dowry, and I'll spend my time painting."

"Don't worry about us anymore, Mother," Leila's daughters comforted her.

"Yes, Mother. Technology has advanced now, and we'll see you face-to-face on the phone," said Narin.

"Oh, my my, you have already settled me in! Look at my daughters, dear God. They've all grown up and will send their mother back to school. What do I know about girls when I can't even smell your scent on the phone and have to talk to you face-to-face?"

When Idris came home in the evening, he, too, had some fruits that Leila had bought from the market in his hand. The twins took the bags from him and relieved him of the burden.

"Uncle, we have news for you. The famous artist, Mrs Leila, is now standing in front of you."

Idris didn't understand, so they told him about the surprise they had prepared. Idris was overjoyed. He hugged his sister and kissed her on the forehead.

"Leila, wow!"

"It's not 'Mrs. Leila,' my daughters. My last name will be my father's name. They will call me 'Leila QASIM'."

Leila had always dreamed of carrying Yausef's surname since childhood. Her eyes clouded.

Benazir said, "Ahmet the teacher always called you 'Mrs. Leila'."

"Poor guy, who knows where he disappeared," Leila lamented.

"When you become famous, maybe Ahmet the teacher will find you," Idris said seriously.

Leila was so pleased with the idea that she couldn't sleep with joy. A peaceful and melancholic feeling engulfed her, the city, the world...

For the first time in a long time, someone who hadn't crossed her mind came to her.

"Yausef!"

Where was he now? Who was with him? For some reason, she imagined herself with him as if she had never been apart. It was as if they were living in a farmhouse in the village together. Sometimes she had perverse fantasies of losing herself in his green eyes and moistening her lips with his. She even believed that her daughters were his. She laughed to herself.

"Oh, goodness… Have you become indecent at this age, Leila? Get a hold of yourself," she prodded herself.

She went to the door of the room where her daughters were working and called out. She went in and made one more plea.

"I wonder… Can we also find my childhood friend from there on the Internet? I don't think there is another name like his. Yausef… I was angry with him, but he never left me and sent me letters. You also heard about it," she said, awaiting her daughters' approval.

One of the twins started searching for the name on her computer, and the others gathered around. She pointed out the mistake in the name with her finger, which contained the letter "A". They quickly searched for Yausef on social media and found him.

In the profile picture, the man who appeared as Yausef was the same man. He looked again and again. "Yes, this is…" Leila's eyes filled with tears. Although she tried not to show it to her daughters, they were old enough to understand and comprehend everything.

They sent him a short message. "Hello, Yausef. I sincerely wish for your well-being. I'm in Istanbul for my daughters' school and if you're around, I'd like to meet up and reminisce about the past… Until we meet, stay with love. Leila."

As if he was waiting for this message, Yausef responded immediately. The message had already arrived when Leila straightened up, and she was both surprised and flattered.

They arranged to meet as soon as possible. Butterflies fluttered inside her, as if she had suddenly turned into a 14-year-old girl again. Yausef had already bought a ticket from Berlin to Istanbul and counted the minutes until the day they met.

"Mom!" Both twins' eyes were bloodshot. They were crying uncontrollably.

"What happened? Did something happen to Yausef?"

"Our father has passed away..." Benazir said. She was acting more calmly than the twins. It was as if she could keep things under control because she was the older sister.

Leila felt nothing; on the contrary, a sense of relief washed over her. However, memories came to mind. Apart from Muhtar's antics, she never remembered him fondly.

She was in silence for a bit, wishing she would like to cry over her memories: when she was beaten, when she was persecuted, when she never got understood. She just said:

"If he's passed away, then he's passed away... We're all going to die."

The twins hung their heads and began to cry even more. They went to their rooms.

"Okay, get ready; let's go to the village. Let's fulfil the customs one last time." Leila sat down next to her daughters, who began to pack their suitcases in a hurry.

"Aren't you going to London right away then? What about Yausef? You were supposed to meet tomorrow..."

"Forget it... Neither of them has been around this long; they can wait longer. Let's go to the village first. Let's see sister Behiye and your stepsiblings. Then I'll come back, and you guys can stay there for a while. It's for the best."

The girls looked at their mother in surprise. "It's for the best, like this: I'll also visit my father. Where else would I have gone to share this joy with him?"

Yausef and Leila's meeting two days later did not happen. Yausef had come to Istanbul the next day, walking through crowded and dizzying streets while feeling disappointed. Then he received another message.

Leila had written that she was going to the village because of the news of Muhtar, the father of her daughters, passing away. Therefore, the meeting would not happen.

The village was dancing in a flood of light, with the long untouched windows of the houses shimmering like tempting pools of molten gold. No calls to prayer emanated from the minarets and spires; no speakers blared out their melodies. The church had been abandoned, waiting to be captured in a tourist's camera frame. Though hardly any Syriac families remained in the village, they occasionally dropped by to use their summer houses. After all, their loved ones were buried here.

The village, which had gone years without visitors, was now being left to the mercy of the two-way highway's exhaust fumes, buried in dust. If Leila had a cleaning brush, she would have wiped the miniature stone houses' surfaces and sides. A dry, lifeless, grey town had replaced the once-green village.

Thankfully, Qasim's house was still standing, about two hundred meters from the road. This was the only favour the headman had ever done for him in his life. The road did not pass through his father's house, and the Abrohoms' homes were also left unscathed.

The asphalt road, belching smoke from the heat, passed between Rivervillage and Greenvillage, separating the villages from each other. The gravel spilling over the edges of the asphalt road shone brightly. The road was clean and quite shiny, as if no one had ever walked on it. It sizzled in the heat of the sun, echoing the sound of large vehicles passing over it. Behind the hill near the village, the quarry was covered in white dust like a flour mill. You could hear the noise behind its faint outline. Like white pigeon wings, the stone was cut from the rocks and carried on the backs of powerful machines towards the workshop. There, the stones were shaped by the craftsmen's hands.

The mourning house also delivered meals to the workers at the quarry. The headman's charity was meant to benefit the labourers too. The tradition of cooking with pots had not changed in the village, but the household population had dwindled compared to before. The villagers usually shared their meals with the neighbouring villages or quarry workers.

Before asking the traveller, "Are you hungry or thirsty?" They insisted that the traveller sit down and food was placed in front of them within five minutes. They had always done so, and they continued to do so. The road passed closest to the headman's house. Workers rested there, used the bathroom, and even filled their stomachs with food and tea before continuing their work.

Behiye's workers were still living in the nearby house, so they had not suffered any harm from anyone. It never crossed their minds that anyone would harm them.

"After all, you always get hit by the one closest to you! Because they know everything about you, your weaknesses, what makes you happy, what makes you sad, where you lack, or where you have excess..."

"What have I done wrong, my daughter, for God's sake?"

"I don't blame you, Behiye Sister. I am angry because they treat you like a sheep." Leila furrowed her brows as she spoke angrily, "I will never forget the advice my father gave me. He once said, 'You will not tolerate injustice and insults like a sheep; otherwise, they will benefit from your wool and meat. You are not a sheep; you are Leila!' I have been standing up to injustice and insults for years with this stubbornness, but I have also been subjected to violence. Fortunately, I never gave in. But how could you do such a thing, Behiye Sister..."

When Leila returned to the village, she faced some unbearable truths. Cemile had been scheming behind Leila's back. Somehow, she managed to convince the village headman with a thousand lies, which wasn't difficult to do. The village headman gave a paper to his first wife, his first official wife, and his uncle's daughter Behiye, and didn't even need to force her to sign it. Behiye did what she was told and put her finger on the divorce petition. Thus, Cemile took over the official documents. She also had the land deeds in the village transferred to her name, even though she didn't have a male child...

Behiye was given the house in the village informally. However, the concrete building in Midyat and the bank accounts would officially belong to Cemile and, therefore her son. The people who came to express their condolences to the headman's family were few and far between. Leila entered the house and found Cemile. She glared at Cemile like an angry bull, and her face turned into a mask of rage. Leila advanced on Cemile.

"You peasant of a sly woman, this was not part of our agreement!" She was about to attack when Behiye grabbed Leila by the arm.

"For God's sake, Leila let it be; let her see what has happened. At least she didn't harm my daughters, she kept her word, and they married whom they wanted and left."

"Yes! What do you want? Didn't your daughters go to school? Thanks to me..." she shouted in a high-pitched voice.

"Thanks to you? What did you do? Your only job was to have children. You horny woman! Where are they? You couldn't even have a girl, or a boy! You took over all of his wealth. There are tears in all the girls' eyes in those presences. May it all be forbidden for you..."

Behiye was overwhelmed, and she acted with Leila. If it weren't for her daughters, saving Cemile from Leila's grasp would have been a serious challenge. Benazir and the twins were serving inside the house with the other stepdaughters. Rukiye was in a distant city due to her husband's mandatory duty and wasn't expected to come to the village for a while.

They took Leila outside to calm her down. According to Behiye, Leila had turned into a noisy woman when she returned from Istanbul.

"Oh, how shameful. The headman has just died, and they are only concerned with money..." She didn't ignore the whispers, but she didn't care.

"All those girls are innocent. That money is forbidden for you..." she repeated.

"For God's sake, my daughter, listen to me. They will talk about you behind your back. All of you will return to your cities, and I will be the one left here. Then I will have to hear these rumours all by myself and feel sad. Please don't say anything, even if it's for my sake. It's already done..."

"Let us suffer so much, but let that woman take everything and leave it to her son! Oh, my goodness..."

Behiye was like a bird who had eaten sour fruit.

"How could you not inform me beforehand, Behiye Sister?"

"I didn't know, my dear. The headman gave me a pen and paper. I can't read or write nor have the power to understand. I just made a scratch. The headman wasn't convinced, and he said I had to put my fingerprint on it, so I did. Then the headman told me I could have a lot of things that could be mine. How could I know? Oh, foolish me…"

"They used you. He divorced you in one session… Of course, their daughters didn't know. Thank goodness we turned our backs and left for Istanbul!"

Behiye's sad gaze softened Leila's steel face.

"Anyway… I have nothing to do with that man or his money anymore. My paintings are in high demand. Look what I'm going to say, they're inviting me to London. I'll come back here as a famous artist from London."

"Where did you say?"

"To London!" Leila raised her voice a little so Behiye could hear it.

"I'm going to England…"

"Are you crazy, my daughter? If you stay there, you won't come back here again…"

Leila laughed and continued, "That's why I don't have time or energy to deal with Cemile. If things go well, I'll return to the village, my home. We'll continue our lives as sisters, won't we, my dear sister?"

"God forbid, don't jinx it. You'll be a big person, won't you!"

"Why not let them work too, like me? Let them have something too!"

"When you become famous, why would you return to the village, my daughter? Stay there. Are you crazy?"

"If things go well, I want to return to my village. I said… I'll have a farmhouse here. I want to raise animals and paint in my garden, under the sun."

Behiye sat there, feeling relaxed. She dreamed of not dying alone and forgetting. Even Leila's dream of being by her side warmed her heart. Leila, her companion whom she loved like a daughter, who could visit her every day and have a chat with her in this village.

Leila, on the other hand, was uncomfortable in her chair. Knowing that Cemile was inside, she couldn't help but look at the house with disdain again.

"But it's not the time yet... I have something else to tell you," said Behiye.

"Say it."

"Mustafa's ex-fiancée, Suheyla, you know..."

The word "ex" pierced Leila's heart.

"Well, what happened to her?" she asked.

"She married the richest man in the village. They have five children together."

"Is that so?"

"Yes, indeed. Our hero is buried underground while she... well, she managed to move on."

"Must have been able to," Leila said.

Behiye's ears weren't working as well as they used to. "Pardon me?" she asked.

"She used to tell Mustafa 'I can't live without you,' and 'I'll die without you'... But she moved on after all. That slut!"

"Don't say such things, my dear. You're going to grow up and become an artist soon," she warned Leila, and then added with the wisdom of her years, "That's how life is, you'll have to accept it. What else can you do?"

"Yes... a life without honour!"

The number of guests dwindled. Leila stayed with her daughters Behiye and Cemile, but Cemile disappeared from the scene.

Just before sunset, the sky once again spread its colours, challenging Leila with the question, "Can you do better than me?"

Leila wandered the village streets with strange but nostalgic feelings and stopped by her father's house. A fountain had been installed in the garden, and she had carried the hose on her shoulder after borrowing it from Behiye. She attached the long hose and turned on the tap. She wanted to quench the thirst of the parched ground. The garden wasn't enough, so she watered the whole courtyard. She stuck her finger on the end of the hose and sprayed water as far as she could reach. As the water soaked into the earth, Leila lost herself in thought, wandering far away.

"It was almost unfair to Yausef. I should have gone to see him; we could have satisfied our longing for each other. The headman could have waited a day or two longer, the late fatso."

She heard a rustling noise and was frightened. Had she imagined the headman and spoken out loud? She listened to the footsteps getting louder and louder. She turned her head in that direction, and her breath caught in her throat. Her emotions were a jumbled mess. Yausef was standing right in front of her. The drops of water spraying from the hose seemed to catch all the colours of the rainbow, shining like a jewel on the young man. He smiled with emerald eyes:

"Hello, Leila, how are you?"

She was so nervous that her words were jumbled. They stood there silently for a while.

They arranged to meet at a venue the next day, and Yausef went home while Leila returned to her daughters. Leila lay in bed with her daughters, and for the first time in her life, she fell asleep with a smile on her face. Her dreams were starting to come true.

"I've lived my whole life for this moment; to meet with you, alone, one last time. And now I am so excited... I don't know how two former lovers behave when they meet after years," Yausef said, spreading his arms without any worry about being seen by anyone.

They hugged, easing the weight of years of awkwardness. They sat across from each other at the table without speaking for a long time. Both blushed, their heartbeats racing with excitement. Leila fidgeted with her fingers shyly while Yausef smiled at her and then looked down at the table. He looked at her, the woman he had loved for twenty-two years, and she was sitting right in front of him again. He had found her again, and they were alone together. They didn't even notice the waiters around them. They had become two innocent, shy lovers, unable to recall ever feeling this embarrassed twenty-two years ago.

"My condolences, Leila. As soon as I received your message, I rushed over," Yausef said.

Leila understood that her daughter had sent the message to Yausef and shrugged. It was clear that she wasn't very upset about the death of the village headman. She crossed her arms. Without waiting for Yausef to say anything else, she spoke up.

"So, you became a surgeon after failing your class in high school."

"I failed for you, Leila."

"My daughters told me about the information on your profile. Honestly, I'm very happy for you. Congratulations."

The two lovers, like strangers, were hesitant to look each other in the eye and afraid to touch.

"Leila, I don't know what to say. I wish…"

"Forget it… looking back at the past wastes our time. Let's look forward," Leila interrupted.

Yausef broke down, tears streaming down his face.

Leila quickly changed the subject.

"How are your parents? And the children…"

He answered her question.

"The children are as big as donkeys. Benjamin never married; he devoted himself to religion. Gabriel has become a huge man and has smart, sweet children. Even the children have grown up. Samuel became a father and is living with his girlfriend at a young age. They are very happy together."

"How nice. May they always be happy."

"My father has gotten quite old. I left him alone with a caregiver… I take care of my father."

"And Aunt Aziza?"

"My mother passed away a few years ago from breast cancer. She had been undergoing chemotherapy for many years, and we thought she had overcome it, but it came back. She never recovered from the pain of losing her children."

Yausef tried to divert his words as if he had broken a pot. "I am glad that Idris has returned and that he is building a new life with you in Istanbul. I hope he is doing well."

Leila remained silent.

"If my father dies, I will be completely alone. I have always felt incomplete throughout my life in Berlin."

"I am very sorry for your mother, Yausef. And what about you? Have you never married? Do you have any children?"

"No... I... I have always waited for you, Leila," he choked.

Leila shuddered at his words, her thoughts and feelings pulling her back and forth. She looked at Yausef with tearful eyes but couldn't say anything.

"And you, Leila? Your husband is died," Yausef said, even using the word 'husband' reluctantly. "I always knew that we would meet again someday. For 22 years, I have lived with the thought of you. From now on, your daughters will be my own. I will never let them miss their father."

"That's great... But Yausef, how will that work? How can we forget our past and move forward? I wish it were that easy, just to take a brush and paint over our memories so they disappear. Is that even possible?"

"Leila... No matter what, we can start a new life together. We can leave the past behind us."

"Yausef, have you forgotten? Our families are sworn enemies! How can we build a life over the blood of our brothers?"

"Before that issue, we were like soulmates. We can be like that again. What they did was a mistake... And they paid the price for it..."

"Yausef!" Leila's voice rose sharply. "Yes, we were like soulmates. But... Our hearts were broken, our souls shattered. Don't you understand? Sometimes we have to let time pass without interfering. We must flow with it as it is. If it's not meant to be, then it's not meant to be..."

Yausef couldn't take it anymore. His emerald eyes turned red; tears streamed down his cheeks. "I won't leave you anymore; I can't, do you understand? I can't breathe without you, Leila. Don't deprive me of yourself, please."

"For all these years, you have lived without me. You can continue to do so. I have grown accustomed to it. Besides, I have other plans. I want to live my life on my own terms. I am going to London soon for an art exhibition at the Tate Modern. This is just the beginning... I want to live my life according to my own decisions. As I said, dwelling on the past will only waste our time."

Yausef's throat was dry; he swallowed hard. He wiped his eyes. His heart burned with pain. He had no more words to convince Leila.

Even if he fell silent for a moment, it didn't mean he gave up on Leila.

"My mother's decisions have shaped my life until now. I am now on the verge of realising my dream. I can't think of anything other than my paintings," she said. Leila spoke with the indifference of a new-born baby.

"You are the strongest woman I know, Leila. I want you to hear that with your own ears."

"How many women have you known?" Leila asked, dispelling the gloomy atmosphere and smiling.

"I can't help but fall in love with you. I can't give you up" said Yausef quietly.

They moistened their throats with a sip of their cold teas.

Istanbul was a bustling city like an ant's nest during the day, and it felt scary and unsafe at night. People who ran around all day would fall asleep without even having the chance to have a chat in their homes, where they longed to stretch their feet. The lights that faded after the exhausting day turned the city into a huge cemetery. It was also frightening to think that millions of people would not be alive after a hundred years, which kept people awake at night.

Clearly, some people could not sleep. A few houses in different parts of the buildings seemed to be floating in the air and would not go out until the morning light. As soon as the twilight began, the noise of horns and human movement started to give people a headache. Beggars were also a part of the scary side of the city. People threw themselves onto the road to avoid them when they suddenly appeared. Avoiding an accident was a matter of chance. With their mouths open and covered in dirt, the drowsy beggars continued to sleep on the sidewalks. Despite being strong and young, begging suited them. Those struggling with stress would punish them by ignoring them when they passed by.

Countless buildings were suffocating people and narrowing the sky. Istanbul changed so fast that sometimes people confused the streets they walked on. If someone fell, everyone would immediately avoid them, but they were not without curiosity. They would enjoy watching those surrounded by a circle after falling or fighting.

Everyone was angry; everyone was so furious... No one gave in; no one showed respect for each other. Nobody was happy with their lives. Their discontent was evident on their faces.

"This is Istanbul, the city they call it!" Leila said. She felt relieved when she came from the village, but the huge city had drained her energy in a day. Idris had picked Leila up from the airport with a friend from the coffee shop. Idris took his brother's suitcase upstairs, and Leila followed him. They went up to the top floor of the building, where there was no elevator, out of breath. Zeynep, their neighbour, appeared as soon as they opened the door, welcoming them with condolences. Leila nodded her head, breathless, and walked inside.

She had to prepare another suitcase for the next day without waiting too long. Leila was a passenger to London.

"In this case, you carried my bag. Who will carry it there? I must be self-sufficient," Leila said to her brother Idris as she unpacked her bag.

Idris went into the kitchen and made some tea. He leaned his head out the window and watched the passers-by as he smoked his cigarette. The cigarette ash was flying and breaking apart in the air. "You're a strong enough woman, Leila," he said.

He had heard this same talk twice this week. Yausef had also said she was the strongest woman he knew while they were sitting at the café in Midyat. Was she strong because she would become famous for her paintings, or were all the figures that made her who she was the source of her strength?

"What is strength, Idris brother?" Leila asked.

"Strength... It means control and mercy. Most empires have done it that way. Showing mercy is the strength itself."

"So, I'm not strong because I don't forgive my mother now?" Leila asked.

"I won't forgive her either. Let's be weak, then. But think about it. If it weren't for your mother, would you live this life here? A life where you're going to Tate Modern as an artist," Idris replied.

Leila didn't say anything. She drifted away in thought. After a while, she said, "I still won't forgive her. I won't be a mother like her, and my daughters won't be like her either."

Leila continued to talk with Idris in the living room from her bedroom. She unpacked her suitcase and started to put her clothes in for a week. She put her floral dress in the suitcase. Her daughters had dragged her out to the market to buy a couple of modern clothes to look stylish. A white, flowing shirt and black, loose-fitting, fabric pants. Leila had never worn pants in her life. It was always floral dresses and a knit vest to cover her rear. Even she couldn't recognise herself in the modern clothes she tried on; there was a completely different Leila in the mirror of the fitting room. She got tired of that image quickly and changed her clothes.

"If I had studied, my style would have changed like this," she daydreamed. Although her daughters admired their mother, Leila did what she knew best and couldn't give up her floral dresses and the crocheted shawls she had made, so she put them in the empty parts of the suitcase.

She had walked around the house all day to get used to the low-heeled shoes. She took them, put banana socks inside so they wouldn't take up much space.

"Is London cold, right?" Leila asked.

"They say it's the country with the sun that never sets, but that means something else of course," Idris said and laughed.

They were still talking without a break. Idris was shuttling back and forth between the kitchen and the dining table in the living room. The tone of his voice sounded different to Leila's ears as he came and went. Leila couldn't relax until she finished her work. Finally, she heard the sound of the suitcase zipper closing, went to the sink and washed her hands again.

"You know, Leila, sometimes we have to forgive people..." Idris said.

"You're still talking about her, our mother. I told you I won't forgive her," Leila said.

"That's right..."

"Is it Leila QASIM?" he asked.

"Yes, sir."

"Wasn't that the name of one of our first martyrs? Where does this name come from? Please, research it immediately."

The announcement of an art exhibition was being made in the local newspaper. The person in charge, who had strong connections with the Barzani family, lived in London and was curious about this name with astonishment. They brought the short paragraph introducing Leila in front of the person in charge. As they read the painter's biography, they couldn't believe it. They read it repeatedly: "Leila, daughter of Qasim from Greenvillage in Midyat…" The person in charge was impatient to meet the young woman. They asked their assistant to remind them of the exhibition time so they wouldn't miss it. They would not only have the honour of meeting her but also see her paintings.

Leila's legs were shaking, and she was speechless with excitement. She was wearing a flowing blue sequin kaftan. An unexpected crowd greeted her. Both foreigners and English people were interested in her. A cocktail was also held for her, and people were waiting in front of her paintings with admiration and drinks in their hands.

"Leila QASIM!"

"Here I am."

The person in charge greeted Leila with a big smile behind their glasses. They introduced themselves and reached out their hand:

"Your father, the late Qasim, was my dear friend... May his soul rest in peace. We are grateful to have found you. You are Qasim's gift to us. You have a special place in our hearts. Welcome... If it is suitable, we want to throw a reception for you tomorrow..."

The balding person in charge was sweating profusely. They were experiencing the excitement of meeting Leila, with their teeth showing in a wide smile.

The curly-haired art lover stood in front of a pale painting of apple trees, dressed in a suit. Children were grinning at each other like a red and yellow apple on the dry, pale-coloured branches. Leila knew who he was and approached him:

"Yausef! What are you doing here?"

"How could I leave you alone on a day like this?"

He looked at a painting, then at Leila:

"You know, that day was a turning point in my life... I will never forget it, and I see that you haven't forgotten either, despite all the experiences you've been through..."

"How could I forget..."

"It's wonderful to see you again."

"Yes, it's a strange feeling. Being together in a foreign land..."

"Watching you from afar, Leila, brought a refreshing feeling to my heart. I never want to be away from you again."

They stood side by side for a long while, looking at the painting.

"Well, that's just it," Leila broke the stretched silence with a sigh.

The mixed media on the canvas had aged and deteriorated, giving it a stale appearance. Leila seemed to want to show how even beautiful things can decay over time.

Despite being under numerous glittering lights, the paintings displayed empty, dilapidated, faded, and tired images. The silence evoked death, a barren landscape, and an empty village. At the same time, the diversity of maliciousness, sin, competition, differences in opinion, and family structures that harboured countless stories were also highlighted. She depicted both the life of her dreams and the reality of what she had experienced in a homogeneous manner.

She had worked on a stone canvas with natural materials such as hay, ginger root, and rust. They brought her the "Stone" painting and asked her to give an interview. She answered the questions while a translator translated her words.

"My paintings translate my emotions, past, and history. My language and dreams would have disappeared if I hadn't created them. However, I have a reason to live. Instead of raising my daughters, I grew up with them, but something was missing. I always wanted to express myself with brushes, paint, and paper. That's how I felt inside... Everyone who has been a part of my life has impacted me for better or worse...

"That 'Stone' represented my entire life, the people who impacted me, and everything I had hidden inside. I couldn't do what it did, hide my truths; I had to put them into my paintings. One day, you would hear me, whether it was one person or thousands. But I knew that one day my paintings would be my language... If I hadn't done that, I wouldn't have been any different from that 'Stone.'

"That day is today... If I hadn't created my paintings, I would have still lived, but I would have died without ever feeling alive. The colours and figures made me strong...

"Today, I also carry my father's name because he raised me. I am Leila QASIM, my father's daughter... After me, there will be other

Leilas, and they will eventually discover and showcase their talents. This world is big enough for all of us...”

Leila had thought she would stutter at first, but as the questions were asked, she answered them rapidly, as if she had rehearsed them beforehand.

Yausef applauded her with pride, and the others in the room followed suit, clapping along with the translator. He took her out to dinner, and they chatted like two new friends.

They walked from Trafalgar Square to Buckingham Palace, then all the way to Hyde Park. They were tireless until they stopped to catch their breath in Soho. Walking along Oxford and Regent Streets in the evening was also a pleasure, as every street corner had different buildings like prizes for the pedestrians.

The day wasn’t enough, so they went to the Portobello Market the next day, admiring the colourful houses.

“These houses are even more colourful than my paintings!” Leila exclaimed, observing people of all kinds of colours. “There are more diverse people here than in Istanbul. And the parks are everywhere... Oh my God, if this were in our country, they would definitely turn them all into wheat fields or concrete in Istanbul.”

“Here, everything is regulated...”

“How nice,” the responsible laughed. He loved Leila very much. “Leila Han (Madam), we will give you a salary for the work and efforts of our late comrade Qasim, and we will do whatever it takes for you to stay here. We are ready to support you for life.”

“I cannot stay here...”

“What?”

Since they did not yet know Leila well, they urged her to stay in London.

"I cannot trade one day of sunshine in my land for all of this," she said, adding, "Also, since you are going to support me, please do it not only here but also in my country. Is it not possible?"

After the trip, they went to the reception address. The responsible presented Leila with a medal of honour at the reception. They granted her a lifetime salary on behalf of Qasim. It was good support for Leila to be able to continue painting. Moreover, her paintings were selling unexpectedly well.

Leila was now the age her father had been when he passed away. She was going back to her hometown, her childhood home. She reunited with Yausef, and they walked and talked, laughing while touring London again.

The villagers who still lived in the village gathered there and waited for Leila. The women started to ululate as soon as the car carrying her arrived. One woman's ululation ended, and another started to make rhythmic sounds by moving her tongue on her palate.

One of the twins held a large bouquet, primarily roses, while the other held a mirrored tray. Their mothers were waiting at the gate of the garden. İdris had renovated the house and the garden for the art school. With the help of his quarry friends, they restored the stone house and placed sculptural stones in the garden. The surroundings of that "famous" stone, to which Leila had given a name even in her painting, were trimmed, and the stone appeared as a living being. İdris had transformed the old family home into an art school, but everything related to the past was preserved.

Idris had painted and varnished the following on a canvas: "Leila QASIM grew up in this house and painted her paintings in this garden."

It was hung at the entrance of the garden like a banner. Leila's return from London was greeted with drums and trumpets.

"Your surprises never end!" said Leila, unable to hide her happiness. Her eyes filled with tears and trickled down her cheeks like pearls. She was even more emotional when she saw the canvas banner. Idris took his sister under his arm and said, "If our father were here, he would be proud of you."

"We're proud of you because you're our mother. Thank you for giving birth to us, Mom," the twins said in unison.

"You both speak at the same time now. Hopefully, your husbands won't get confused," she joked, making the crowd laugh.

"We have one more surprise for you," Benazir said.

It must be Yausef; yes, it must be him. She had seen him everywhere she went, so it was no longer a surprise.

At the entrance of Yausef's beige lace-embroidered house, she saw two silhouettes approaching her quickly from the arch. She recognised one of their faces. Then, with a smiling moustache and slightly tousled hair, it was Ahmet, the Teacher.

"Ahmet Teacher!" she exclaimed.

There was also a pregnant woman beside him. The modern woman extended her delicate hand and said, "It's an honour to meet you, Mrs Leila."

Leila could no longer hold back her tears. Instead, she covered her face with her hands like a child and cried loudly. Her face was drenched as if water had been poured on it.

"When I couldn't find you in Istanbul, I thought something had happened to you, Teacher. Your number was also never available," Leila said through her sobs.

"I had my phone stolen in Istanbul. I'm so sorry, Mrs Leila... I also tried calling you but couldn't find an account under your name."

"Is this beautiful woman your wife, teacher?"

"Oh yes, her name is Sevda… She's also an art teacher. I was appointed to a small town in Izmir, where we met and married." Ahmet took Leila's hand and placed it on his wife's belly. "We're having a daughter, Mrs Leila, and we'll name her after you. We hope she'll be like you."

"Ah, could there be a better compliment than this!" Leila exclaimed.

"You made it possible. We hope that many more Leilas will achieve this…" Ahmet said.

"And the reason you came here to see me is?" Leila asked, confused by his negative response.

"Not that," Ahmet replied.

"We didn't come just to see you, Leila. My husband and I came to ask for your permission to give art lessons and continue where you left off. Do we have your consent?"

Leila chuckled with childlike glee, "Well, where were we?"

Arm in arm, they walked towards the ribbon-cutting ceremony at the art school. Her heart ached, thinking she might see Yausef there. But he always liked to surprise her, showing up unexpectedly. Despite her telling him she wouldn't marry him, Yausef never gave up on Leila.

She stopped and examined the branches sprouting from the apple trees. "Yausef gave us the key to his house. We'll be staying there for a while. He's also set aside a large part of the house for important occasions."

"Important occasions?" she asked.

"He asked if we could use it for exhibitions. How could I refuse such an offer? Even if we didn't put anything in there, it looks like a museum… He took care of it himself, pruning and treating these trees."

Leila wondered how he managed to do it so quickly after returning from Berlin. The memories of those trees, with all their joys and sorrows, came flooding back. She sighed and turned her gaze towards the teacher, squinting from the sun as she looked at Ahmet.

Yausef always found a way to meet with Leila and continue their friendship, writing to her frequently and calling her from Berlin.

Despite Leila refusing his marriage proposal, she couldn't escape their friendship. They both knew they couldn't have a romantic relationship again. Yet, she still searched for Yausef with her eyes.

Arin handed her the scissors from the tray, and she cut the red ribbon, which stretched from one side of the door to the other. The villagers, including the headman, applauded until their hands were sore. Idris' co-workers from the quarry had come too. Narin handed her mother the flowers.

A group of women from neighbouring villages arrived, hugging Leila and crying joyfully. She had become a source of hope for them.

Tea was served in delicate, thin glasses from the samovar. The cookies were distributed to guests, villagers, and children. The responsible person in England had provided her with all kinds of help; her salary was enough for ten people and more. The Barzani family had sent a thank-you card for their contributions and expressed excitement for the continuation of her paintings.

She still planned to educate women who hadn't had the opportunity to learn according to their talents and interests. But, as Yausef had said, she would instill solidarity, culture, and good morals in them.

The next day, Idris returned home with his glasses again covered in white dust. Leila laughed and said, "You couldn't see me before; can you see me now in this state?"

"Oh yes... Leila, I have good news for you," Idris replied.

Leila crossed her arms and patiently waited for Idris to share his news.

"From now on, I will stay here too. They gave me my job back at the quarry. I'll work with my friends, and we can walk back home together. Imagine that! I'm not cut out for the chaos of Istanbul. Plus, this is a great place to read books! I'll repeatedly be reading all the books on the shelves in my closet."

"Okay," Leila said.

"And the girls have become adults; they no longer need us. They are strong and independent women who can stand on their own two feet..." Idris said, swelling with pride and paternal feelings.

"Yes, that's true," Leila replied. "Our neighbour Zeynep said they will become responsible, and she was right."

"You know, I can realise my dream here too," Idris continued.

"What dream?" Leila asked.

"I wanted to work at the library. I'll create my own library here. Anyone who visits us can read books in our house while listening to the sounds of the village," Idris said, his face glowing with excitement and triumph.

"That's a wonderful idea," Leila said.

They sat on the ancient-looking stone statues near the art school. Idris sat on one of the outdated chairs, playing the trumpet with his fingers on the armrest. He was thrilled to live his dreams in this village, and his triumphant smile shone brightly.

Leila sat in her chair, stretching her arms and fingers, saying, "Well, then we'll continue just like the old and beautiful days. Will you help me with the varnishing work again?"

Idris accepted with a smile, "Of course... Varnishing is my job!"

"And, as they say, I would rather be the servant of my land than endure someone else's bad breath," Idris added.

"That's exactly what my father used to say," Leila replied.

The sun was painting and shaping the sky in its own way. The bride-like clouds were separated into fragments and hung limply in the sky. It made people want to touch those clouds. The greenery in the garden had come to life, and countless types of plants turned the garden into a paradise.

Leila put her hands together, turned them upside down, raised her arms and stretched them like a bow, then relaxed them by snapping her fingers. "Wow, my father was right... A person's heart and soul will always be where their loved ones are buried, this is where their homeland is..."

THE END